F
Tho

Distortion

Published in 2018 by Lethe Press, Inc.
6 University Drive, Suite 206 / PMB #223 • Amherst, MA 01002 usa
www.lethepressbooks.com • lethepress@aol.com

isbn: 978-1-59021-353-7 / 1-59021-357-2

Set in Bembo
Cover design: Inkspiral Design.
Interior design: Frankie Dineen

DISTORTION

BY LEE THOMAS

dis·tor'tion *noun*

1 The action of distorting or the state of being distorted.

1a A distorted form or part.

2 The action of giving a misleading account or impression.

3 Change in the form of an electrical signal or sound wave during processing.

— Oxford Dictionaries

For John Charles Perry, as always

DISTORTION

1

I imagine if the average guy received a phone call from a stranger halfway across the country, telling him his daughter was in "terrible trouble" and needed him "immediately," he would respond with desperate questions while preparing a hasty rescue. As for me, I looked for my cigarettes. Scratched my head. I figured the idiot on the other end of the phone was calling the wrong number or the wrong Mick Harris. The guy may have made any number of mistakes, because while he was certainly talking to me, he couldn't be talking to *me*.

I'm not a complete idiot. I mean I knew about my daughter, but she was never part of my life. Her mother wouldn't allow it, forbid it actually. So I couldn't be blamed for doubting the information.

The call came early on a Wednesday morning about the time I was getting my second cup of coffee. For me, that's the best time of the day. Quiet. Usually too early for the phone to start ringing. Work was still an hour off. Just me and the news. Coffee. Cigarettes. I was reading the headlines from the screen of the laptop I kept on the kitchen counter when the phone rang. I stared at the device like it was a big, nasty crack in the drywall that had appeared overnight. Second ring.

Shit.

"Hello?"

"I'm looking for Michael Harris."

"Sorry," I told him, thinking it had to be a telemarketer. It seemed a bit early for one of those sales-pitch harpies to be calling, but telemarketers were the only ones that called me "Michael."

So, I said, "He's out."

"Do you know when he'll be in?"

"Nope." I hung up and made it back to my chair, my coffee, the news. The phone rang again.

"Yeah?"

"It's very important that I speak with Mr. Harris," the man said. This guy's voice was one of those razor thin nasal jobs that doesn't hit the eardrum quite so much as slices it. He was obviously worked up about something, and apparently, it had something to do with me.

"About what?"

"His daughter."

"Wrong number, buddy." I felt around my robe for the pack of smokes I always kept with me. Found the box. Pulled it out and stopped, noticing that my heart was beating a little faster.

"Mr. Harris?"

"Not the one you want."

"Mick Harris?"

"Look, who is this?"

It took a split-second for the caller to hone his blade of a voice, but once he did, he came at me slashing. "My name is Dalfour, Aaron Dalfour. I'm a friend of your daughter's. Well, of her mother's actually. But I'm her friend, too. She doesn't have many of them. No. No, she needs a friend these days. Or a father. She's got some terrible trouble. Terrible…"

"Hold up," I said. I heard what the guy was telling me, and I figured he was wrong, but if he wasn't, I was going to need some nicotine support. I lit up a Marlboro and carried the phone with me back to the counter where my coffee waited.

Dalfour kept talking, his sharp voice cutting with rapid babble. I wasn't ready to listen.

"Dalfour." I said. "Dalfour. Breathe for a second."

"Right. Yes. Fine."

Once I was seated with a bit of smog in my chest and some coffee on my lips, I asked the most obvious question I could think of, hoping it would put the guy squarely in the mistaken zone, freeing me up to get back to my life.

"What's this girl's name? The one you think is my daughter."

That seemed to do the trick. Dalfour didn't answer. Nothing but breath on the phone.

"Uh, Dalfour?"

"I… oh dear… I have to go. Goodbye." And the phone went dead.

As practical jokes went, this one was lame and tasteless but somebody had obviously done his homework. Though a lot of my life was public knowledge (at least much of my history was available on the web), the fact that I had a daughter was gratefully absent from those accounts. I almost admired this asshole's resourcefulness. He'd done a good job of digging up obscure info. That's not to say that Dalfour's call hadn't done the trick if his intent was to unnerve me, but I'd received phoners from some major league whack-jobs over the years, so I knew the procedure. I tapped the recent calls button, and wrote down the number. The area code wasn't familiar. Not local at any rate. Putting the phone down on the kitchen counter, I considered calling the jerk back, giving him a bit of a scare. He had interrupted my morning and gone in a little too deep on the personal history. Why not call and threaten some retaliation?

And the answer was simple: it wasn't worth it.

A lot of these goofs had come and gone, leaving a bit of annoyance in their wake but causing no real trouble. I've always found it best to let them get their grins and then go away. If anything, I'd learned not to poke the crazies.

Upstairs, I showered and put myself together, dressed in my usual work outfit of old jeans and a beat up cotton shirt stained with paint and varnish and cleanser. I grabbed my wallet and keys off the kitchen counter and powered down the laptop before closing it up and tucking it under my arm.

The whole time, I listened for the phone.

A second impulse to return Dalfour's call hit my neck like an electric wire. I even lifted the phone and pressed a couple of numbers. But it ended there.

The phone went back in its charger. I loaded up my truck and headed to work.

★   ★   ★

The morning was clear and warm with silver blue sky above, and the sun radiated in the rearview like a quarter reflecting a nuclear blast. A warm, dry breeze pushed through the truck's open window, and Denver stood tall and shimmering to the north. The radio played at a respectable volume. I tried to put Dalfour's call out of my mind, tried to put my daughter back in the mental crate where I kept her memory, but the possibilities teased me, excited and angered me. I turned the radio up and tried to lose myself by following the chord progression of an Aerosmith tune.

The song ended. I didn't want to hear the one that followed.

When the opening notes of "Alone With You" began to seep through my truck's speakers, I shot out a finger and killed the radio's power. The song was too familiar and hit all the wrong nerves. It wasn't a bad song (At least I hoped not. I'd written the fucking thing) but like many songs, it took me back to places I didn't want to be…

… and Ricky Blaine was always there, waiting.

Ricky: the poster child for late-80s excess, a blond howling banshee and the ghost in my broken down machine. Ricky and I had spent fifteen years in the same band, and made some decent music together. From the early-80s until the mid 90's, I was marginally famous, particularly if you were a rebellious fourteen-year-old suburban kid. Granted, the recording industry operates on dog years, so it might as well have been a hundred years ago, but my band made a pretty good run during the days of Aqua Net, spandex, ripped tank tops, and fringe jackets. We called ourselves Palace. Put out seven records. At least they were called records when I was a kid. CDs by the time we were actually recording. I still call them records. Whatever. Three of those hit the top ten, but these days, we're relegated to shows like *Whatever Happened 2* and oldies stations (and that's a shiv to the ribs, I'll tell you) but for a while, we were at the top of the heap.

Ricky Blaine was Palace's lead singer, and he didn't end well. Low. Ugly. Broke. Where are they now? Right? Better question: Where are they buried?

I didn't want to end up like Ricky.

Fortunately, I didn't have to. All of that was behind me. The hair, the lycra, the ongoing party that was only interrupted by blackouts and court ordered rehab, were history. These days, I look like any other blue-collar Joe with conservative hair, just short enough to be shy of having any real style to it. A bit more weight in my chest and maybe a bit too much in the gut. Mustache. I'm one of those guys you see walking down the street with a metal lunch pail and chambray shirt who looks like he's given up on the American dream and has settled for taking home a paycheck.

I called myself a contractor but didn't have a license for it. My business partner, Edwin Brett, and I bought and renovated houses. Resold the properties for a decent profit. Flippers, right? I hired out the serious work like plumbing and wiring and anything structural, but did a lot of the cosmetic work myself—the painting, the tiling, hanging the wallpaper. It was quiet. It was something I could do alone. Me, my smokes, some coffee. Peaceful.

After so many years of noise, peaceful was good.

If Dalfour proved legit, I imagined peaceful would be a memory, but he hadn't called again. Whack-job. Nothing more.

My current project, a house on Wendell Drive, looked pretty sad when I pulled the truck into the garage. Edwin and I had closed on the property eight weeks before, but other projects had kept me busy. Instead of letting the place just sit, I'd had the plumbing completely replaced and hired my electrician to rewire the house.

Hauling a gray tackle box with assorted tools and my laptop under my arm, I walked into the shadows of the house, entering from the garage to the kitchen. With the lights on, the kitchen looked more depressing than usual, which I attributed to Dalfour's aggravating call. The linoleum countertops hadn't aged well, and the cabinetry had buckled. The nook where the refrigerator belonged was foul with water stains on the wall and curling linoleum on the floor. Once white, the nook's flooring had darkened to the color of cooked spinach. Observing the unappealing details, I could still imagine what this kitchen would look like with polished nickel pulls on laminate-faced

cabinets, granite countertops, new appliances and a clean floor of
white ceramic tile. My imagination put my daughter in that room
(though of course, I didn't know what she might look like). She was
beautiful in my mind, fixing a meal for a family she would one day
have. Pots boiled on a shining stainless steel range and steam poured
toward the range hood.

Isley. That's my daughter's name: Isley. Her mother's idea.

I leaned on the counter, felt the sharp edge dig into my lower back.

The imagined domestic scenes came and went, with different faces.
My first wife, Paulette, leaned over the counter, wearing a sheer negligee,
her head moving in a slow pass to inhale a line of blow before climbing on the countertop and spreading her legs. Other women followed,
some demure, some coarse, some barely remembered and merely shapes.

My imagination failed me then, and the kitchen dissolved into its
squalor as the last woman, my mother, entered the thought-drama. Her
hair was short but kinky and graying; her face looked as if someone
had taken a razor blade to every crease and wrinkle, so that scab and
not shadow accented the advancement of time. She drank deeply from
a two-dollar bottle of vodka. When the bottle was empty, she shrieked
and threw the bottle across the kitchen to shatter against the wall. Her
hands, like claws, clamped over her ears, tore at her hair, and she kept
screaming and screaming as if the nightmares would fly away on the
surface of a harsh, high B-flat.

All of that mind movie stuff threw me. These days I don't think
about women much. They were very much a part of a time and a place
for me, acceptable accessories to a grand fiction played out on an arena
stage, most of them as easy to wipe away as makeup following a show.

No longer entertained by the imagined phantoms in the kitchen, I
gathered up my computer and my tackle box, and left the room. In the
master suite of the house, I plugged the laptop into a bathroom socket,
powered it up and sat on the toilet seat to make notes on the floor plan.

My daughter's name was in my head. The last time (in fact, the only
time) I'd seen her played like streaming video: a short clip. Looped.
Blurry. Too brief.

An eight-year-old girl.

Her hair back in a white elastic tie.

A conservative but pretty dress covering her from throat to shin.

A look of fear in her eyes.

★   ★   ★

As always, my partner Edwin made an appearance. (Not my partner in the romantic sense, just so that's clear). Edwin dabbled in real estate and a number of other ventures. Our renovation business was a minor player in his financial portfolio, but he always made a point to show interest in the projects, even if he didn't care what color I painted a room or what lighting fixtures hung there just so long as a hipster couple would sell their soul to Colorado National for keys to the front door.

I was in the living room when Edwin arrived. Edwin was a big beefy guy, and he wore a gray jacket over black slacks. He had dull eyes, a plump nose and little if any neck separating his earlobes from his shoulders. Basically, Edwin looked like a gangster from a forty's film noir.

"So when will this shack be ready for the market?"

"A few weeks. Maybe a month."

He didn't like my answer. He never did. "But it's a crackerbox. We could build them faster than that."

"So build them. The walls have to be taken down to the plaster and resurfaced. Same with the floor."

"Why did I let you talk me into this money pit?"

"You're the one that bought it from the bank."

Edwin lit up with a smile. "And I got it for a steal."

"Then shut the hell up."

"What are you going to do in here?" he asked, pulling his head back to look at the ceiling.

I didn't know. After two hours in the house, staring at my laptop and paint chips and surfing the web for fixtures and flooring, I had thought little about the house on Wendell Drive. Aaron Dalfour was in my head, and my daughter accompanied him, pressed firmly behind my eyes. Did he really know her? Who was she, now? As the day progressed my desire to find out escalated, and the last thing I could concentrate on were the details of the renovation.

Edwin picked up on some of my distraction. He commented on it.

"Weird thing," I said. "I got a call this morning. Some guy told me that my daughter was in some kind of trouble."

"You have a daughter? When did that happen?"

"I've mentioned her before."

"You haven't."

"Edwin."

"I'd remember."

"Anyway," I said to get back to the subject. Then I told him about the call and how Dalfour seemed eager to get off the phone the second I'd asked for proof.

"Well, there you go," Edwin said, throwing his hands wide like a game show host. "Just an asshole yanking your chain."

"Right."

"Except you don't want to believe that. You want to believe that your daughter is out there, needing you. You want to see her."

He knew me better than anyone else.

"It was a bad joke, Edwin. Christ, I'm not going to tie myself in knots over a crank phone call. I find it hard to believe that Noelle has had a sudden change of heart and wants me to meet our daughter."

"But you want to believe it," he said.

Yeah, I wanted to believe it.

★   ★   ★

Edwin stayed in the house for thirty minutes before excusing himself for a lunch date. I managed to stay for about an hour myself before I decided to go home. The work could wait. The downswing in the market hadn't shown any signs of letting up, so the place could sit empty for another year, regardless. On the drive home, I picked up some food from a drive-thru and ate in the truck. I finished the meal as I pulled into my driveway.

I'd bought the large Spanish style house because it was spacious and simple, and it sat back in a cul-de-sac in a quiet neighborhood in south Denver. The house was L-shaped with a turret at the elbow and an open and airy floor plan–living room leading to dining room leading to kitchen. Thick tiles ran beneath brightly patterned southwestern rugs of cotton, wool and jute. A staircase with a carved rosewood banister descended between the dining and the family rooms. High ceilings were drawn with exposed beams and held wrought iron light fixtures that seemed to disappear in the nighttime shadows. The place was too big for one person; I knew that, but I isolated myself at home much of the time, so I wanted my hermit's retreat to be comfortable.

I'd built a recording studio in the basement and fiddled with song writing in my spare time, but I hadn't sold a tune in nearly four years and hadn't completed one in over a year. Still, when I needed another layer of separation from the world, more walls and insulation between myself and mankind, I followed the stairs down to bang out some frustration on my bass or the drums or the piano. But that day I stayed upstairs, listening for the phone and pacing the rooms, noting chores that I had no intention of doing.

I called the number that I'd jotted down for Aaron Dalfour that morning, but no one answered and there was no machine to take the call. Thinking that I'd dialed wrong, I tried again. Same nothing.

I crashed out for about thirty minutes. While dozing, Isley drifted through my thoughts. She pushed her way in no matter how hard I pushed back.

I'd seen her once. In her seventeen years of life, she had been mine for a total of thirty seconds.

The memory was far more vivid than it should have been, and my imagination took some liberties with the incident, but it came back so clear and cold that I shuddered as I stared at the spinning blades of the ceiling fan.

The remembered afternoon seemed only a handful of days behind me, rather than the full decade past it was. The memory hurt, so I went further back into my history, and realized the pain began long before I decided to see my child. In fact, pain drove me to see her in the first place.

2

In the city of Celebration, Arkansas a man named Herbert "Baby-leg" Kole signed the register at the Celebration House, a quaint inn just off the town square. Mr. Rowley Twain, who owned the pleasant hotel with his wife Suzanne, noted his guest's square and serious face, a weathered overnight case, and two cigars jutting from the pocket of a cotton shirt that stretched tightly across Baby-leg's shoulders but wept with wrinkles over his midsection. Kole could have been a salesman. Rowley Twain knew the look well. Until the Quality Inn went up off the freeway north of the medical center, all of the salesman that stayed in this part of the state had signed their names to his register.

But Baby-leg Bert was not in the sales business; "Collections" would have been a more accurate description of his trade. He worked for a man named Ryan, a mid-level bookmaker who'd set up shop in Shreveport, Louisiana, and though Ryan had made it a practice to only work with those men or women whom he knew could cover their losses—corporate execs, bored trophy brides, trust fund sponges—every now and then one of Ryan's clients came up dry. That's when Baby-leg Bert went to work.

After signing his name in the book—a tradition Rowley Twain loved too much to let go, even though computer records were far easier to access—Baby-leg Bert climbed the stairs to his room on the second floor. Twenty minutes later, when the guest returned to the lobby, Mr. Twain asked if he needed directions to one of the local attractions, but his guest merely smiled and waved on his way out the door. Twain bid his guest a good night and returned to the office to eat his dinner and watch game shows. He did not see Baby-leg return at seven-thirty that evening.

At twenty-past eight Baby-leg called room service and ordered a smothered pork chop plate with fried okra, mustard greens and two colas, which he used to dilute shots of Jack Daniels, poured from a bottle he kept in his battered leather bag. Clara Ronson, the room service waitress found Baby-leg Bert pleasant enough, if a bit flirtatious. ("He smiled at me and winked a couple of times," she later told the police.) Before leaving the hotel for the night, she made the rounds of the halls to collect trays and found Baby-leg Bert's just outside his door. The plate was clean and the silver neatly placed across it.

Police records indicate that Baby-leg called his employer at ten thirty-three and spoke for two minutes. He made no other phone calls while staying at the Celebration House. To the best of the staff's recollection he had no visitors.

But at a little after one in the morning, Baby-leg started shouting. Soon after, his guttural cries rose from threatening barks to high-pitched shrieks that tore through the halls of the Celebration House. The screams were so sharp that a guest down the hall felt certain that Baby-leg was brutalizing a woman in his room. Even from the small apartment on the first floor, Rowley Twain could hear the ruckus.

Twain hurried from his bed and snatched for his robe, while his wife mumbled in her sleep. Rowley first visited the office to snatch up the skeleton key, and then dialed nine-one-one while climbing the stairs toward the source of the dreadful noise. The privacy of his guests was sacred to Rowley, but this level of caterwauling in the middle of the night was simply too much.

Two guests stood at their doors, peering out with questions. Rowley held up his hand to assure them that all was under control and continued to the far end of the corridor where a final cry peeled out and was quickly silenced. The emergency operator kept him on the line, so Rowley said, "Excuse me a moment," and rapped on the door. He called his guest's name three times and then rapped again, but there was no answer. Readying to open the door with his passkey, Rowley stopped himself. Instead of opening the door he backed away from it and waited for the police to arrive.

Officer Doug Richmond was present when Rowley Twain opened the door to Baby-leg Bert's room. The hotel owner inserted the key and twisted it, then quickly stepped back, allowing the policeman access.

Baby-leg Bert was found, sprawled naked on the floor, his eyes staring widely yet vacantly at the ceiling fan. Mouth open. Tongue drawn back from his teeth. His torso was twisted awkwardly as if frozen while in the throes of a seizure, and his fingers dug into the carpet.

The official cause of death would be determined natural causes. A heart attack. Nothing in the room seemed amiss. There were no signs of a struggle. In fact the only oddity Officer Richmond discovered was a partially burned note resting in an ashtray next to the still smoldering tip of one of Baby-leg's Dominican stogies.

3

Aaron Dalfour finally got me on the phone a little after five that afternoon. I was in the studio running scales on the bass to lose myself in something familiar when the ringing pulled my attention away from the fret board. I set the instrument down with the care of a mother putting her baby to crib. The Washburn was my first "real" bass, over twenty-five years old and in mint condition. It wasn't the best instrument ever made, or even considered in the running to be a classic, but it was a clean, powerful guitar, and I always kept it close.

"Hello."

"Mr. Harris," Dalfour said, "I'm so sorry I was interrupted earlier. Isley came in while we were speaking, and I didn't want to upset her. She's been through so much already."

And there was her name. There was the proof I'd requested.

"Where are you calling from, Aaron?"

"From my home."

"What city? What state?"

"Celebration, Arkansas. Why?"

"Call me curious."

"Mr. Harris, I know how odd all of this must be for you, but I only have a minute. I think you should come down here. There's been some trouble."

Though curious about Dalfour's definition of trouble, I was more interested in learning why I was being contacted by this stranger rather than by Isley's mother, or Isley herself for that matter. It struck me as incredibly unlikely that I had ascended from leper outcast to savior in Noelle's eyes, and while I was certainly willing to help, my efforts weren't likely to be greeted with any measure of gratitude unless Noelle had undergone some tremendous change of heart.

"What does Noelle say about this? I mean, does she even know you're calling?"

"I…well…no. She's dead, Mr. Harris. That's part of the trouble."

Dalfour's news hit me hard. An inexplicable combination of sadness and loss (after all, I barely knew this woman) met in my chest like blades that cut and tore their way to my throat. Dalfour kept trying to move the conversation ahead, but I couldn't respond. I hadn't heard from Noelle in nearly a decade; the last time we'd spoken she had demanded that I stay away from her home and our daughter. She was in my life for three months a very long time ago and then hardly at all through the intervening years, and yet, I felt as if I'd just lost someone extremely close to me.

"What happened?" I asked, swallowing hard to dislodge the knot · from my throat. Aaron was already five steps along in the conversation, talking about where I might stay when I arrived in Celebration. I cut him off and repeated my question.

"She took her own life, bless her soul," Aaron said. "I'd rather not go into the details just now. I really only have another minute or two. I can tell you everything when you get here. You will come won't you?"

"Yeah," I said. "Just tell me where to book a room."

★   ★   ★

In the aftermath of Aaron's call, I felt emotionally drained and considerably lost. Even punching the keys on the computer in my office to make flight arrangements exhausted me. My daughter, a girl of seventeen, just lost the only parent she'd ever known, and now I was expected to step up and take responsibility?

I had spent years trying to be part of her life, though I can't say that I *fought* to be a part of her life. I never took Noelle to court or attempted any legal coercion that would have allowed partial custody—even simple visitation—of Isley. But I did try. Letters and phone calls—ignored or greeted with barely concealed hostility. I tried, but Noelle wanted me as far away from her and her child as she could get me. My nerves were shot. My daughter, a girl I didn't even know, needed me. Her mother, a woman I had loved within the parameters of my nature was dead. Nothing could have prepared me for Aaron's news and what it would mean to my life.

In recent years, my social interactions were limited in the extreme. My family—mother, father, brothers—were old wounds. Nothing there but scars. I kept a small list of people I worried about. Very small. The remaining members of Palace, Clyde and Rudy; my business partner, Edwin; a few well known figures in the music industry whose names I don't need to drop here: these were the people in my life. Isley and Noelle Vale were strangers. They were nothing more than old melodies I'd nearly forgotten, but now they were playing in my head. Infectious. Persistent.

I carried these thoughts with me to the kitchen where I brewed a fresh pot of coffee, hoping the caffeine would help clear my head and burn away the lethargy that had gripped me after Aaron Dalfour's call.

Noelle committed suicide? Took her own life? It made no sense.

A lot folks have a taste for suicide in them. Some people need just a sprinkle of it, daring mortality for a bit of savory adrenaline; they cross against the streetlight, drink a little too much, eat artery clogging diets. Others find they need a little more flavor, and add more and more zest; they become firemen or cops and the suicide spice becomes part of their every meal. Then there are those who coat their lives in the seasoning, to block out all other scents and tastes—for them it's the razor blade, sleeping pills, a hose running from the tailpipe.

For me, it's cigarettes, in addition to a history of drug and alcohol use, which has probably put a couple of nails in the coffin. For Ricky Blaine, former lead singer of Palace, it had been needles holding an elixir of heroin and cocaine, no longer meant to enhance the party, but designed, rather, to anesthetize the pain of his expulsion from it. He'd found his place in the world, and it had eaten him whole.

Back on the road. We gotta get back on the road.

How had Noelle managed it? I wondered. What could drive her over the edge?

★   ★   ★

That night I dozed restlessly. At one point I imagined something covering my head. Convinced that I was suffocating, I shot up in bed, scratching at my face and trying to remove the dream fabric from my nose and mouth so I could breathe again. Such dreams came and went, one colliding with the next. Ricky Blaine screamed at me, his corpse-thin face twisting impossibly as his jaw unhinged to release a shriek designed to call demons. His clawed fingers dug into my shoulders.

Back on the road, he screamed.

Back on the road.

Then I was in the bathroom of an arena—maybe in Pensacola, maybe in Mobile—and two women were taking turns sucking me off. They wore clouds of teased blonde hair, had narrow waists and exaggerated breasts. The details shifted and the bodies expanded with muscle; the hair withdrew into distorted scalps; the breasts receded. The figures, now masculine, continued their hungry business. Their faces elongated as if formed of melting wax. Their eyes were sealed; their noses were flattened and shoved out of joint, leaving only lumpy, wet holes with which they entertained my cock. Standing in the open bathroom door, Noelle leaned against the jamb and cried, watching the two grotesque men going down on me. Ricky stood behind her screaming. I was embarrassed and I tried to get away, but the men melted into the wall and into each other, forming a barrier to keep me from escaping. Their flesh bubbled and fused, as if welded where arm met arm, shoulder met shoulder, hip met hip. My ex-wife, Paulette turned to me with a film of white on her nostrils and told me to fuck her before a torrent of opalescent fluid shot from her open mouth and from between her legs. The discharge pooled like liquid pearls on the floor, and Ricky Blaine kept screaming *Back on the road.*

We have to get back on the road!

At just after three in the morning, I opened my eyes and noticed Ricky Blaine standing in the corner of my bedroom. Only the tips of his nose and chin caught the light from the window. His siren-high demand for a tour was finally silenced. He didn't move. Didn't speak.

He just stood there, in the corner, looking at me.

My eyes adjusted so I could see more of his lanky body and emo-
tionless face. Slowly, Ricky lifted his arms, bringing them above his
head and clasping his palms together, the way he had always done on
stage during the final refrain of "Alone With You." Then his fingers
spread wide and grew like vines. They climbed up the wall, around
the window. His cottony wisps of hair turned to creeping tendrils
and fanned across the glass like webbed cracks. The transformation
continued until Ricky was completely replaced by writhing filaments.
He covered my walls, my ceiling and floor. Then, he was gone, and I
woke up for real.

I went into the bathroom and took a sleeping pill. Something
moved across the mirror, a flicker of light.

I took a second pill and went back to bed.

4

So the gay thing.

If you caught the Behind the Music special you might have heard that monotone jackass say, "But Mick Harris was living a lie," like I was a serial killer with a freezer full of heads. Then they flashed a blurry picture of the exterior of some gay bar called The Tool Box (and no, I've never been in that particular bar). Yes, I was in the closet, and no, I didn't handle it well. You could say I came out swinging, carrying aggression and arrogance in equal measure, all but daring people to give me shit about my personal life. The lie of bisexuality–far more acceptable to my peers–gave way to a jaded honesty, and in the end, no one really cared. By the time I'd made the proclamation no one was left to care. The days of Palace's relevance had ended. No one gave a fuck what I did with my dick anymore.

The morning following my terrible dreams, I woke and looked around the bedroom, realized I was alone and walked down to the coffeepot and my laptop on the kitchen counter. I sat there and read the news. In theory, I was becoming a father today.

Time for a Cuban.

Light 'em up boys. It's a girl.

Suck on this.

Reading the news, scanning the various headlines, I kept wondering what Isley would be like and how she would react to me, and very little of what I pictured was good. Oh, in between reading severed phrases about the latest NFL star being charged with rape, I could almost imagine Isley running into my arms, calling me daddy and telling me how so very badly she'd always wanted to meet me. More often though my imagination fed me clips of my daughter wearing her mother's face, telling me what a useless oxygen sponge I was, and what the hell did she want me around for when she'd lived seventeen perfectly good years without me?

And suddenly I didn't want to head south. What in the hell was I getting myself into, and how did I get out of it? Flying to Arkansas was not a good idea. No way. Not even close to a brilliant plan. Maybe I could just wire her a few grand, send her a birthday card or have my lawyer make some calls to take care of her parking tickets or whatever trouble she might have.

Christ, she was seventeen; what kind of trouble *could* she have at that age?

I went through a couple more cigarettes than usual and surfed the web, hoping to find an adequate distraction. I even went to the Palace website, saw my face, nearly twenty years younger staring back at me, saw Ricky with his perfect pout and narrow features all but jumping out of the screen to be noticed while the three guys around him acted as little more than background for his striking presence.

Back on the road, I thought.

I clicked the window closed and shut down the laptop. It was time to go.

★   ★   ★

At the airport, I picked up a paperback from the gift shop, sat on a hard chair and waited for them to announce the boarding of my flight. Before discovering music, I had used books to escape. They were usually stolen from the library or the drug store down on Merringham Ave., and they got me through the days before I picked up a bass. Later in life when I was on tour, I'd bring about a dozen paperbacks with me. Sometimes on the road I just needed to be left alone. When I felt that way, I'd do the isolation thing with a book while the other guys were playing video games, playing cards or just playing with whatever harem was hitching a ride to the next town. Back then when I finished a book I'd dump it in a dressing room or a hotel room or out the window of the bus. When they were gone, I stocked up on more. For a while there, Ricky had called me "Shakespeare," which was a refreshing change from "Runt."

I got on the plane at about ten a.m. It was too early to start drinking, so I popped a couple of xanax and dozed through the flight all but bol*ting* awake when the captain announced we were on final descent.

Daddy's home.

★   ★   ★

In the rental car, headed down the highway toward Celebration, Arkansas, I considered my first trip to the city. That resounding mistake came back with humiliating clarity.

Ten years gone, right?

Palace was no more.

The band had broken up. Rudy, our guitar player, made the announcement but it wasn't a surprise to anyone. Grunge had seen its coronation day and sales were down and after a lot of years on the road, it was time to put the toys away. Time to move on. Time to grow up.

We'd been pretty frustrated over the last couple of years anyway. A lot of fighting. Ricky and I could barely make it through a rehearsal without coming to blows. Our drummer, Clyde and our guitar player, Rudy were burned out. Despite the obvious descent of our star, Ricky's ego remained inflated and soaring. Deluded to the end.

I accepted our demise without blinking–no argument, no questions. Even so, I was fucking lost. At the time, I was thirty-four, and suddenly retired. With any luck, that meant being bored out of my mind for the next forty, maybe fifty, years. I started using cocaine again, something I hadn't done for a couple years, and something that I never committed to the way Ricky or Rudy had. I'd been out of the band for a few months, and could not find a new groove. Two or three bands asked me to tour, but I wasn't interested. I sat in on a few studio sessions and found that playing what other people told me to play had a freeing aspect to it, even if it wasn't as satisfying as writing and performing my own material. I moved from Los Angeles to New York and from there to Paris, having some bizarre notion that I would meet a pack of similar expatriates on the *Rive Gauche* like something from a Hemingway novel.

I met no one.

I never learned the language but in the most fundamental way my ignorance served as a comfort. In a foreign country, I could explain why every moment felt wrong and hollow, why I never felt integrated with the people with whom I shared the streets, why I felt so completely out of place.

But after two months, I needed to be back among Americans so I returned to the states and to Los Angeles and the house in the hills.

And that's where I stayed, morning, noon and night after night, ordering food in, ordering alcohol in, sitting on my terrace next to the swimming pool looking over the lights of the city, drinking martinis and snorting coke and trying to figure it all out.

In my mind, I was a failure. I'd followed celebrity as far as the road allowed but was alone and unwanted and unnecessary to the world. Nothing I did was good enough, and nothing I possessed meant anything because it was not *exactly* what I wanted.

Where was my family? The loving partner? Where were the friends— the real friends who wanted nothing but to drop by to shoot the breeze and have a beer and talk about their lives? Where was the sit-com fantasy of normalcy that I'd wondered at as a kid? Even as an adult and knowing that such perfect existences did not, in fact, exist, I wanted it and wondered how I'd ended up so very far away from anything even resembling my mind's vision of happiness.

It made no sense. It made me nuts.

So, I took another trip. I had a daughter in the south, and I wanted to see her.

Seemed like a good idea at the time. Sadly, at the time I'd been dosed up on coke for two days and squeezing the last drops from a case of Absolut.

I arranged the flight and landed on a Saturday afternoon. The heat was oppressive, working into my pores like hot grease. I was sickeningly hung over. My hair was still long, erupting like a fountain from my scalp, and my clothes hugged every inch of my body. And four minutes after I stepped out of the airport, I felt like complete shit.

The rental car's AC was on the blink and a weak stream of air, barely a child's breath, came from the vents. So I baked and sweated and felt like my clothes were made of sudsy brillo, slipping and scraping over my skin with every movement of my arms on the wheel or my foot on the pedal. Following a map I pulled off the Internet, I stopped at a convenience store and bought a six-pack of beer, guzzled two before I got out of the lot. Opened a third. Rested it between my legs while I struggled to find Amaryllis Street in Celebration, Arkansas.

When I got there, my defiance was flatter than my hair. I caught a glimpse of myself in the mirror. My eyes were red, swollen and rimmed with dark skin. My cheeks were sunken in the manner of the diseased. I looked like I'd just stepped out of the shower after a boxing match—one I'd lost.

I was no one's father.

That's when I saw my daughter. The door to the small yellow house opened and two little girls walked out onto the porch. One girl was blond with glittering green eyes and a short, white dress with blue flowers on it; she was a stranger. But oh, the other one—the girl with the long brown hair, pulled back in a white elastic tie with her proper and pretty summer dress—she was mine. The smile was purely her mother's but we shared the same eyes, (though my child was being much kinder to hers). They were bright and alive, not the scratched and chipped marbles I carried around in my skull. I rolled down the window. The two girls turned to me, and their smiles faded.

Isley.

My God. She was real, and I knew it. But then, she was seeing me. The girls, so pretty and fresh with energy, stopped skipping. The blonde girl made a low hissing sound in her throat and pulled Isley back a step. I tried to smile. I wanted to say "Hello, baby. I'm your father." But Isley turned to her friend, and they clutched each other as if in the shadow of a monster. Then, they ran back toward the house, ran like the devil was on their heels. A moment later, shouts erupted inside.

Sitting outside of a small yellow house on Amaryllis Street, thousands of miles from my place in the Hollywood Hills, I hit that legendary location–rock bottom. I gave my monstrous reflection another disdainful glance, realized how I must have looked to those two children and started to cry. The front door slammed open. Noelle stomped onto the porch, and I gunned the engine. Drove away.

A week later a bald guy with oily skin served me with a restraining order signed by Noelle Vale and some judge.

The first thing I did when I got back to Los Angeles, before I even went home to get unpacked, was had my hair sheered. I told the stylist to take it down to the scalp, giving me the appearance of a West Hollywood bartender. The girl who cut it ooed and tsked, saying it was a shame to lose such beautiful hair, but she didn't understand that the hair was only the beginning.

I wanted it all gone. I wanted to put the party behind me because the caterer had run out of food and the guests were starting to feed on me, and there was very little left.

At home, after downing half a bottle of Stoli, I went to my closets and threw everything I owned into bags–every shirt, every jacket, every pair of tight and shiny pants–and hauled them to the curb. I did more blow, got more fuel in my system. Worked through the night until all I had to wear were the clothes on my back, and the next morning, going on four days without sleep and feeling a cottony electric haze like a thunder storm in my head, I went shopping and bought new clothes, respectable boring suburban clothes that I imagined were the type worn by the Ward and June Cleavers of the dot com age. Next, I called a real estate agent and told him to come appraise my house, and then I passed out for two days, only waking when that real estate agent leaned into the doorbell for the eighth time.

I admit that the whole thing was insane and desperate, but it was the only way to escape. If I had to change, then it was going to be final. No going back. No backsliding. End it. Get rid of the image and the costume and the people. Leave the party before the hungry celebrants devoured me.

   This transformation occurred a decade before my second trip to
Celebration. My life had changed, slowed, evened out in the intervening years. I didn't know if any of that qualified me for fatherhood,
but I was driving the rental car over the county line and into the city
of Celebration, and I was about to find out.

5

During our phone conversation, I had asked Aaron Dalfour about accommodations. I figured a gay bed and breakfast wasn't likely, so I didn't broach the subject. He suggested I stay at the Celebration House Hotel, which was a boutique property in the middle of town. It sounded precious and homey, with lots of interaction between myself and the owners and the other guests–"Good folks," Dalfour said. Just as cozy as you please.

"What about motels?" I asked.

Aaron suggested a place a few minutes out of town called Faye's Inn. It was popular with fishermen, and I'd have a lot more privacy.

On the two-lane highway, two miles north of Celebration, the pine trees lining the road opened to a clearing and the shacks comprising Faye's Inn appeared, crouching below them. You'd expect a place called Faye's Inn to be inviting, maybe even quaint, and I'd imagined something out of Currier and Ives, but I should have been thinking *Psycho*. Faye's was a series of squat, square buildings, maybe a dozen of them, that huddled like a pack beneath the branches of the pine forest.

Inside the office I met Faye LaMarche, a bent woman with hair two shades lighter than Windex and glasses as thick as highball bases. Her face was perfectly smooth as if the skin had been stolen from a much younger woman and grafted onto the aged Faye. Her voice cracked when she spoke, and she did little to hide her dislike for me.

She smiled tightly when she told me how much the room would cost for the night.

"Excuse me?" I said.

"One hundred and five a night. That includes towels and sheets."

I looked out the window at the tiny wood-sided boxes and wondered how in hell the woman could charge so much. She couldn't have had but a handful of visitors in the course of a year, and her prices seemed a good way to keep anyone from coming back.

"That's pretty steep," I said, opening my wallet.

"Only folks that can afford it come here. A lot of businessfolk from Little Rock come on out for the bass. City-ots, I call 'em. But that's the price, and you don't get a discount just because you ain't fishin'. That's your business."

City-ot that I am, I gave Faye my credit card.

"Where you in from?" Faye asked.

"Denver."

"Oh sure," Faye said. "That's up north."

I smiled and nodded. The compact woman with the light blue hair pulled a key off of a hook and said "Cabin 4. It's got a nice view of the river."

Again, I looked out the window at the huddle of cabins, peered through the breaks between them, but saw no water. "The river?"

"It's a walk," Faye said. "But it's one of our preferred cabins. There's a path between cabins 9 and 10. It'll take you on back. Hope you don't got a lot of luggage."

"Is there a phone in the room?" I asked.

Faye looked at me like I'd just spit on her floor. "Course they got phones. We ain't hicks Mr. Harris. Your cabin is fully appointed. Even got cable TV."

"Sorry," I said. "And where was that path?"

Faye walked out of the office with me and jabbed a finger at the two cabins in the center of the enclave. "Just go on through there. We keep the trail clear, so it's easy enough to find your way back. If you walk into the river, you've gone too far."

Retrieving my luggage from the trunk, I noted the quiet court-yard. Maybe the other guests were out for the day, doing god knows whatever it was people did out here, I found the path easy enough, and it was cleared just as Faye had said it would be. It twisted and turned between the thick pine trunks and after a five-minute walk, sweat poring down my face, I came into a clearing. I didn't hear the sound of the river up until that point but once I took the final bend in the path and the curtain of needled branches pulled back to reveal silver-blue sky, its roar struck my ears.

It was beautiful; I'll give Faye that. The cabins were situated along the bank. I counted four of the white boxes. The first cabin I came to wore the number 2. Rods and reels stood stacked on the tiny square of porch at the front. A large Igloo cooler squatted beneath them. A light burned beyond the filmy white curtain. At the next cabin I heard a soft jazz song playing and something else. The mellow, smooth melody, played with expert grace on a saxophone was occasionally punctuated by grunts and the sound of wood hitting wood: headboard to wall.

Sex. Nothing else sounded like it.

Somebody was having a very pleasant afternoon. And why not?

Once I got over my initial apprehension of Faye's set up, I had to admit that between the swaddling forest, the soothing rush of the river and the relative isolation, she had herself decent if not fancy accommodations.

I moved on. The sounds of sex and music fell behind me. At my cabin, I put down my bag on the narrow porch and fitted the key in the lock.

Inside was about what I'd expected. The room was a perfect square, maybe fourteen feet by fourteen feet with an L-shaped wall to section off the bathroom. The walls were painted a nicotine-stain yellow and the bedspread picked up this color scheme with a day lily print. The smell was also familiar.

For the first few years, Palace spent a lot of time in motels while touring smaller venues. Not yet able to afford real hotels, we'd made do with a series of motor lodges that usually included a number in their name. Every single one of those places had the same scent—a dull mildewed odor like wet socks that fought its way through the cleansers and room fresheners. All in all, I'd stayed in worse rooms than the one at Faye's Inn, but not in a lot of years.

I dropped my bag by the desk beneath the river-facing window and unbuttoned my shirt, which I hooked on the front doorknob. The shower was a small stand up jobbie, the kind Ricky Blaine had always called "coffins with nozzles," but the water pressure was decent, and I scrubbed the airplane atmosphere and the sweat off myself and again, felt a dull pang of terror at the prospect of meeting my daughter. I lingered in the shower, soaping up a second and a third time, and let the jet of water hose me off.

I was stalling.

I couldn't help but wonder what Isley would think of me, wondered if she'd remember seeing me sitting in a rental car outside of her house, looking like a monster in the blazing afternoon sun. Maybe even worse, she might only know me through the media—the *Behind the Music* show and *Top Metal Moments* clips. If that was the case, I can only imagine what she would think. Of course, the worst thing to my mind was that she knew absolutely nothing about me at all, that I was a blank column beside the word *Father* in her personal dictionary.

Dressed and dry, but already feeling fresh sweat breaking out on my neck, I looked around the cube-room as if I might have forgotten something. The compulsion to check my e-mail account thrummed in my head, but it was nearing four o'clock so it would have to wait. Outside I marveled at the river for a moment too long, locked the door and stepped out onto the dirt track running in front of Cabin 4.

As I neared the main path that would lead back to the parking lot, a chipper voice said "Good Afternoon."

Two men sat in plastic chairs on the porch in front of Cabin 3. The front door was open between them, and they looked like matching statues, guarding the entrance. They weren't identical but they complemented one another and offered symmetry. The man on the left had a salt and pepper mustache and green eyes while the one on the right was clean-shaven with brown eyes, but below the neck, they might have been photocopies of the same body. They were moving well into middle age, but had the burly fit bodies of older men who took care of themselves. Dark hair fanned out over their chests and bellies. Both looked amused and relaxed. Friendly.

"Hey," I said in greeting.

"Are you our neighbor this year?" the guy with the mustache asked.

"For a couple of days, anyway."

"Well, you got time for a beer to get us acquainted?" This from the clean-shaven guy on the right.

"Sorry," I told them. "I've got a meeting in town." Only then did I realize that this was the cabin from which I'd heard the impassioned grunts and the thumping of a headboard. I cast a glance inside to note the rumpled linens on the bed.

The last thing I'd expected to find at Faye's Inn were a pitcher and a catcher from my home team.

"Well, you stop by later," Clean Shaven said. "I'm John Palmer and this is Tony Martin. The cooler is always stocked and open."

"I appreciate that. Take it easy," I told them and continued down the path.

★   ★   ★

Aaron Dalfour suggested that we meet someplace public to keep things from exploding into a scene, but he didn't want it to be *too* public. He picked a diner situated halfway between town and Faye's. I'd noted it on the drive out, so wasn't worried about finding the place. In fact, I was there in just under five minutes.

But I wasn't ready to go in. My nerves were frayed; it felt like I'd done a couple bumps of blow and was on the down side, needing more. Anxiety clenched my belly in a fist and I leaned back, took some deep breaths and tried to get my head in a place where I could handle the meeting ahead.

Before Palace had hit, I'd worked for Clyde's father, doing contract work around Portland. Nothing too severe, just drywall, house painting, papering and finish work. I was on a job, wallpapering a bathroom when Clyde threw open the door and grabbed my arm, started dragging me out of the place. He said we had a gig that night in Seattle, and we needed to get on the road. The guitar player of a band called Cujo had taken a swing at the lead singer of Engine an emerging speed metal act out of the Bay Area. Cujo was the opening act, and they got canned on the spot. So, our manager received a call and took the gig. During the drive up, I didn't think much about it; it was another show.

But it wasn't. We were playing the Moore Theatre and it seated something like fifteen hundred people. Up to that point we'd played small clubs, high school gyms and roller rinks, and yeah we filled those places, but it was nothing like this. Opening for a band like Engine in a place like the Moore, the music thing started to feel real in a way it hadn't before. When I got there and saw the size of the place, I made it through the sound check and the meet and greet with Engine, and then found a bathroom and threw up. Sitting in the rental car outside the diner, I felt pretty close to puking again.

I rolled down the window and smoked a cigarette, noticing that a dozen pickup trucks lined the drive. In fact, mine was the only car amid the heartier, functional vehicles. I played little mental games to work up my courage to enter the diner.

When I did manage to work up the courage, at least enough to get out of the truck, I stopped in front of the diner, looked to the right of the door and noticed a vending machine. The device struck me as an odd thing to have in front of a restaurant, and I wondered why they would be distributing food or drinks from a box out front instead of pulling customers inside. That quandary was cleared up pretty fast when I read the front of the machine.

Live Bait, it read. A backlit graphic of a jumping bass ran across the left panel, and along the right such tasty delights as night crawlers and minnows and bags of something called spawn were listed. I stared at this oddity for some time, realizing that things lived and squirmed within that box. Someone had dug these creatures up and dumped them into an old soda pop machine, waiting for Bubba to slip a few quarters in so he could have hook meat for the day. The vending machine chilled me, really messed with my head, but I didn't have time to figure out why, exactly. I had to get inside to see Aaron Dalfour. To see Isley Vale.

They were easy enough to spot. Aaron looked exactly the way I thought he would: a neatly dressed twig with a very proper haircut. I put his age somewhere between thirty-eight and forty-five. He wore a pumpkin orange polo shirt, and his skin was the color of cream cheese.

Nervous and squeaky clean, he looked like an insurance agent who never quite met quota.

He peered up with a bit of surprise in his eyes. That's when Isley turned. That's when she saw her father for the second time in her life.

And she didn't like what she saw. She still had her mother's mouth, now turned down in a disapproving frown, and her eyes narrowed, tightening the scope so her fury would hit its mark. I tried to smile. Failed miserably. From the moment I saw her face, I was imagining what that kid must be thinking:

Oh you think you're something special, Mick Harris, don't you? You used to be a rock star back when they played that meaningless glam-pop trash. But you're not a star; you're a selfish, no-talent loser, a bass player, a nobody in a band of nobodies. Lame. Your only hits were sappy pieces of over-produced cheese with no more resonance than moth farts.

Pathetic.

And what about me? And what about my mother? We weren't good enough? You couldn't be bothered to include us in your little rock and roll fantasy?

Aaron Dalfour rose from his seat at the booth and gave Isley a cautious glance before hurrying down the aisle toward me. "Mick? Mick is it? I'm glad you could make it," he said. "We're down here." As if I couldn't see twenty feet away.

We walked back to the booth, and I shoved my hands in my pockets. Isley looked at me with annoyance. She was an attractive girl. *Maybe too thin.* A fall of rich brown hair cascaded to her shoulders. Her face was heart shaped with a slender nose, and she still had my eyes. They were big and green, and currently, filled with loathing.

"Mick," Aaron said. "This is Isley Vale. Isley, this is your..."

"Don't even," Isley snapped. She looked back at her soda, lifted the plastic cup and sucked noisily at the straw. "Are you going to sit down?" she asked, never looking up from the beverage in her hand.

"Maybe I should go," Aaron muttered.

"Maybe you shouldn't have come in the first place," Isley said.

I watched this exchange and grew cold inside. Aggression does that to me, it hardens and freezes me. Some people mistook this reaction as bravery, even cool indifference. I didn't know what to make of it. It just happened.

"Why don't you take off?" I suggested to Aaron. "We'll be fine."

I sat down in the booth and faced Isley as Aaron made his way to the far end of the diner. He chatted with the waitress, pointed at our booth and then at himself. Isley never looked up.

"I imagine this isn't easy for you," I said.

"You mean, it's not easy for you."

"Yes. But I'm not imagining that." I tried to laugh, made it through the first chuckle, let the second die in my throat.

I expected a long silence to follow as Isley put together her attack, but it came rather quickly. "How many kids do you have?"

That one took me off guard. *Where were you? Why'd you leave me? Who do you think you are?* Accusations and questions about my absence I had considered, but this… this threw me. I told her what I knew. "One."

"That you know of."

Well, that was true enough. Though, unlike some of my band mates, I'd never been served with paternity papers or been contacted by a one-nighter to announce my fatherhood. I wasn't nearly as active as they were. Even so, there had been women and a lot of stupidity and reckless behavior.

"I have a daughter. You."

"That you know of," she repeated.

The interrogation needled me. I threw a casual glance to the side and noticed the other diners, who were doing their best to appear disinterested in the third degree I was enduring. Two women in awful, floral-print dresses stared at their plates, forks poised over chunks of meat, swimming in brown gravy. Neither moved, fearing any sound they made might block out my response. A man in a trucker's cap and a sweat stained blue button down, held a plastic cup to his lips, but didn't appear to be drinking.

Clearly, the audience was waiting for a show.

"Fine," I said, looking back at Isley. "I have one kid *that I know of.*"

"Classic."

"Did your mother ever tell you about me?"

"Not really. Not until… " She let the sentence drift off and stirred her cola with a straw.

"What did she say?"

"She said you ran off with your band. Said you didn't want to settle down because you were famous."

"That's not true."

"You didn't even marry mom," she said. "You had two other wives, but I guess mom wasn't good enough for you. Considering everything, she probably lucked out."

"That's enough," I said.

A second after the warning was out of my mouth, she set in on me like a starving dog. What followed was a complete deconstruction of me as a human being, delivered with such a belief in my fundamental perversion as to be ludicrous. According to my daughter, I was a drug addict, an alcoholic, a sexual predator, and a devil worshipper, prone to violence. Christ, her description was worse than that lousy *Behind the Music* program. Watching that, most people would have thought that I spent my life tweaking on blow so I could fuck a college football team under the bleeding carcasses of a goat herd.

When she finished her ridiculous condemnation of Mick Harris, I just nodded my head and tried to smile. If I had been cold during her scolding of Aaron Dalfour, I was now absolutely frozen inside. Granted, she was a hurt little girl. A child. Apparently, she had nothing but some sensationalistic television programs and maybe a few words from her mother to judge me by, and God knows, I wasn't around to prove myself to her, and yeah, there were some wild times, maybe even shocking for mom-and-pop-Iowa, but I was not the man Isley Vale described; that man didn't exist.

"And you believe all that?"

Silence.

"Look," I said. "You're very hurt and probably confused. You certainly have a lot of bad information about me. We'll get to that later."

"I know that…"

"No," I said. It was my turn to talk about Mick Harris. "I did not desert you or your mother. Some things happened. Things I had no control over, and Noelle didn't want to have anything to do with me. Fine. She had an idea about what her life was going to be like, and I didn't fit into it. My absence was her decision."

"Right," Isley muttered with rich sarcasm. "Because you're all Husband of the Year and shit."

A bolt of anger cut through the numb but was quickly suffocated. She was goading me for an answer I couldn't give her. Telling Isley what had happened between her mother and I would have been as effective as slapping her across the cheek. I couldn't say that I appreciated the young woman across the table from me. In fact, I could barely tolerate her sour expression and bitter self-satisfied tirade, but I wasn't going to be cruel. Not if I could help it.

"I'm not going to sit here and argue with you."

"Then you'd better get the check."

"Look, I flew out here..."

"Why? Because you felt guilty about running off and wanted to make it all okay so you could feel better?"

"I assure you, I felt a hell of a lot better at home."

Isley stabbed her soda with the straw. "Then go home," she said. "I don't need you here. I don't need you at all."

"That's not the way I hear it."

"I don't care what you heard. You think just because you were famous once and you've got a ton of money lying around you can just show up?"

"I'm not rich. I work a regular job."

"Right. Sure. You're such a martyr. When I was twelve, mom had to get a job at the Tasty Cone, working nights, so she could afford to have my teeth fixed. But that's okay because she only had to teach during the days and tutor kids after school. No biggie that she had to put on a fucking paper hat and serve food *we* couldn't even afford to all of my friends."

"So what am I supposed to do? You want me to apologize for something I had no control over?"

"Do what you want," she said. And then under her breath, just loud enough for me to hear, "It's what you're good at."

"You don't know a thing about me."

"You're all over the television. *Your parties and your tours and all of those girls and then all of your boyfriends.* Did you care about any of them?"

Chick-question. No way to win. Fuck it. I was tired.

"No," I said. "I didn't care about them, and they didn't care about me. Okay? I was a guy in a band. They were perks of the job. That's it. No matter what lies went through our heads, that's as deep as it went. It was all a predictable sitcom, and everyone played his or her part. They got a story to tell their friends, and I got a little distraction and some fuel for my ego."

"Pathetic."

"Yep," I said. "Absolutely empty and sad, and the best fucking time I've ever had. A hell of a lot better than this."

"Well I'm so sorry."

"Don't even try and play that shit with me. If your mother worked three jobs or four jobs that was her business. Her decision. I sent checks. I tried to help, and she wouldn't let me, so if you've got a problem with wearing K-Mart clothes or eating Hamburger Helper every Sunday night, bring it up with her, not me. Yeah, I was a fuck up. Big deal. The world's full of 'em. At least, I *tried* to be there, even when she told me what a piece of shit I was. I kept trying because I thought you deserved that."

"Now you're blaming mom?" Isley delivered a condescending chuckle. "She was a better person than you'll ever be."

"I couldn't agree more," I said.

With no response to that, Isley stood up and stormed down the aisle, threw open the door and ran into the parking lot.

Fuck. Kids, right?

★   ★   ★

I once fucked a girl against an ice machine.

It was Palace's first tour. We were staying in dive motels and playing at clubs along the West coast. The girl and some friends had followed us back from the gig, and she caught up with me when I went out to get a soda to dilute the cheap whiskey our manager had scored. The fluorescent light in the outdoor hallway flickered and buzzed like a squadron of trapped fireflies. The ice machine crunched and rumbled.

When we were finished she wanted to talk, told me how much she loved Ricky Blaine and Rudy Trevino. They were so cool. They were awesome.

"So what are you doing out here with me?" I asked, seething and ready to be rid of her.

"Oh, that's cool. You're in the band too."

And there it was.

I was in the band. I wasn't her first or even her second choice, and she knew nothing about the person under the hair, but I stood on a stage with a guitar strapped over my shoulder. Who could say if she even found me attractive? My only value was the colored-lights reflecting off of my face, the noise pumping from the amps at my back and the PA towers on either side of the stage. I was one of a hundred, maybe a thousand different guys who were "in the band."

Later in life, I came to a similar realization about men. Oh, they didn't care if I was a musician, but the illusions were comparable. Maybe I wasn't "in the band," but I was "there:" convenient, available, a machine of distraction to assist in the illusion of intimacy. It was a fair enough trade.

Isley wanted to know if any of them had mattered to me. They all mattered, but they meant nothing. Just as meals I'd had two months ago meant nothing, and breaths I'd taken ten years ago meant nothing. Sustenance mattered and oxygen mattered, but the details didn't stick. You ate. You breathed. You fucked.

That was life. The rest was just drama.

★   ★   ★

In the aftermath of my daughter's exit, Aaron climbed out of his booth, grabbing his glass of iced tea with both hands and worked his way down the aisle to where I sat. I waved at the waitress and pointed to Aaron's glass. The waitress nodded. Smiled at me. Winked. Dear Lord.

Aaron opened his mouth to start babbling, and I lifted my palm. "Don't."

When my drink was delivered, I looked at the nervous little stick across the table from me and asked, "Why the hell am I here?"

"Well, I thought that since…"

I saw him gearing up for a detailed monologue and interrupted. "Okay. Let me rephrase. You said that Isley was in some trouble. Does she need money? Is she in trouble at school? *With the law?* What?" I was already giving up, and it didn't feel all that bad. If she needed money, I'd write a check. If it was the law, I had a good lawyer, or I could hire somebody local. Whatever her problems were, I could help, but I'd be damned if I was going to hang out and play piñata for her to cane.

"Mostly financial. But there are other things," Aaron said. "Noelle left her in a rather bad place."

As I sipped through my first glass of tea, Aaron laid out the financial problems, and while I could see where they might be daunting for a seventeen-year-old girl, they were, in reality, rather minor. Noelle died, leaving her mortgage in arrears to the tune of eight hundred dollars and the bank was starting to yap about it. Her life insurance was enough to cover her funeral with maybe enough left over to buy a cheeseburger. No bank accounts to speak of. No real assets. Isley was broke and would soon be losing her home to the bank.

"I'm doing what I can to help, but I'm a teacher, Mick. Do you have any idea what that means in the south? It means poverty. If my parents hadn't left me a house that was fully paid for I'd be renting a room and eating bologna sandwiches at every meal."

"She doesn't have any other relatives? No other friends?"

"No relatives left. As for friends, well, she's got a lot fewer of those lately."

"What do you mean lately?"

"There was a boy," Aaron said, casting a glance through the window. "I'd better drive her home. We can talk later."

"Wait a minute," I said. As far as I was concerned there wasn't going to be much in the way of later, so I wanted to get some things clear. "Does she have anyone looking after her? Did the authorities appoint a guardian for her or is she just alone in that house?"

"Well that's one of the reasons I called you," Aaron said. "The courts have made her a ward of Darrell Wertimer; he's the judge's cousin. But that's a real bad place for Isley to be."

"Bad?"

"He's something less than a gentleman," Aaron said. "Especially when young ladies are involved."

Great. The courts appointed some perv as my daughter's guardian, and from the looks of things she'd rather stay with him than spend another minute with me. Since I didn't stand much of a chance with her in the near future, I decided to check out this Wertimer guy. "I'd better go over there and have a talk with him. I can at least let him know I'm around."

"No point in that. He's out of town for the next couple of days, and his wife isn't a problem, really. She's got some broken toys in her attic, but she isn't dangerous. Hopefully by the time Darrell gets back from Shreveport, you'll have everything taken care of."

Though neither comforted nor convinced, it seemed the Wertimer issue would have to wait. So, I told Aaron that I could help with the money.

When Isley was born, I had set up a trust. Since Noelle wouldn't let me be involved, it was something I put together to feel involved. Technically, Isley couldn't access the money until her eighteenth birthday, but she'd be in good shape. "Until then, I'll make sure the bank and her bills get paid. If she won't take any money from me, I'll go around her."

"That's very good of you," Aaron said. "Now, I really should go before she tries to hitch back to town. She's already been picked up a few times, and the Sheriff is losing his patience with her."

Imagine that.

6

On the steps of Cabin 3, I sat with my back against the railing, looking up at John Palmer and Tony Martin, who again flanked the door in their lawn chairs. Though evening settled, it was still hot, and the breeze, scented by pine and the river, barely moved the air. I couldn't remember the last time I had sat outdoors and chatted, but my neighbors caught me on my way back to Cabin 4 and invited me for a beer. Considering the day I'd had, their company struck me as a pleasant distraction. So I was trying to make conversation. Small talk.

I suck at small talk.

"You know, Black Sabbath had a singer named Tony Martin," I told the mustached guy who was handing me a beer. His smile faded a bit, pushed out by an attempt to show interest.

"That so," John Palmer said. "I thought that Ozzy guy from the television sang for them."

"Yeah, he's back with them, but they had another guy."

"Oh," Tony said, but he couldn't have cared less, or he simply didn't know how to respond to such a stupid comment. Either way, I was feeling like an ass.

"What brings you to the sticks, Mick?" John asked, trying to bridge my clumsiness. "You don't sound like you're from around these parts."

"Neither do you," I said.

"Well, that's the point isn't it?" John said. He threw a playful look at Tony who turned a marked shade redder and looked down at his beer can. "Oh stop it," John said with a laugh and reached out to slap Tony's shoulder. I was missing something in this exchange, but it seemed to be a joke they both understood. "I actually used to visit here when I was a kid. My uncle had a place in Celebration, so my dad would bring me down for fishing excursions. We'd make a few trips every summer. It's a great place to get away."

"From everything," Tony said into the mouth of his beer can before taking a drink.

"It's beautiful country," I said. After a pause to sip my beer, I added, "I'm down visiting my daughter."

"That's nice. Our kids are all grown and moved, too," Tony threw in. "Finally have some quiet in the house after twenty-eight years."

"So you guys used to be married?" I asked.

"Used to? Hell, we still are," John said. "And no, not to each other."

"John," Tony said with warning in his voice. "I can't imagine that Mick gives a damn about our situation."

"Christ," John said. "If he doesn't, he'd be about the only one we ever met."

"Well, I'm not going to sit here and listen to this again."

"I thought we agreed we weren't going to be assholes about this anymore."

Tony was obviously agitated, taking great care to examine the printing on his beer's aluminum can. "Call it what you want, just quit telling everybody."

"Have another beer."

Maybe these two weren't married to each other, but they certainly sounded like they were. I kept my mouth shut until they stopped pecking at one another and turned their attention back to me.

"So how old is your daughter, Mick?"

"Seventeen."

"Living with her mother, then?" John asked.

"Not exactly. Her mother passed away a couple weeks ago."

Both shook their heads and tutted under their breaths. "That's a shame," John said.

"So you'll be taking custody?" Tony asked.

"That remains to be seen. I'm basically just here to help her through the worst of it, but after that, I don't know."

"Now, this sounds like a story," John said, scooting his chair a little closer to me.

"Oh for God's sake," Tony muttered. "Give him some room. Maybe he doesn't want to talk about it. Not everyone has to spill their guts to every person they meet."

"You'd think this guy would get some grins from having a stick shoved so far up his ass," John said, nodding his head in Tony's direction.

"Okay, that's enough for me. I'm going to catch the news." Tony reached into the cooler for a fresh beer, snapped the top, stood up. "Night, Mick. Nice meeting you. Hopefully we can have a civilized conversation one of these evenings when this one isn't around."

"Night," I said.

Tony stopped in the doorway and turned. He tipped his beer can at John and lowered his head in a gesture that was overly stern. "You be sure and get your ass to bed early."

"Go watch your news," John said. "I'll be in before you turn into a pumpkin."

The cabin door closed, and John stood from the plastic chair, rolled his head on his shoulders, then shrugged. "You feel like a walk? We still have about ten minutes of light left, let me show you the place."

"Fine with me."

A minute later, we were walking past my cabin and along the path, deeper into the woods, farther up river. I was aware of the darkness behind the tree trunks, how the woods wove together into an ever deepening night, layer after layer until the forest was nothing but a black sheet. To our right the river gurgled by in a soothing *shoosh* that worked its way into my stride.

"I hope I didn't say anything to upset him."

"Not at all," John said. "Tony is still pretty uptight about our situation. He's just wired that way. It's fine. As for me, I decided to quit worrying about it."

"How long have you two…?"

"About thirty years now."

His reply ran through my head, looping and tangling with other thoughts. Thirty years seemed like an impossible span of time, particularly in light of my history with relationship breakdown. My first partner Glen and I were together for just over six years before we both looked up one day and decided to call it quits, and I was with him considerably longer than with either of my wives or any of the men that followed. In a way, I was envious of John and Tony. No. That's not right. I *was* envious without reservation. I'd never had anyone in my life for thirty years, let alone someone intimate. "That's great," I said.

"Yes," John said. "It is."

"But you're both married?"

"Two beautiful women."

"That's got to be quite a balancing act."

"Not at all. They have us through most of the year, and we have each other for two weeks. What happens here, only happens here, and it stays here."

The path eased us closer to the river. On the left a picnic table and benches sat in the middle of a clearing. To the back, an iron grill stood. Its once-black body was faded and veined white by weather and use. The river gurgled by on the right, and frogs had begun a late evening chorus. Wind shushed through the treetops and our feet crunched over twigs and needles. Pine scented the air like Christmas, and I felt the tension of my encounter with Isley finally easing from my shoulders as I wandered along, letting John talk.

"Back home, we're pretty conservative. We seemed to have hit a groove about twenty years ago and found it comfortable. Everything just kind of froze. Or maybe it was just us that froze. When you add that to the fact that the town we live in is a time warp itself, something straight out of the seventies only with Internet access, we miss a lot of the world's turning. But we get out here, away from what is expected of us, away from the mortgage and the wives and the church socials and the potluck dinners and we get a chance to be something else. I mean we're still ourselves. It's just different."

We took a curve on the path and the river fell behind a low fence of bushes with the occasional column of pine trunk standing grandly above. The burping frogs grew louder, more frenzied. Crickets and some buzzing insects joined the chorus.

"So what about you, Mick?" John asked. "What's life back home for you like?"

"Not bad. Not great," I said.

"I'm sorry to hear that. You seem like a nice enough guy."

"My own fault," I said. "Just can't seem to get the whole normal life thing down."

"Maybe you weren't built for a normal life," John said.

"That's depressing as hell."

"Why? What did Aristotle say about beasts and gods?"

"You're asking the wrong guy."

"Well, look it up one of these days. I can't remember exactly how it goes. Must've had one too many of these," he said, shaking his beer can in the air. He turned his head toward the river and seemed to be looking for something. Checking over his shoulder and back down the path we had just walked, he stopped and turned. "Yep. We missed it. *Me and my big mouth*. Not paying attention."

"Missed what?"

"You'll see," John said, retracing his steps on the path.

We walked for a few minutes and then John veered off the track into the dense brush that separated us from the river. Standing on the trail a few feet from where he disappeared into the brush, I hesitated. Though John seemed harmless enough, the fact remained that he was a stranger. Besides, it was nearly full dark now, and it was getting tough to make out the trail, let alone pick my way through underbrush.

"Come on," John called. "I ain't gonna bite ya'."

A moment later, not wanting to offend my guide, I walked off the path. Bushes scraped over my arms and a branch poked at my neck before springing back into place. I only covered about twenty feet when the foliage opened up to reveal an incredible scene.

I stood on the river's edge looking at an outcropping of stone jutting twenty feet into the current. Across the river, the forest stood like a black fence with ragged edges cutting across the plum-purple sky. Above this, the moon glowed full and orange and perfect. The river, several shades lighter than the tree lined bank crept by, giving the scene a sense of soothing movement. John stood at the end of the rocky pier, hands on his hips, head thrown back to take in the moon.

Below me, a pool caught the saffron disk in a reflection. Further down river, I saw the lights of Celebration twinkling through the trees.

"Not bad, huh?" John asked.

"It's just about perfect," I said, turning my attention up river. Once my eyes adjusted, I could see a good ways and noticed something on the river's edge far up from where we stood. "What is that?"

John left his place at the end of the outcropping and picked his way back to me, keeping his eyes on the uneven stone surface. When he reached me, he followed my gaze toward the strange blue glow upriver and said, "Freak Town."

"What?"

He laughed and clapped me on the shoulder. "Just an old story my Uncle used to tell to keep us in line when we were kids."

"So what is it?"

"Don't know," John said. "It's always there though. At least, it has been for as long as I can remember. I tried to find it once, but came down sick before I got there. Haven't thought about it much since."

"Does somebody live up there?"

"Could be. I haven't seen any houses up that way. For all I know, there's a bar up there, and that's just some neon hitting river mist."

John's explanation made some sense. It didn't look like reflected light, however. It looked like a blue flame, rippling and flaring in the forest but it didn't cast light on the tree trunks or the ground near it. Though curious about this phenomenon, I eventually traded the mysterious light for the river, the moon and my guide.

"So you come out here every year?" I asked of John, who knelt down to scoop river water into his hand.

John rubbed his neck with a dripping palm to cool himself off. "Every other year. Sometimes we end up in Chicago or New York."

"Good fishing there?" I asked with a smile.

"We fish our brains out," John replied. "This place is special though. Quiet."

"It is that."

"I imagine it wouldn't be terribly exciting for someone like you."

"Excitement is over rated. But you're probably right. I don't know if I could do the small town thing."

"So, you probably wouldn't move out here. For your daughter?"

The thought had never occurred to me. I was in the habit of thinking in terms of hours and days ahead, not weeks or months. And my meeting with Isley had been something less than successful. She didn't want to share a soda with me, so it seemed unlikely she would be willing to share a life with me.

"I doubt it will come to that."

"You never know," John said. He knelt down and scooped more water from the river and again, rubbed it over his neck. "I suppose I should get back before Tony has a tantrum."

We walked back along the trail. The conversation was mostly John's responsibility. My head was too full, and I couldn't hold a coherent thought, so I let him talk about his kids and his wife—Gretchen, "A real fox"—and tried to keep things cordial with the occasional grunt or question. Back at my cabin, we said goodnight. John continued on down the path, and I opened the door.

Two steps into the room I froze.

Someone had been in my cabin.

Carefully, I searched the place. Nothing was missing. Nothing was broken. In fact, my visitor was rather tidy. The shirt I'd left on the doorknob had been moved; whoever had broken in had hung it on the hook sticking from the back of the door. I probably wouldn't have even noticed this minor rearrangement of the scene. I rarely kept track of where my clothes landed. I might not have known that anyone had been there at all.

Except, they'd left a note.

7

The patter of rain woke me the next morning. The drops didn't pour down, just a light shower, but it hit the siding of the building like BB shot. After a full night of dreamless sleep, I felt considerably better and even-tempered. The note waiting to greet me on my return the previous evening sat on the small oak desk in the corner of the room. I lifted it and read the two words there again. They made no more sense than they had the night before.

Jody Mayram?

Upon finding the note, I'd felt a strange kind of paranoia, like the person who had written it stood in the room right behind me. Obviously, the sense of violation had been playing with my head. It occurred to me that Faye might have left it. Maybe it was a message from someone in town, but I hadn't thought so. Before going to bed, I'd checked the room again, made sure nothing was missing. Made damned sure no one was hiding in there. Then went back to the note.

I studied the ragged scrawl of the letters. A shaky hand. Thick rusty brown ink.

On Palace's third tour through San Antonio, a girl left Ricky a note, calling him a "God." She'd written the note in blood. Ricky and the other guys laughed about it. The thought of it still makes me sick. The note that had been left for me appeared to have been written in the same substance.

I didn't bother calling the police for a lot of reasons. Mostly it came down to prejudice. When I tried to imagine what kind of cop would be employed in this part of the country, a lot of unfavorable images ran through my head. I pictured pot bellied rednecks with guns, gnawing chaw and making racist slurs for giggles all the while looking at me like I should be modeling a feathered number with a tar lining. Add to that the fact that the note meant absolutely nothing to me and could have been from anyone (about anything), and it was easier to just let the whole thing go.

Still, first thing in the morning, I returned to the scrap of paper, but reading that name (and I assumed it *was* a name) with a night of sleep behind me made it no less of a mystery. I sat at the small desk in the corner, just staring at the shaky red lines, wondering if the ink had come from a factory or some animal's veins.

Jody Mayram.

I refolded the note, set it on the desk's corner and set up my laptop to go on line for e-mails. The urge for coffee settled in my brain and belly, and I searched the room for one of those one-cup makers a lot of motel rooms offered, knowing it wasn't there, but driven by addiction to look. Once satisfied that the appliance didn't exist, I worked through my messages, erasing spam, jotting quick responses to acquaintances or saving the notes until I felt I had something to write to the sender. Edwin sent me an email, joking around and wondering if I had found any other lost children. The president of the Palace fan club sent me an official update on the status of the website and the membership. Not surprisingly, membership was down. The fact that any membership remained was the only real surprise. Once, Palace's fan roster consisted of over a hundred thousand names, but that was in ninety-three before the full force of Cobain's Crusade swept out of Seattle. Most of the current "fans" lived in Japan, Germany, and the Netherlands but it was nice to know someone was out their listening.

The ever-dedicated captain of this sinking ship, Debbie Deeds, self-appointed president of the Palace Guard, always couched these numbers with phrases like "natural attrition due to over-saturation, maturation and mortality of the audience." Which was to say that my fans were bored, old, or dead. At the end of her report, Debbie made the rather predictable request for a new song. In some ways, she was like Ricky Blaine: Debbie was convinced that Palace was just resting in a cocoon, waiting to break out and take flight as something new and wonderful.

The eternally deluded. You gotta love 'em.

She wrote:

Despite the unfortunate passing of Ricky Blaine—God rest his soul in Heaven with Jimi, Janis, Phil, Bon and "Steamin'" Steve—Palace still has great music to offer the world. Perhaps a tribute to Ricky, a requiem if you will. His fans deserve that.

Debbie Deeds ended most of her notes with something along these lines. It was never going to happen. Oh, the song she thought the fans "deserved" was written. I'd composed "The Street" over a year ago, even recorded the song in my basement studio, playing all of the instruments myself and croaking out the lyrics, but even if I'd wanted to release that song or any other song, there was the little problem of having it actually distributed by a record label. Debbie wanted it to be an exclusive, an MP3 file downloaded from the website. That idea struck me as wholly pathetic.

But yeah, the song was written, recorded, shoved away in the storage closet with a hundred other disks. The world didn't need to hear it; I didn't *want* to hear it. The song was the most depressing thing I'd ever heard, let alone ever written.

And the streets around you are empty.
Locked doors, the roar of silence all around
They've gone home, the party's done
And there's nothing
left on the sidewalks
Nothing left but tears

The tapping of the rain worked its way into my head, brought me a few steps lower. I wrote a brief note thanking Debbie and signed off.

After taking a long shower, mostly just standing under the spray, hoping the beads of water would get deep enough to dislodge the glum running under my skin, I dressed. As an afterthought, I put the note that was left for me the night before in the back pocket of my jeans, grabbed my checkbook (because I figured, if nothing else, I could get Isley's money troubles under some control before I left town) and decided to give the city of Celebration a look.

Without an umbrella, I was wet if not soaked by the time I finished trudging over the muddy trail through the morning drizzle. In the car,

I pulled out the maps I'd printed and set off toward town. Starting with the familiar, I navigated the rental car to the yellow house on Amaryllis Street. When I first pulled up, I thought I'd driven to the wrong address. I didn't remember the house being so small, but I checked the numbers on the siding, squinting to make them out through the gloom of the porch. This was the right place, but my heart sank to see it.

Vandals had paid Noelle Vale's house a visit. Rocks had shattered one of the windows in front and a lantern-shaped porch lamp. The word, "witch" screamed diagonally across the front door. The red letters drooled and spattered as if the word were hastily drawn in blood.

A twinge of anger, the dull cousin of true rage, snapped behind my ribs as if this desecration had happened to my own home.

What had Aaron said about a boy? Isley's involvement with the kid had cost her friends? Apparently, she incurred some local peer wrath. The injuries to the house's façade certainly looked like child's work.

Despite the graffiti and the damage, I could tell that the house was clean and neat, but hardly spacious. Could they have been comfortable living there? I hoped so, but suspected not. I wanted Isley to be there, so I could catch another glimpse of her. My anger at Isley's verbal assault the previous afternoon had faded considerably by then, and I was almost ready to try again, but Isley wouldn't be at this sad little house with its shadow-black windows. She was staying with a judge's reprobate cousin: a guy named Wertimer.

With Noelle's house in the rearview, I drove around the neighborhoods on the outskirts of town, looking at towering mansions and crumbling shacks, depending on how far east or west I traveled. Apparently, the money was kept to the east, whereas poverty was allowed to roam free along the western edge of the city charter. Here were trailer homes, ancient rotting shotgun and camelback houses, some tilting to the side as their foundations gave way. Discarded toys and tools littered yards. Cars, broken and rusted, mounted cinderblocks like exhibits at a museum for the apocalypse. I was glad to see that Noelle and Isley didn't live in this ragged village. They did not live in the pricier part of town either. It seemed they existed right in the middle.

Eventually, my need for coffee sent me looking for a café. I drove to downtown Celebration. The city stood around a town square with all of the predictably quaint buildings in place: a courthouse with a clock tower above its Corinthian columns, a library flanked by a couple of stone lions (reminding me of my neighbors in Cabin 3), a large old fashioned bank that was the distinguished grandfather of the modern glass and plastic quick-serve institutions dotting the country. A block-square park sat in the middle and two-story retail establishments faced off on the courthouse to complete the "square." I found a bakery along this row and entered to the scent of sweet, baked dough.

Behind the counter stood a pleasant looking fat guy with a bell-shaped head and thick brown hair combed back from his brow. He wore a wide grin and a white shirt and his skin was so dark and evenly tanned that it appeared airbrushed on. Looking at him reminded me of cartoon bears dancing around with rolls of toilet paper.

"Mornin," he called joyfully, as if I were standing across the street and not less than fifteen feet away. Against his almond skin, his teeth radiated white.

"Good morning."

"You look about like you need some coffee and one a' mah crullers. No. Make that two a' mah crullers and about a vat of coffee."

"Just the coffee, thanks." I took a seat at a small metal bistro table by the window where I could look out on the square. Checking my watch, I found that it was a little after nine in the morning, but the streets were deserted.

And there's nothing
left on the sidewalks
Nothing left but tears

"Where y'all in from?" the baker asked, setting a mug on the table in front of me.

"Denver," I told him.

"Aw yeah. That's up north. What brings you on down to Celebration?"

"Just visiting," I said lifting the mug and taking my first sip of coffee. Oh, that first sip. That's the addictive one. The rest of the day, it's just habit, but that first taste is a pure shot of blissful amphetamine.

"Well, welcome. My name's Bump Carter. Carter like the president."

"Bump?"

The big guy chuckled and shook his head. "Mah folks were a bit touched up top. I got a sister a-name-a Chunk and a little brother a-name-a Hog. I figure ah got off good in that mix."

"Nice to meet you, Bump. I'm Mick."

Bump reached out a hand the size of a deflated football and wrapped it around mine, gave it a good pump and released. He fished in the pocket of his black slacks and pulled out a pack of Lucky Strikes. Lit one up.

I could get used to this place.

"Where is everyone?" I asked. "Town looks deserted."

"Ever'one's already got to where they going," Bump said. "With the rain, they stayin put. It'll pick up round lunchtime." He drew deeply on his cigarette and eyed me with narrowing eyes as if he might be trying to recognize me. The baker pointed his cigarette at me and bounced it in the air a couple of times before saying, "Yah look kind'a familiar. Do I know yah people?"

"Couldn't say."

"Well, yah said yah was down visiting folks. Yah got family round here?"

"Something like that."

"Well, either yah do or yah do not have family down hear," Bump said with a laugh. He looked around the small shop, spotted an ashtray on the table behind me, leaned his bulk to grab it. "This here's a simple true or false question."

"There's a girl that lives here. Her name's Isley Vale, and..." I stopped.

Bump's face went from dark to darker, and his smile disappeared, replaced with a stern setting of the jaw, drawing his lips into a frown. He nodded his head slowly, ashing his smoke in time with the motion.

Aaron had warned me that Isley was not terribly popular these days—something about a boy.

"You okay?" I asked.

"No, suh," Bump said. "Now, I feel nothing but sad for that girl's loss, her mother'n'all, 'cause Noelle was a fine woman and done nothing but goodness with herself right on up to the time she died, but what that Isley did to Sandy Winchester was nothing short'a evil."

"What did she do?" I asked over the lip of my coffee cup.

"I'm not one for gossip," Bump said, looking over his shoulder as if to see if anyone was around to contest the claim. "Sandy was nothing short a a miracle, that boy was. He had him the good looks and the charm of a movie star. Gonna be a lawyer one day and put the bad ones behind bars, he used to say. Oh sure it helped he come from the right people and had himself a leg up from the moment he was brought into the world, but he didn't let it get in his head. No suh, Sandy was a levelheaded kid with a good heart and a head full'a brain. He took the Celebration High School Rockets to the championship game and won it for 'em all by hisself. He was a star that boy was. No doubt about it. He might a been president one day, just like William Jefferson Clinton, but then that Isley came along."

By this time in Bump's story, I'd finished about half of my coffee. I found my own pack of cigarettes and lit one up.

"It did not end well, son," Bump said. "That's all I'm saying."

"I don't follow. What do you mean it didn't end well?"

"Just that. It did not end well. Sandy Winchester was found curled up on his bedroom floor as dead as Elvis."

"He's dead?"

"That's what I said."

"When did this happen?" I asked

"The late part of July. 'Bout a month now."

"And her mother died two weeks ago?"

"Yes, suh. And you don't think it's funny that the two folks closest to that Isley Vale just up and got dead? No suh. There's no coincidence there. Girl's got some badness in her."

Though I had initially liked this Bump guy, the baker bear was verging on pissing me off, and the funny thing was I probably knew the baker better than I knew my own daughter, and yet a deep inner need to protect her, defend her, boiled up in my throat. Normally, I would have let such bullshit roll right off, but Bump believed what he was telling me, and my guess was, a lot of other folks in Celebration believed it too. The vandalism of Noelle and Isley's home was a nasty, childish attack, but it made some sense in the context of Bump Carter's world. The residents of Celebration had been wounded. They looked around for answers to the loss of their golden boy and a woman they admired and came up with superstition and folklore and a monster: Isley Vale.

"Yah best steer clear of that girl, yah know what's good for yah. People around her go ass to dirt pretty quick."

"I'll keep that in mind," I said. "What do I owe you?"

★   ★   ★

Outside, the rain took a break, but heavy clouds blanketed the sky. The air smelled fresh, and for the moment if felt comfortably warm, but soon enough it would start to stew. I looked across at the library and then to the bank, wondering if this was the place that held the note to Noelle's house.

I called Aaron on my cell phone to find out.

"Oh Mick," Aaron said. "I'm glad you called. I just feel terrible about yesterday."

"Not your fault, Aaron. There's a whole lot of bad history between Isley and me, and it doesn't look like we're going to get past it."

"You're not leaving are you?" He sounded desperate.

"Well, I wanted to take care of a few things first, but yeah," I said. I asked him about the bank, and it turned out that it was indeed the institution holding the mortgage on Noelle's house.

"I've got some of the paperwork here, bills and statements and what not," Aaron said. "Isley didn't know what to do with everything when

Noelle passed, so I did what I could. Why don't you come on by, and we'll go over everything."

The thought of spending more time with Aaron didn't thrill me. He struck me as a nice enough guy, but he made me uncomfortable. He was just a bit too eager to please. Even so, having the paperwork on Noelle's place would help, and I could get more details about Isley's troubles, maybe even some information about Noelle.

I agreed.

"Good enough," Aaron said. "I'll put a fresh pot of coffee on."

Well, that was something anyway.

★   ★   ★

Aaron's house stood to the East of town, not quite out to the plantation mansions, but still in a good neighborhood with some fine antebellum architecture. The house itself was a simple three-story yellow con-struction with brown shutters and a narrow porch running across the front. A window on the second floor was cracked from upper corner to lower in a jagged diagonal line. Otherwise the place looked homey and well maintained, having been painted in the last couple of years.

Aaron greeted me at the door with a broad smile, ushering me into the house with a quick, "ignore the mess," which I took to be a reflex-ive deprecation, as the place appeared spotless. He guided me to a large sofa covered in knobby crimson fabric and asked me to sit. Coffee was set out on the table: two cups with saucers, cream, sugar and a modern thermal carafe that looked wrong in the extremely traditional home.

"I really can't apologize enough for yesterday. I know you must have felt just awful, but I didn't really know what to do."

"None of us knows what to do," I said. "But thanks for trying. Right now, it might be best to just take care of what we can."

"Perhaps. I wish you'd reconsider and stay on though. I think Isley will come around. I really do." Aaron sat in a dirt brown armchair and leaned forward to lift a saucer from the table. "But I understand this is all very odd for you, me calling up out of the blue like that."

"I'm glad you called."

"I just think Isley has so much going on in her head and her heart right now that she isn't thinking real clear. I'm sure she wanted to meet you and would like to get to know you some, but everything's a storm with her right now."

A storm sounded like an understatement. A hurricane maybe. That got me to thinking about what Bump Carter had told me about Sandy Winchester. I imagined Aaron knew more about that situation, so I asked him.

"How'd you hear about Sandy?" he asked, seeming quite surprised that I knew the name.

"Your local baker told me."

"Bump?" Aaron asked, his mouth twisting as if around a lemon drop. "That's easy enough to believe. After Noelle said her goodbyes to that man, he's been nothing but nasty to the both of them."

"Noelle dated that guy?" A twinge of jealousy jabbed me, so unexpected it made me cough on the film of coffee in my throat.

"Long time ago," Aaron said. "Maybe seven or eight years now. Bump's first wife died of cancer, and I think it soured him some. Don't get me wrong. From what Noelle tells…told me, he was a fine gentleman and nice as he could be to Isley. I think Isley saw through it though, knew Bump was hiding the way he really felt. Whatever the case, Noelle broke things off. Bump's remarried, met a nice woman named Suzanne from the grocery up in Grevespoint, but from what I can sew together, he's still got some grudge in him."

I nodded my head at this. I didn't mention that Bump had described Noelle in nothing but complimentary terms, which seemed to contradict Aaron's story. Instead, I turned the conversation back to Sandy Winchester.

"Well, that is a plain and simple tragedy."

"How so?" I asked.

"A boy that age just up and dying like that. Might be one of those hereditary conditions you hear about."

"Any idea what might have set him off?"

"Lord no," Aaron said, lifting his coffee cup for another sip. "The night it happened he was up to the river with Isley. They had themselves a picnic supper, swam a bit. From what Isley tells me, it was just as nice as you please, but that night at home in his own bed Sandy woke up screaming. He just screamed and cried, and before his parents could get to him, he was dead. His heart gave out, God bless him. Sad, sad business. Now, if you'll excuse me for just a moment."

Aaron returned his cup and saucer to the table and stood. He walked across the room and into the front hall, leaving me with a shitload of questions. The most infuriating being: How could a town, even if it was filled with backward idiots, believe a girl had the power to cause a boy's heart failure and her own mother's suicide?

I looked around Aaron's living room, hoping to find a distraction from my growing anger. The room was spare to say the least. It contained the sitting area—the sofa, table, and chair—but nothing else of any note. The bookshelves were nearly bare, with only a handful of paperback novels on one shelf and a framed photograph on another. A couple of low, red candles decorated the fireplace mantle. At my feet, an inexpensive carpet, something you'd find at a Home Depot or Wal-Mart, covered the polished wooden floor.

Aaron's parents may have left him a house that was fully paid for, but it didn't appear they'd left him much else in the way of domestic comforts. The place looked stripped clean by robbers, and it occurred to me then, maybe Aaron had been forced to sell off some of his family's belongings just to stay afloat. I couldn't tell you how many musicians I'd known over the years, Ricky Blaine among them, that had found their castles crumbling and were forced to pawn or auction their fast lane accoutrements just to put food on the table, or in Ricky's case, drugs in their veins.

When he returned, Aaron poured more coffee for us and took his seat. He spoke rapidly as he did so.

"I'm sure you must be curious about what my interest in all of this is. It's perfectly natural for you to wonder. I mean, here I am, not family at all, and I've taken on the role of unofficial guardian for your

daughter, but considering how close Noelle and I were, it's really not
such a mystery. And no, we weren't a romantic item. Lord no. Far from
it." Aaron paused to sip some coffee, wiped at his lip. "Noelle and I go
all the way back to grammar school. Truth be told, I carried a flame
for her on and off, but I knew nothing was ever going to come of that,
and the friendship was just too important.

"We fell out of touch for a lot of years, when she went off to college and for a few years there after she came home. By then, she had
Isley, and something about Noelle had changed. Part of it was being
a mother. No doubt there. But there was something else, something
I couldn't put my finger on. For those first few years, she stayed with
her mama, rarely left the house, just focused on mothering. Oh, if you
saw her at the grocery, she was nice as could be, but she didn't go in
for social outings. I got the idea that she was ashamed, having that
girl out of wedlock, you understand? But of course, I got that wrong."

"Wrong?" I asked.

"Lord yes, Mick. So wrong. Noelle rejoined the community after a
time. I suppose Isley was about three years old. I saw them frequently
around town, at picnics and church and what not, and Noelle and I
picked up our friendship, dusted it off and got on with it. We had long
heart to hearts at her mama's house and the way Noelle acted had nothing to do with shame. She just seemed content. You know? She seemed
whole, like she didn't want for a single thing in the world. She had her
baby and a comfortable little house and that seemed to do her fine."

I reached for my own cup of coffee, a series of emotions flashing
like lightning, bolting from brain to chest, chest to brain. Whether
intended or not, Aaron's message carried a good amount of cruelty.
Though glad to know that Noelle was happy in the years following
our relationship, I couldn't help but read between Aaron's words and
find Noelle neither needed, nor wanted, nor missed me. I don't even
know why I cared so much. Looking back, I would have made a terrible husband, even if women were the right fit for me. But it all goes
back, all the way back, to a child's need to be wanted, to be important,
to be connected.

My earliest memory is of my mother. We stood in a kitchen staring down at a puddle of purple juice with bits of glass like ice floe littering the fluid. My mother's voice came at me shrill and merciless like an eagle diving for prey, and the words, "You should never have been born," punctuated her tirade. I imagine she said a lot of hateful things to me in that kitchen, but that is the only line I remember—maybe because it was repeated so frequently in my youth.

"Did she ever mention me?" I asked. "Did she tell you what happened?"

"No and no," Aaron replied. "I'm sorry, Mick. All she ever said about Noelle's daddy was that he traveled a lot and a relationship wasn't possible."

"Oh. Okay."

"I'm sorry, Mick."

"No problem," I said. "I'm sure Noelle had her reasons, and she isn't around to explain them. Let's forget about it. Tell me about Isley. This trouble of hers. You said that money was part of it, and you mentioned her guardian, Wertimer. I got the impression from that Bump guy she wasn't exactly welcomed around here anymore. Is that the bulk of it?"

"Yes and no," Aaron said. He reached for his coffee again then stopped and pulled his hands back to his lap. Even in that momentary gesture, I saw the tremble in his hands. "The trouble really started about six months ago when she and Sandy Winchester started seeing each other. Up until then, Isley's best friend was a girl named Gloria Jones. Of course Gloria, like most girls in town, had her eye on Sandy herself. There was a falling out and some poisoned words, and Gloria started stabbing at Isley's back. It was all very childish and ugly. Needless to say, when Sandy died things got worse. Then when Noelle died… Well, things became unbearable. Kids are like sharks and they got the scent of blood in the water, and Isley didn't really stand a chance."

"What happened?"

"Have you been by Noelle's house?"

I nodded my head, remembering broken windows and the word "witch" drawn sloppily in red paint across the front door.

"The adults are little better, I'm afraid. Human nature, I suppose. A lot of folks think that ignorance and superstition are part and parcel of living out here where it's quiet, but it's the same everyplace, I imagine. Something bad happens and people need to know why, even if there is no *why*. They need villains to beat up so they feel a little safer. Hell, some folks still believe in ghouls and goblins."

And witches, I thought.

"Around here, we got ourselves a couple of haunted houses, a gator-man that lives downriver in a cave somewhere near Plenty and the Trash Boy haunting the woods out by Faye's place where you're staying."

"Trash Boy?" I asked with a chuckle. "What's he do? Punish people who don't recycle?"

Such a bad joke but Aaron laughed anyway and reached for his coffee.

"No, the Trash Boy is said to wander those woods along the river night and day. He just minds his own business until someone says his Christian name. If someone does that, well, Trash Boy comes for them in their sleep, steals the breath from their bodies."

"Why do they call him Trash Boy?"

"Who can say? Why do they believe a man-gator lives in a river-bank cave? It's just local legend, regional mythology. Like I said, folks need villains."

"Like there aren't enough of those in the real world."

"True enough, Mick."

I spent another hour at Aaron's house. During that time we discussed Isley and what could be done about her current situation. I didn't even know if I'd see her again. Not this trip anyway. I wanted to, but every time I thought about it, the same emotional walls shot up, making it impossible for me to see a clear and effective approach.

As for Aaron Dalfour, I never did feel comfortable around the guy. Truth be told, a lot of that was me. Over the years, surrounded by the gods and acolytes of the music industry, I learned to keep a good distance from people. Generally, people wanted something from you. You were someone to be seen with, someone to market, someone whose name had a bit of cache that could be leveraged. I hated feeling that way. The whole jaded thing–while completely warranted during my "career"–had faded little over the years. Being around someone like Aaron, a guy that always seemed two seconds from pissing himself with excitement, made alarms clang in my head.

Still, there was nothing for him to gain by helping Isley, nothing I could see at any rate. Maybe I'd been away from regular people for too long.

★ ★ ★

After leaving Aaron's house, I drove downtown and parked behind Arkansas First Trust. The sky was clearer, though gray clouds still hung to the south. I stepped out of the car into a damp boiler-room heat. Sweat was running from my brow and armpits by the time I took my third step.

Inside the bank, bright, shining smiles from the suited tellers and officers greeted me. As with Bump Carter, those smiles faded when I mentioned Isley's name.

"Oh, I see," said a woman named Beatrice in a powder blue skirt suit. "I'm sure Mr. Bowden will be glad to help you."

Bowden, one of the bank's officers kept me waiting for about ten minutes. When he emerged from an office to my left he looked around the lobby as if searching for a familiar face. He found Beatrice who nodded and pointed at me, thinking I couldn't see her in my peripheral vision. Then, she spread out that phony white smile and turned back to her customer.

Bowden was a narrow man with his hair slicked back to his scalp. The tortoise shell glasses that balanced on his nose looked like they belonged on a much bigger face, and his suit hung too short in the sleeves. His smile was tight and wholly insincere. He crossed the lobby in long determined strides. He eyed me up and down, my shapeless blue shirt, my baggy jeans, my Rockport walking shoes, and wrote me off as a nuisance before he made it halfway to where I stood. I ignored his attempt at small talk and got down to business. "I understand payments are running behind on a property owned by Noelle Vale. I'd like to take care of that."

"Very good," Bowden said.

I asked how much it would take to cover the mortgage for the next eight months. Isley would turn eighteen in six, but she'd need some time to have the trust worked out before it was fluid for her. The banker's tight, smarmy grin flicked at the edges as if his mouth were being teased by a fisherman's line.

"And may I ask what your interest in this transaction is?" Bowden said.

"No. You can ask me for two forms of ID, and I'd say that's about the only conversation we need to have."

My answer didn't please Bowden but his financial training had taught him a good bit about obsequiousness, and he made a sort of spastic bow before saying, "Of course."

"And what was that amount again?"

He told me. I wrote the check, and Bowden *did* request my identification, even questioned the driver's license because it said my eyes were green, and they appeared more of a blue to him. Pinhead asshole. Once we got the whole matter sorted out and he accepted the check, I left.

On the walk, looking out at the square, I got a queasy feeling in my gut. To my left were the row of shops and Bump Carter's bakery. Ahead stood the library, its twin stone lions growling eternally. On my right stood the courthouse and its clock tower. For all of the years I'd lived alone, worked alone, and sat at my computer, interacting more with usernames than with real human beings, I couldn't remember ever feeling quite so lonely.

I knew it was because of Isley. My daughter was close and needing me. But I couldn't reach her. She wouldn't let me.

8

I sat at the small desk in Cabin 4, writing checks. The curtains were open so I could see the river flowing by. Sunlight dappled its low crests. Next to me, the air conditioner alternated between a soothing hum and a crunching grind. Despite the noise, the machine did its job, cooling the shack to an acceptably frigid level. Even so, I removed my shirt before sitting down to make additional headway on Isley's financial crises. Before I'd left his place, Aaron had given me a low stack of bills and statements and half a book of stamps. I killed some time, putting the bills in order, wondering at the low balances on everything from utility charges to credit card payments. In fact the balances on Noelle's Visa and MasterCard were so low, I decided to just pay them off. Ultimately, the damage to my bank account was nominal. Between light, gas, phone and credit cards, the checks I wrote amounted to less than a single month's mortgage payment.

I sealed up the envelopes, stamped them and left them in a neat pile at the edge of the desk. By this time, I was getting hungry, so I went into the bathroom and cleaned up. I was drying my face when my neighbor John knocked on the door.

"Want to join us for some lunch?" he asked, standing on the small porch of my cabin, wearing a Boston Red Sox baseball cap and a white t-shirt.

Over his shoulder, down the trail, Tony stood in front of the weathered barbecue; smoke engulfed him like dragon's breath and then cleared. He swatted the air with his spatula, waved his hand in front of his face. His voice rolled over the path in staccato growls. He was too far away for me to decipher the content, but I imagine curses and accusations wouldn't have been a stretch.

"I know it looks dire," John said. "But he's actually a rather good griller. You feel up to some gab?"

"Just let me put on a shirt."

John and I sat at the picnic bench under the shade of the surrounding pines, observing Tony's continued battle with the barbecue grill. Between the cooking meat, a sweet basting glaze and the pervasive scent of pine, reminding me of Christmas, I didn't much mind the humidity. Outdoors just smelled too good. Besides, the beer was ice cold and a light breeze took the edge off the heat.

"The flames are too high," John said. A cloud of smoke rolled over the both of us. "You're going to burn this whole place to the ground and us with it."

"If that'll shut you up, I'm all for it," Tony said, again beating the air with his spatula.

"Pyro."

"Bitch."

I laughed at their exchange and drew deeply from my beer. A sense of accomplishment was about me as I sat there; the visit to the bank that morning and taking care of a handful of bills had given it to me. I wasn't fooling myself though. The accomplishment was minor, but it was something—a hell of a lot more than I'd done for my daughter in the last seventeen years.

"So, how's Celebration treating you?" John asked. "Noticed you were out early this morning."

"Interesting place."

"Uh oh. That's considered the kiss of death by a tourism board. Did you run into trouble?"

"Not at all," I said. There was no way to explain my encounters with Bump Carter or the employees of Arkansas First Trust without going into details about Isley, so I avoided the whole mess by saying, "I really didn't see that much."

"Were you visiting your daughter?"

"Hey, Snoop," Tony called from his place at the grill. "Why don't you let our guest enjoy his beer? We didn't invite him over for an interrogation."

John turned on the bench to face Tony. "We're having a conversation here. You just mind the meat."

This set off a round of affectionate bickering that lasted up to the point Tony scraped the hamburgers off the grill, loaded them onto a plate and set them down in the middle of the table. They had a good spread of condiments, lettuce and pickles laid out, and John pulled a tub of potato salad from the cooler where the beer was kept. We loaded up plates and then loaded up our burgers, before the conversation came back round to Isley.

"So, things aren't going so well with your daughter?"

I was surprised that this question came from Tony. After he asked, he chomped down hard on his burger, squirting a blob of ketchup out the back end to dribble onto his plate.

"You could say that."

"We've both been through it," Tony said. He looked at John and smiled. "Tell him about Olivia's flirtation with tattooing."

John was in mid-chew and started laughing, which turned quickly to choking. I slapped him on the back until it passed.

"You tell him about Laurie's European adventure," John said.

"Oh God," Tony laughed, shaking his head.

This was the kind of thing that made me jealous when I spent time with couples. They had a shorthand. The simple phrases, even single words, that carried entire histories like tips of icebergs, denoting a great mass of support below. I shared that with Palace to some degree but never managed that kind of intimate code with a lover.

"You want a parental nightmare?" Tony asked, wiping at his mustache with a napkin. "Suffice to say, she no longer finds France terribly romantic."

John laughed and gave the table a quick slap. I had no idea what story lay behind the comments, imagined my situation with Isley was far different than that of Tony and his daughter.

"I don't know if I'm going to be around long enough for any kind of breakthrough," I said.

"You will be," John said. "I get the impression this means something to you. If that's the case, you'll stick around until you make it work."

I didn't know what to say to that. Honestly, I thought he was wrong.
I was not intending to stay in Celebration. Though, it immediately
occurred to me that there was nothing at home calling me back.

"Maybe."

John, sensing that I wasn't comfortable with the conversation,
changed the subject.

"So, how's your cabin?"

"Fine, I suppose. This is all a bit rustic for me." I thought about
the note left for me the night before. John and I were out walking
but Tony had remained behind, maybe he'd seen or heard something.
"Someone was in my cabin last night. You didn't see anyone did you?"

"No," Tony said, a look of surprise on is face.

"Did they take anything?" John asked.

"Nothing was taken. They just hung up my shirt and left a note."

"Maybe Faye was cleaning the room," he said.

"A few hours after I checked in?" I asked. It was a possibility, but
Faye didn't strike me as the sort to make any extra effort on behalf of
a city-ot from "up north."

"What did the note say?" John asked.

I reached into my back pocket and produced it, handed him the
paper. John shook his head and pointed across the table.

"I don't have my glasses. Let Tony have a look."

"Jody Mayram?" Tony said. He shrugged. "Just the name? You might
want to ask Faye if this is a phone message."

"That could be, but there's no number, and I don't know anyone by
that name, and the only people that know I'm in town are Isley and
a guy named Dalfour. Plus, the ink."

"It looks like blood," Tony said, casually as if noting the color of a
vaguely interesting pair of socks.

"Did you lock your door?" John asked, sounding worried. "Before
we took our walk, was your door locked?"

"I think so."

We speculated for several minutes, John working himself into a
froth every now and again, only to be calmed by Tony telling him,
"Relax, Pal."

I helped John round up the plates and bottles, deposited them in a plastic sack while Tony organized the condiments and scrubbed the grill with a wire brush. We were about to leave the barbecue clearing when a branch snapped just beyond the tree line. Leaves rustled like someone walked through the forest toward us.

But no one emerged from the woods. Even so, the crunching of footsteps was as clear as the gurgling of the river, the caw of birds in the treetops.

"Hello?" Tony called into the woods, leaning a bit to the side to get a better look between tree trunks. "Anybody there?"

"Probably a deer," John said. "Come on."

"Sounds like a two footer to me," Tony said.

"Maybe it's the Mud Witch," John said with a laugh.

"The what?" I asked.

"Local fairy tale," John said. "Supposedly, she lives in the woods but if you say her real name, she comes for you. People say that just looking at her is so terrifying it freezes you like seeing Medusa. Your heart and lungs just stop working. My uncle used to tell me about her to keep me in line when I was a kid."

"I heard the same story earlier today," I said. "Only it was supposed to be a little boy who sucked the air out of your lungs or something."

"Sounds like Bloody Mary to me," Tony piped in. "That was the story we told back in St. Louis. Only Mary had an axe and you had to say her name into a mirror a dozen times."

The rustling along the tree line continued. All three of us looked at the woods. Then, adults that we were, we walked very quickly away, following the path to our cabins without looking back.

9

Ricky Blaine recorded his suicide note. He was staying with friends in Hollywood and used their Radio Shack am/fm tape deck to lay down the last tracks of his life. His hosts, being junkies in a persistent state of semi-consciousness, recorded over the bulk of the message with a Stone Temple Pilots song. All that remained of Ricky's last performance was:

Back on the road. If we just could have gotten back on the road. Fuck. We were fucking legend. Legend. Nothing but shit now. Shit. Whatever, man.

You've been a great audience. See yaaaa!

★   ★   ★

I woke from a deep sleep at three in the afternoon. The grinding of the air conditioner met my waking ears and a bright shaft of light, sun reflecting off a metal thermometer that hung from the eaves of the cabin, cut my opening eyes. Before drifting off after lunch, I'd done a lot of thinking about Isley and about her mother. I felt I owed Noelle nothing at this point, except perhaps mourning. Maybe I didn't try hard enough, but I had tried.

Every letter I sent was returned. Every check went uncashed. She wanted nothing to do with me. What I needed to remind myself of, in that hour lying on the bed, staring at the pale yellow ceiling, was that those were her decisions, not Isley's. My complete expulsion from the lives of both mother and daughter were of Noelle's construction. Isley shouldn't have to pay for that.

So, I decided to see my daughter again. If she blew me off, I would try tomorrow and the next day. She would have to come to accept me on her own terms, but she needed to know I was there.

I drove to the only address I had and found Isley at the house on Amaryllis Street. She sat on the porch, back in the shade on a white wooden bench placed beneath the shattered living room window. She watched me climb out of the car and then turned her head away, staring down the block.

Witch, the door read.

"Hey," I said, standing under the shelter of the porch. I noticed a bucket of sudsy water sitting beside the doorjamb with a fat wad of sponge floating amid the bubbles. Isley intended to clean off the insulting graffiti. Apparently, she'd been too upset by the word to get started because both painted word and door were dry.

"Aaron told me what you did," Isley said through a tight jaw. "Mom's house. The bank."

"You've got enough to worry about without rent," I said.

"Yeah."

"Is it okay if I sit down?"

Isley flashed me a look so full of disgust that I didn't take the chance of sitting near her. Instead, I parked my ass on the porch railing.

"You can't buy me," she said.

"I'm aware of that."

"It's not like you can just show up with a checkbook and make everything okay."

"I know that, too. That's not why I came."

Isley crossed her arms dramatically over her chest and gazed down the street. Apparently, she'd finished talking.

"Look, I can't make you not be angry with me, but I'm going to be around for a while. I'm staying out at Faye's Inn. I'm in Cabin 4. If you want to talk, you can call or come by any time you want. I'll give you my cell number. You shouldn't be alone with all of this."

"You didn't care if mom was alone."

"That's not true. I cared a great deal about your mother."

"Please," Isley said. "You ran off after three months, and she never saw you again."

"I did not run off."

"Mom wouldn't lie. Not about that."

"Well, she had it wrong."

"Then, what did happen? Where were you?"

I couldn't answer the first part of that question, not just yet. There was no way I could explain her mother's flight from my life without doing more damage.

"Your mother thought it was best if I wasn't in the picture."

"And now that she's dead, you figure differently?"

"Yes. I do. I think you've got a lot of shit coming down on you right now and not a lot of places to find cover."

"You don't know anything."

"Well, I assume you didn't plan the design elements of the door or that window," I said, pointing over her shoulder at the shattered pane of glass. "And I know about your mother. I know about Sandy. You're telling me it gets worse than that?"

Isley looked up. Her wounded expression tore through me even before she started to cry. But then her lower lip was trembling, and her eyes moistened, and she hunched over, sobbing into her palms. I crossed the porch and put my arm around her shoulders, sat down, took her in my arms.

She didn't pull away. She pushed in close to me, and I held tightly, feeling her body shaking against mine.

Now generally, comforting people fell pretty low on my list of talents. I figured the best thing I could do when somebody was upset was just keep my mouth shut for a while, which I did.

Finally, Isley pulled away and wiped at her eyes.

"I have to clean the door off," she said. She sniffed, wiped at her eyes again, and stood up.

"Do you have a phone book inside?" I asked.

"Why?" Isley asked, suddenly defensive.

"The window. The place shouldn't stay open like that."

"Well, I can't afford to have it fixed, so it'll have to wait."

"I'll take care of it," I told her. "Let's just get the place fixed up."

Though she accepted my offer, Isley wouldn't let me in the house. She dug the keys out of her pocket and opened the door and then turned on me with an upraised palm. "Just wait," she said. A minute

later she stood on the threshold holding out a slender phone book. I
took it from her and crossed to the bench. She started washing the door
as I thumbed through the book. While she scrubbed at the cruel graffiti,
I found that two companies vied for the glass needs of Celebration.

I called Glass Hopper because they advertised fast turnaround,
though I admit the name made me cringe. The woman I spoke with
told me that they couldn't get anyone out this afternoon but could
have a truck over first thing in the morning. I thanked her and hung
up, then tried the number for Celebration Windows. They told me
the same thing the woman from Glass Hopper had. Apparently, broken
windows were something of an epidemic these days. I scheduled the
repair for the following morning.

"Isley, can you meet me in the morning to let the repairman in?"

"If the Wertimers will let me out of the cage."

"How are things over there?"

Isley glared at me and went back to scrubbing. The worst of the
slogan was coming off, but it was going to leave a pink stain on the
white door. I could already see it would need paint. I could do both
door and jamb in about an hour, maybe in the morning while the
windows were being repaired.

I was about to run the idea past Isley when she started crying again.
She dropped the sponge in the bucket and gripped her thighs with
wet hands.

"It's never going to come off," she said her voice cracking with sobs.
"It's fucked. Everything's fucked!"

"It's okay."

"Nothing's okay. Not any more."

"I'll get some paint and take care of it in the morning."

"You don't get it. You don't get anything. Just leave me alone."

My first inclination was to go to her, to hold her again, but something told me she wasn't going to allow that a second time. Instead, I
went to the railing and waited.

I grew uncomfortable watching Isley cry. Every sob jabbed at me,
worked between my ribs into my heart. Usually when someone started

crying, I left because I was either the cause of the tears or because I just didn't understand what was wrong. With Isley I understood, whether she believed it or not. Like Ricky Blaine, Isley was watching her world crumble, torn at the seams and pulling away and no matter how frantically she tried to hold the pieces together they continued to separate. First Sandy Winchester, then her mother. Suddenly she was very alone, or at least that's how she saw it. I was there but I was a stranger, just a guy intruding on and adding to her misery.

"Do you want to get some dinner?" I asked once she seemed to have her emotions under control. "We could talk, maybe figure out what we're going to do."

"*We?*" Isley asked. Her voice carried ice. "You paid some bills. Good for you. You can go home and pat yourself on the back."

"I'm not going anywhere," I said.

"Well, I don't want you here."

"Okay," I said as evenly as I could manage. She was pissing me off again, and I knew I had to keep that under control. "I'll be back in the morning. You'll have to let the window guy in unless you want to give me the keys."

She didn't say anything. Instead, she reached into the bucket and grabbed the sponge, then attacked the door with it, scrubbing at the painted word as if it were a magic symbol that once gone, could take all of her bad luck with it.

"Take it easy," I said and walked away.

★   ★   ★

Committed to remaining in Celebration, I made a few stops on the way back to Faye's. At the hardware store, I bought sandpaper, a can of primer, good white paint, a brush, and a drop cloth. Yeah, I know I could have slapped a couple of coats of satin finish on the door and been done with it, but I figured I needed to put in a little effort. Penance, right? Rows of small appliances sat on shelves behind the cashier's counter. A black and chrome coffee maker caught my eye, and I had the guy behind the counter add it to the bill. On my way out, I noticed a massive blue cooler that rode on wheels and decided I needed one of those too. At the grocery store I picked up some food, mostly salt and grease in the shape of snacks, but also coffee and filters, a loaf of bread and some ham to slap between slices. I bought a couple of six packs of beer to share with my neighbors and three bags of ice. Faye's Inn was going to be home for a while, so might as well make it comfortable.

But I wasn't going to be comfortable at Faye's. I knew that even before I turned into the parking lot of the motel and saw the police car and ambulance parked there, both in full bubble-light boogie.

10

A small man in a police uniform leaned on his cruiser, smoking a cigarette and appraising the world through mirrored shades. He barely stood five and a half feet tall, but he was wrapped in confidence as surely as if his uniform was made of armor and not beige cotton. The officer looked at me, made a quick appraisal, obviously found me less than interesting, and took another slow drag off of his cigarette.

I crossed the gravel in four quick, stone crunching strides.

"Hold up," the diminutive cop said. "You staying here at Faye's?"

"Yeah," I said. Leaning forward, I noticed his nameplate read *Richmond*. "What's going on?"

"It sounds like cardiac arrest," Officer Richmond replied. "Damned shame. A couple of boys out for some fishing and just enjoying themselves and this kind of thing happens. Terrible thing to happen on such a nice day."

My firmly established prejudices again southern law enforcement flickered and died away. Now, I have reasons for feeling less than comfortable with these guys. Mobile. Atlanta. Tallahassee. I'd met their cops under unfriendly circumstances, and I had no reason to believe Richmond had been cast in a different mold. I'd expected him to be all bluster and cold-hearted stupidity, but Richmond fell outside of my limited perception. There was something very grounded about this guy. I felt it. Even with those silly mirror shades, a good dose of sincerity and compassion came through.

"We got an old fella back there who collapsed, and his buddy called it in. I'm along to escort the EMS boys up to County General."

Already I was wondering which of my neighbors, John or Tony was lying on the stretcher. It wasn't a difficult piece of fortune telling.

The gurney appeared from between the cabins a few seconds later, and John clutched the side of it. Tony lay on his back with a sheet spread over him from foot to midsection. An oxygen mask clutched his face like an alien. The two paramedics picked up a little speed once they were off the dirt and guided the rolling cot to the back of their van. John's face was puckered. He had a thumbnail firmly clamped between his teeth, and he looked around the lot, back at Tony, back around the lot. I could feel his panic from fifty feet.

"Excuse me," I told Richmond and set off toward the ambulance.

Tony was loaded inside, and John stared into the back of the vehicle, rocking from side to side, clutching himself with one arm while he gnawed on his thumb. He looked up at the sound of my approach, seemed to barely register my face and returned his attention to his lifelong friend, strapped into the belly of the van.

"John?"

"Yeah. Oh, Mick. Uh… hi."

"What happened?"

"I think it's his h-heart."

"Oh, Christ, man. I'm sorry."

"I've got to go with him."

"Of course. Do you need anything?"

"Luck," John said. He took a step toward the ambulance, then paused and looked at me. "Uhm… Gretchen and Molly will be coming down. I already called them. I probably won't get back before they arrive, and I-I need you to do me a favor."

"We gotta go," a paramedic called from the front of the ambulance.

John stepped forward. "In the cabin. There are… there are, things. You know? I don't want the girls to see them. Could you… in the cabin… could…"

I understood. He and Tony had certain party favors their wives wouldn't appreciate, and he wanted me to "straighten up" the place.

"I will. Go."

"Yeah… thanks…. Uh, yeah." And he climbed into the ambulance. A paramedic slammed the doors and ran around to the front. It peeled out in a spray of gravel, and I noticed officer Richmond was on their tail and then taking the lead before they'd disappeared down the road.

Back at the car, I pulled all the way into the lot and parked, locked it up, wandered down the path toward the cabins. Though I had initially

wondered how two people could possibly have meant as much to each
other as Tony and John, it had never occurred to me what losing such
an intimate companion might mean.

At Cabin 3, I pushed open the door. The bed was rumpled and
clothes were strewn about the floor. I hung a couple of shirts on the
bathroom doorknob, straightened the sheets and bedspread and then
looked around for the "things" John was so concerned about. On the
nightstand, I found a blue plastic bottle of Wet lubricant and figured
that needed to go. Next to the bottle, I saw a folded scrap of paper
and lifted it.

It was the note that had been left for me on my first night in Celebration, the note I gave Tony to read at lunch. Something tickled
the back of my mind, something about a boy, a witch, and a woman
named Mary.

"Jody Mayram," I said. "Who the fuck is Jody Mayram?"

I folded the note and put it in my pocket, returned to my chore. I
opened the nightstand drawer and actually took a step back, startled.

There was nothing in that drawer that I hadn't seen before, but
these were not things I'd expected to find in the middle-aged couple's
possession: poppers, butterfly nipple clamps, a studded cock ring, a pink
butt plug and a perforated leather paddle. On the scale of things, these
were pretty lightweight items, but when attributed to the conservative
guys I'd shared some beers with, they were startling. John and Tony
took their playtime seriously.

Everything went onto a towel. I rolled it up and carried the party
favors back to my cabin. Once I dropped the rolled towel on the chair,
I scrubbed my hands in the bathroom sink and realized I should check
the bathroom next door. When I returned to Cabin 3, I kicked the
rest of John and Tony's discarded clothes, socks and jockey shorts, into
a pile by the bathroom door. Checked the tub and medicine cabinet
for anything provocative, and found a prescription bottle of Viagra,
which on its own wouldn't warrant much interest, but Tony's wife
might indeed wonder why he needed the pills for a fishing trip with
his best friend. I pocketed the prescription bottle and continued the

search, but nothing remained to indicate any extracurricular activities. I closed the door behind me and stepped onto the porch. Next to me sat the cooler, reminding me of the groceries in the trunk of my rental car. That's when I noticed the footprints.

They were large, captured like plaster molds in the drying mud. Somebody had been out here in bare feet, but the prints were too large to be John or Tony's. They moved in from the direction of my cabin, my own shoe prints smeared several of the marks at the bottom of the stairs, but no prints seemed to go the other direction.

Someone had walked to the cabin, traveling downriver on the trail, but they did not go back that way. Interested in this oddity, I stood up, dropped down to the trail. The prints I saw to my left, those leading back to the parking lot, were all from soled shoes. I checked the trees, took a few steps into the woods but found no other tracks.

Curious, I followed the footprints. They played out on the river trail only a hundred yards from camp. Disappeared. The large prints started at this point, and I figured whomever they belonged to had come onto the trail from the woods or the riverbank. My minor investigation ended there, but I continued down the path.

Standing on the rocky outcropping John had introduced to me the night before, an uneasy feeling, that sensation of being watched fell on me. It was daylight so I couldn't see the blue flame upriver, but I remembered the spot where it had blazed. Something moved up there. I figured it was only my imagination. I could barely make out anything from such a distance, but I felt certain dark shapes moved in the woods. Shadowy forms darted back and forth, some leapt, and others crouched. It was just the movement of light reflected off of the river and shadows cast by wind blown branches, but I imagined monsters.

Jesus Christ, what a miserable day. More than anything, I was hurt but it felt like anger. Just punched-the-fuck-in-the-face angry about Isley and Tony and my whole damned life. I wanted to yell at someone or something; throw my voice in with the frogs and the crickets and all of the quaint and shitty wildlife and let the whole damn forest know that I was not in the least bit happy with the way god had chosen to treat me.

I came to the rocky pier hoping to feel better. I thought the sight of the trees, the shore and the river would wash over my eyes and through my body to calm the pain in my head and the thrumming of my nerves, but the beautiful scenery was lost to my mood; it was just wood and water and rock.

So, I left it behind, walked back to the trail. I still needed to unload my car.

11

That night, Ricky returned to my dreams with the violent insistence of a thunderstorm. It was the last night I ever saw him; he'd broken into my house and was skittering about like a roach on crack. His tongue danced over his yellow teeth and his palm combed frantically through the wisps of platinum jutting from his pink scalp. His eyes, the varied colors of raw meat, were wide. Searching. Panicked.

Back on the road.

I sat on a pile of naked people. Their limbs wove and clutched at me, nails digging into my legs, my chest and my shoulders. Ricky sang– *nothing left on the sidewalks… nothing*–and his voice thinned, became sharp and piercing. Syringes like finger bones jutted from his neck and arms. He leapt up on the wall of my living room, clung there, defying gravity and sanity, shrieking and spitting at me.

Back on the road.

"I have to leave," a woman whispered in my ear.

Turning, I saw Noelle push through the knot of bodies, emerging like a phoenix from the tangled torsos. Hands reached out for her, nails hooked into her skin, tore and shredded her flesh.

"I can't live like this," Noelle said. Her voice was hollow and bland. "It's not you, Mick. I don't like what I'm becoming."

I tried to say something to get her to stay, but teeth bit into my thigh and a thatch of short hair settled over my crotch. I knew that if I saw the face of the man in my lap, it would be melted, but the feeling of his mouth on me, the wet heat and dancing tongue, so perfectly attuned to my pleasure, pulled the words back into my throat.

Then, Noelle was free of the human nest. Already she faded into the air. Vanishing.

"She's history, man," Ricky squealed in a tight falsetto. "Best get back on the road. Put it behind. Put it all behind. Nothing but history. On the road, there's nothing but now and then, and *then* don't mean shit."

I woke up, panting and drenched in sweat.

And someone was turning the doorknob, trying to open my cabin door.

★   ★   ★

I called, "Hello," while climbing out of bed, rubbing the sleep and
remnants of the terrible dream from my eyes. The doorknob rattled
as if my guest was trying to tear it out of the jamb. "Hey," I called,
searching the floor for my shorts. "Ease up."

At first, I thought Faye LaMarche might have been checking the
locks or doing god knows what. Then, I figured John was back from
the hospital, perhaps a little drunk and needing to talk. Maybe Tony
died. I wasn't sure. But such reasonable explanations were knocked
away a moment later. Someone wanted in my cabin, and they weren't
waiting for me to invite them.

A hollow boom, a fist on the door, startled me so badly I nearly fell
off the bed's edge. Shorts in hand, I stood and slipped them on. Another
thunderous pounding and the snap of cracking wood filled the cabin.

"Who the fuck is it?" I yelled, sounding as pissed off as I could muster.

When no answer came, I stepped forward, then thought better of it.
Standing in the center of the room, I just looked at the door, which
suddenly held the malevolent possibility of a gun's muzzle. A chill ran
down my back, and my skin pimpled.

The hand fell again. It felt like the entire cabin shook on its foundation from the force of the blow. A thousand tiny needles of fear
jabbed into my skin, each carrying a shot of pure adrenaline. My guts
trembled violently, working their way toward my throat and my chat-
tering teeth. For all I knew, I was alone with a killer on this trail at this
river's edge. A dense wood of pine and shrub separated me from the
nearest occupied cabins, and even if those patrons of Faye's Inn heard
the battering of my door and my shouts of protest, how long would
it take them to get to me?

Too long, I decided. Of course, there was no weapon at my disposal.
No real weapon. I ran to the desk chair and hefted its inadequate
weight.

The cabin quaked with another violent punch at the door. Wood
creaked against hinges and jamb.

"You've got one fucking second to get away from that door or I'm gonna start shooting!"

The bluff felt foolish on my tongue. My only weapon was a collection of sticks that felt about as light as my laptop computer. The chair's only real damage would likely be in the form of splinters. But what choice did I have?

The lie seemed to work though. Heavy footsteps moved across the porch. Then the sound of a great weight dropping into the foliage at the cabin's edge. My guest worked his way along the side of the cabin, to the window at my back. I stepped away from the glass, gripping the chair as tightly as I could, my eyes fixed on the sheer curtain, separating me from the pane.

When the glass shattered, I leapt back a good three feet. Hands swatted at fabric amid a shower of glass. But no one came through. I did a quick calculation and figured the window stood about six feet off the ground, maybe more. The cabin itself was raised nearly three feet by support beams, likely intended to keep the shelter from flooding if the river ran high. If my guest wanted to get in, he'd have to climb.

I caught flashes of a head as the curtain whipped away from clutching fingers, but the face was impossible to discern. The attacker wore a dark mask or a cowl of long hair. Either way, he was beginning to clutch at the windowsill.

With chair raised and cocked back, I raced forward, bringing the insufficient weapon down on the gripping hands. The chair struck the fat fingers and the sill, sending an aching vibration through my hands and up my arm. Ignoring the pain, I struck again, and the fingers withdrew, though my assailant made no sound of protest. The joints in the chair, loosened by the blows, creaked when I again lifted the furniture.

Silence then. I can't say how much time passed. Seconds. Minutes. The quiet gnawed on my nerves as badly as the attack on my door. I listened for footsteps in the weeds, the squelching of mud, the snapping of twigs. During this time, I tried to imagine who might want to do me harm. Certainly the citizens of Celebration carried opinions of Isley. Perhaps those spilled over onto me. Some deranged country

boy might have decided that the witch's daddy needed some hurt, or
they'd simply heard that I had a thing for guys and that was cause
enough for a funeral. It might have been random, just some thug in
the woods, looking for a festival of pain with me as the headline act.
That's as far as my limited imagination took me. Toothless rednecks.
Inbred cannibals. The stuff of drive-in films and direct to DVD movies.

Well, I couldn't just stand there all night, holding the chair over my
head, so I used the legs to pull back the curtain and looked outside,
but nothing moved there. Letting the fabric fall, I worked my way
across the room to the switch for the overhead light and flipped it. I
set the chair down and retrieved my cell phone off of the end table.

I dialed 911. An operator came on. As I gave the woman my location and described what I believed was happening, a new sound rose.

My assailant was outside the south wall of the cabin, beyond the
boards that separated him from the head of my bed. He scraped something over the siding, drawing a line to the corner. To me, it sounded
like nails on a blackboard. It went straight to my gorge making me
gag on the words I spoke to the operator. The sound continued to the
wall on the trailside of the cabin, beneath the window there, to the
porch. I followed the progression, thinking at any minute a scythe or
some other sharp weapon would penetrate the cabin's meager skin. A
heavy step landed on the porch, and the scratching sound persisted, a
monotonous melody played over the rhythm of footsteps.

Over the siding. Across the door. Siding again.

I was seconds from losing it completely. Even the operator's voice in
my ear, so calm and soothing, struck me as the stuff of surreal terrors.
The thud of weight on the riverside of the cabin drew my eyes to the
shattered window.

I dropped the phone on the bed and reached for my trusty chair.
This time, I didn't wait for the hands to appear. I slammed the chair
against the sill until it came apart. I took the longest piece, a piece
with a jagged point and stepped toward the bed.

Out of my mind, I picked up the phone, heard the operator droning
on through the tiny speaker. I interrupted her monotone chatter with,
"This fucker's dead," then once again dropped the phone on the bed.

I stomped to the cabin door, turned the lock and stepped onto the porch. Quickly I checked the planks on either side of me to get a bead on my attacker, but he wasn't there. Just the river. Just the trail. Just the forest.

"Come on," I said, gripping the length of wood with white-knuckled force. "You want to fuck around? Let's fuck around."

My courage lasted nearly thirty seconds, right up to the moment I saw him.

He stepped from the side of the cabin with the moon-dappled river at his back. Even in the meager light, I saw enough of him to shrivel my confidence and snuff my courage.

He wore black pants, held up with matching suspenders that stretched to accommodate his bulging chest and shoulders. In the gloom, his skin appeared the color of pale dirt, but smooth, making me think he wore makeup and not muck. His face seemed to confirm this belief. Black strands of greasy hair striped with gray fell over a broad face, with a strong brow and a square jaw and no eyes at all.

Smooth unbroken sheets of skin ran from the arch of his eyebrows to his jaw line. Only dents in the flesh indicated the sockets where his eyes should have been. I told myself that I was looking at a mask or some other illusion of disfigurement but the voice died in my head the moment he moved.

He reached up and planted his hands on the porch, hoisting himself to the planks, moving more like a spider than a human being. I backed into the cabin, no longer concerned with the nature of his facade, only knowing I never wanted to look at it again. I closed and locked the door. Backed away from it as a fist again cracked against the wood. I walked into the bathroom, closed and locked that door, and knelt down, still holding the useless weapon in my hand.

12

I didn't move from my place on the bathroom floor until I heard Officer Richmond shouting for me from the porch. Sitting there, staring at the floor and occasionally looking up at a stain vaguely the shape of New York state on the wall beneath the sink, I kept my back wedged against the narrow partition of the shower with my feet against the door.

The first raps, announcing the arrival of Officer Richmond, were barely audible. They still scared the shit out of me. Then his muffled voice came through the wall, and I lifted myself from the linoleum.

"We meet again," Officer Richmond said when I opened the door. Without the reflective sunglasses, I saw that Richmond was older than I'd first thought. Deep lines ran beneath his eyes and spread out into pronounced crow's feet at the corners.

"Come on in."

"Are you okay?" he asked, surveying the wreckage in the room.

"Maybe." I was about to offer Richmond the chair when I remembered what I'd done to it. Furthermore, in my haste to arm myself, I'd neglected to remove the towel from its seat—the towel holding John and Tony's party favors. So, there was Richmond, gazing down at the broken chair, a white towel and its spilled contents, including nipple clamps and a fist-sized butt plug. "You can sit on the bed if you want to."

The officer gave me a curious look. His eyebrows arched. "Nah. I'm good," he replied.

With the bulb of latex wrapped back in the towel and the whole thing shoved into the corner, I considered explaining why I had such items in my possession, but decided that no one was going to look good at the end of the story, so I let it go. If nothing else, he'd have an interesting tale to tell his buddies at the station.

"I was asleep," I said. "I woke up about thirty minutes ago. Somebody was trying to get into the cabin."

"Was he armed?"

"I don't know," I said. "Maybe. He was using something to scrape the side of the cabin. It sounded like metal, could have been a knife."

"Well, the kids from town don't usually hang out up here. The fishermen ran 'em off enough times to get the point across. They go down river to The Hollow or into the scrub on the west side of town for their parties."

"This was no kid," I said forcefully, again picturing the eyeless face draped in dark tangles of hair.

"Can you describe him?"

"I'm not sure."

"Excuse me?"

"He might have been wearing a disguise. The light wasn't good, so it's hard to say. But I think he had a mask on, maybe wearing makeup."

"Then just tell me what you saw."

I did the best I could. Officer Richmond cocked his head to the side when I described the gray cast to the man's skin. He did it again when I mentioned the eyeless face, only that time he actually smiled.

"Amusing, is it?" I asked.

"I'm sorry," he said. "I know you've been through a shitty night, and I didn't mean to make light of it. Really. But it does look like someone from town was trying to give you a scare. From the sound of it, they did a real good job. Don't get me wrong. I'm not saying I wouldn'ta shit myself. Hell, I've seen enough of those zombie movies, damn things creep me out so bad, I'd likely-a blown the fucker's head off without so much as a warning. I will say that we don't have anyone that fits your description running around town. If the guy was seriously crippled, he's likely a drifter of some sort, and we'll catch him fast enough."

Richmond's words did nothing to alleviate my fear. If anything, they just made things worse. It was bad enough being a stranger in Celebration, but to be a target on top of it?

"What now?" I asked.

"I'm going to give the place a look over. You can come with or wait inside."

I decided to go along.

The air was thick with heat and moisture hung heavy in my lungs. The night song of crickets and frogs was still in full swing with the gurgle of the river playing a mellow rhythm beneath. With a powerful lantern, Richmond searched between the two cabins, and we both saw trampled plants and footprints. A couple of steps farther down the path, Richmond stabbed his light at the porch of Tony and John's cabin. The door stood open, a black sheet of shadow beyond.

"I closed that," I told him.

A low questioning grunt rolled in Richmond's throat. "You better wait here a minute." The officer climbed onto the porch and moved his flashlight in a quick swipe like a swordsman testing his blade. At the door he paused, ran his light up and down the jamb, presumably look- ing for signs of forced entry. He walked into the cabin, and his light climbed the far wall and then swept across the floor. Two minutes later, Richmond appeared in the doorway. "Nothing here. Place looks fine."

"You want to follow me back to my car?" he asked, stepping onto the porch. "I gotta get something."

We walked quietly for a minute. I didn't like it.

"Do you have any word on Tony?" I asked.

"The guy we pulled out of here?" Richmond asked. "Don't know. They got his heart going, and he made it to the hospital alive, and that's always a good thing when the ticker is involved, but that's about all I know."

We walked to the parking lot, Richmond killed the light from his lantern and holstered it in his belt. "Got more action out here in the last day than we've seen in the last few years."

He clearly wasn't counting the death of a young man or the suicide of one of his town's teachers.

At the car, Richmond climbed in and called up a dispatcher on the radio. He spent two minutes downloading what I'd told him to the woman on the other end of the signal, then signed off. He got out of the cruiser, locked the door and walked to the trunk where he popped the lid. Reaching in, he lifted a long tackle box from the compartment and slammed the trunk closed. "Gonna check for prints. Don't know what we'll check them against, but we should do this right."

"Sure " I said.

"You in town long?" the officer asked.

"Hard to say. Depends on a few things."

"Like your daughter?"

Embarrassed and feeling my cheeks redden, I looked away, noticing that a few fishermen had gathered on a porch across the lot. Their faces were obscured by shadows. Not so with the eager expressions pressed against windows all along the row of cabins. Finding no comfort in these curious onlookers, I turned toward the office and saw Faye LaMarche standing on the porch, smoking a cigarette and eyeing me like I'd just slept with her virgin child. (And yes, I've seen that expression used in context over the years).

So, I returned my attention to the cop and asked him how the hell he could know anything about me.

He stopped and waved a hand up and down his torso. I almost expected him to say *voila.* "Cop. Remember? I asked around about you. You're Isley's daddy. Good thing you finally took on some responsibility for her. She needs it these days." He started walking again, leaving me dumbfounded. "I imagine Noelle could have used a bit herself."

"Look, I'm not really in the mood for a lecture. It's been a tremendously fucked day."

"Wasn't lecturing," Richmond said. "Wasn't accusing either. Just stating a fact. I got a call about two weeks back, about a woman wandering around in her nightgown. It was just about half a mile up the road from here. Turned out to be Noelle Vale. She was a bit out of her head that night, and the next night, she killed herself."

"What was she doing up here?" I asked.

"Couldn't say. She wasn't too coherent when I picked her up."

"Is anything around here, besides Faye's?"

"Not a thing," Richmond said. "It's just more woods and river. Like I said, when I picked her up, Noelle was a bit confused. After about ten minutes in the car, she kind of snapped out of it but couldn't explain what she was doing. She looked embarrassed and wanted to know if she was being arrested. Poor woman." Richmond's voice turned soft

and thoughtful. "I thought quite a bit of her. Can't believe she'd just go and kill herself like that."

"But you don't know why she did it?"

"Nah," Richmond said with something close to a laugh. "Who knows why someone goes from sharp to fuzzy. The idea that it could happen to me is just about the scariest thing I can imagine. My granny had the Alzheimer's, and I used to wonder what she went through. It's got to be awful not knowing who you are, or who your kin are when they come to visit."

"But you don't think there's any connection between Sandy and Noelle do you?"

Richmond laughed. "Of course there's a connection: *your daughter*. But that doesn't mean she had anything to do with it. Just bad luck on her part, is my guess. Unfortunately, a lot of folks don't see it that way. We aren't big on coincidence down here, I suppose. But there's nothing else to explain this. Neither Sandy nor Noelle had a speck of drugs in them. Well, Noelle had the sleeping pills, but you know what I mean."

By this time in the conversation, we were back in front of Cabin 3. Richmond again released his flashlight's beam on the woods, the porch and the gloom within the cabin, taking them all in with a long sweep of the lantern. Inside, he removed a pen from his pocket used it to lift the light switch. As he worked on dusting the doorknobs and the frames, the desktop and the switch, he said nothing, except to move me out of his way when he needed to get across the room. He worked with great efficiency, and had retrieved prints from nearly a dozen different surfaces. All of these were filed in his tackle box.

Once finished with John and Tony's place, he followed me to Cabin 4 and set about dusting the doorknob while I sat on the bed and watched.

"You're a musician," Richmond announced, sweeping a brush over the handle.

"How'd you know that?"

"Still a cop," he said with a laugh. "Nah, I used to listen to Palace a lot in my hell-raising days. Had all your disks. Folks around town are kind of buzzing, and they told me you were *that* Mick Harris. We all thought that Ricky guy was the coolest thing to hit earth since Donkey Kong."

"He would have agreed with you," I said.

"Yeah," Richmond said. "He struck me as the sort. Kinda arrogant. Great voice though."

"He did have the pipes."

"He killed himself too, didn't he?"

"He did," I said. "A couple of years ago."

"Yeah. That's a shame. Like I said, great voice." He finished working over the doorknob, filed more slides in his tackle box and stood up. "That's about it."

I met him at the threshold of my cabin.

"Thanks for coming out," I said.

"That's my job. You got someplace else you could stay for the night?"

"Hadn't thought about it," I said. "But I'm not staying here."

"Fair enough. There's a Quality Inn out on the interstate, about two miles up from the hospital."

★　　★　　★

Following Richmond out of the parking lot, I checked the rearview mirror. There was a cold black moment when I felt certain I saw a man, a large gray man, standing several feet inside the tree line between two cabins. After the jolt of fear passed, I realized it was nothing more than a canoe leaned up against a tree, drying out from a day's use.

13

The Quality Inn proved adequate, and it was really the kind of place I should have checked into upon arriving in Celebration. I imagine Aaron Dalfour thought Faye's was in some way more charming. Who could say? When I woke the next morning, I realized that I'd been in such a hurry to get away from the fishing cabins, I hadn't brought any of my toiletries, and I'd left my laptop on the small desk. Though certainly willing to leave some shampoo and soap–hell, even the limited wardrobe I'd brought on the trip–behind, I wouldn't last long without my computer, not to mention the cord to charge my cell phone. I'd have to go back before the day was out.

But first, I had an appointment to meet my daughter. We needed to get her house fixed up, needed to remove the signs of vandalism and make the place look like a home again. So first thing, I drove out to the house on Amaryllis Street.

Isley sat on the porch, staring at the street. I wandered up the walk, carrying a tall Styrofoam cup of coffee.

"Morning," I said.

"Morning." Her attitude didn't seem to have changed much.

Inside my head, I let loose a deep, loud sigh. After my encounter with that crazy fuck the night before, my conversation with Officer Richmond and almost no sleep, I just didn't have it in me to grapple with Isley's angst. I put the cup on the porch railing. Back at the rental car, I popped the trunk and hoisted the white plastic bag holding the sandpaper, brush and primer. With my free hand, I retrieved the can of paint. On my second trip, I grabbed the drop cloth.

Isley watched me through narrowed lids. Her mouth was drawn tight.

That's right, Honey, I'm still evil, I thought. *I came down to Arkansas to fuck with your head and your life. Just some middle-aged has-been looking to make points with a mistake he made seventeen years ago.*

Since I was awake most of the previous night, alarmed by every damn sound in the motel courtyard my determination to stay in

Celebration met a worthy adversary in my sense of futility. Add to that the absolute strangeness of the events that befell me since checking into Faye's Inn, and my resolve was nearly in retreat.

None of it made any sense, but I was getting the feeling that Celebration's welcome wagon was overflowing with freaks, and the only things in their baskets of goodies were apple-wrapped razor blades and arsenic frosted cookies.

I must have been completely zoned out, because I didn't notice Isley was off of the bench and walking toward me. Her face seemed softer just then, prettier. Maybe it was a trick of the light.

"I can't stay," she said. "Mrs. Wertimer is having one of her bad days, and she didn't want to let me out of the house in the first place."

"Okay," I said.

"I'll give you the key to the front door," she said. "But it's just to let the window guy in. I hope I can trust you not to go snooping around."

She delivered her misgivings awkwardly, as if she were trying to sound more adult. It almost made me smile, but that would have assured me another ass chewing, so I told her that I would let the man in, paint the door, and lock up when we were through. She hesitated for a moment, then pulled a key from her ring.

"Can you bring this back to me?" she asked. "Back to the Wertimer's?"

"Sure."

"Do you know where they live?"

"No."

She told me, giving me somewhat vague directions, the kind you gave someone who was familiar with a place. I paid attention, nodded my head. She told me the address. I repeated in my head a few times until I was certain it was memorized.

"I'll see you later," I said.

"Maybe we could talk a little," Isley said. "I mean I know we should talk."

"I'd like that. We can go someplace for lunch or take a drive. You decide."

She tried to smile then, but the cut of her lips was made with a dull blade, ragged and unfinished. Isley walked down the stairs and along the drive. I watched her until she disappeared behind a house on the corner. My heart beat fast, giving me a sense of elation. A nighttime of worries fell from my shoulders.

I turned to the job of painting the door, and saw a blond boy staring at me through the porch railing.

Though a good distance away, the kid startled me. Only half of his head and part of his torso were visible. He stood against the wall of the house next door. The corner of Isley's house and the rise of the porch blocked most of him from my view. Shade draped him. Long strands of greasy blond hair hung over his brow, nearly obscuring the one eye visible to me. His chest was bare.

"Hey," I said and lifted a hand in a half wave.

The kid hunkered down like a crouching animal. His face pinched tight as if tasting raw lemon. "Jody Mayram," he said, his voice little more than a growl.

Upon hearing that name, seemingly the origin of a mystery, I turned for the stairs. I hit the lawn running and picked up speed, trying to keep the kid in my sights, but the side of the neighbor's house played like a bad film through the porch spindles. By the time I got to the grass alley between the houses, the kid was gone.

Movement from above caught my eye. I thought I saw something disappear over the eaves of the house, a squirrel, a bird, a little boy's foot.

Since this last wasn't possible, I put the thought away and turned back for the porch.

Little brat, I thought.

Jody Mayram.

There was something bad about that name. Every time I thought about it, and the couple of times I'd heard it spoken aloud, it struck the wrong note with me, leaving me cold and off balance. That name had meaning, and it was supposed to *mean* something to me, though I didn't have a clue what that might be. Despite the dumb ass nature of my thoughts, they came on pretty strong. After all, Tony said the name at lunch and nearly died a few hours later. I said it myself while clearing out Tony and John's cabin. Later that night, a deformed visitor had paid a visit and about broke the cabin walls down around my head.

Jody Mayram.

The name clung to me like sweat as I returned to the front of the house.

14

The window guy fell distinctly into the classification of "slammable."

His name was Sidney Tierney. He stood over six feet tall and was so broad through the shoulders, he didn't climb out of the truck, so much as disgorge from it. His skin was black and taught with a gleam of youth about the cheeks, though he could have been my age or a few years older. His features and the twinkle in his eye were so striking, I found myself flustered. My brain had already gone into retreat, assuring me that the chances a guy like Sidney swung my way were next to nil. I'd already had my small-gay-world moment with John and Tony, and the law of averages suggested I'd met my quota for the foreseeable future, even if I spent the next year in Celebration.

"So, you're the famous guy," Sidney said even before introducing himself.

"Word travels fast around here. Most people just call me Mick, though."

His face broke into a winning smile, and he shook my hand quickly before placing his palms on his hips like a superhero as he surveyed the front of the house. "That the only one broken?"

It never occurred to me to check the rest of the house.

"I think so."

"Well, we'll give the place a once over. I'm pretty caught up on things around town, so I can give you some time."

I was very glad to hear that.

We stood there, looking at one another. It was an awkward moment, but a good one. His brown eyes sparkled in the morning light and his lips, full and turned upward in a pleasant smile, were just mesmerizing. I caught myself eye-groping and forced my attention back to his face. This vertical ping pong happened a couple more times, and I knew I better get moving before making a complete ass of myself, or worse yet, pissing the guy off.

"Let's give it a look," I said.

Sidney followed me to the side of the house, where the blond boy had stood minutes before. I peered up at the eaves of the neighbor's place, imagining I might catch the dirty kid glaring over the edge of the roof, but he wasn't there. The windows here were intact. We walked to the back.

"Are you always this quiet?" Sidney asked.

"Sorry. I'm not a morning person."

"Still, burning the night down, hm?"

I laughed at that, blushed. "Burn the Night Down" was one of Palace's least ingenious, yet most successful tunes. A typical party anthem with three chords and a chorus that got stuck in my brain every time I thought about it. God, I hated that song, and I generally got really annoyed with anyone who brought it up—and a lot of people brought it up—but I didn't mind Sidney making the predictable joke.

"That was stupid wasn't it?" he asked. "I bet you hear that kind of thing a lot."

"Some," I said. "It's flattering."

"I promised myself I wouldn't say anything stupid."

"Compared to some of the shit I've heard, that's Einstein. Really. No big deal."

So, we stood quietly again, looking at the back of Isley's house. The windows were dirty, but intact.

I wasn't used to the nerve jangling that standing next to Sidney gave me. God knew there was no way for me to claim inexperience. For years, beautiful women were a given and were no more intimidating than a mint on a pillow. Hell, they were written into the job description. After I came out, it became clear very quickly that you didn't even have to be a rock star to rack up bedroom numbers; you just had to have the internet, the interest, and the energy.

"Looks like the one in front is it," I said, butterflies doing a full-on tribal dance in my belly.

We walked to the alley on the other side of the house. The windows here were also undamaged, so we kept walking and ended up at the foot of the porch stairs. Sidney climbed the stairs and crossed to the broken window without speaking. I went to the door and unlocked it.

A blast of air, musty and hot, rolled out. I walked into the entry, looked around. Intending to keep my promise to Isley I went no further, though an urge to see how Noelle and my daughter had lived pulled and worked at me.

"This won't take long," Sidney said at my shoulder.

"Take your time. I've got to paint this door, so I'll be around for a bit."

With that, he turned away and headed to his truck for tools or gloves or something. I didn't care. I just liked watching him walk.

My only long-term partner, Glen , broke up with me because he thought I was "disconnected." He hated that I spent so much time on the computer and almost no time out in the world meeting "real people." I told him that the more "real people" I met, the less I wanted to be around them. Problem was, I'd met very few "real" people over the years. The people surrounding me through my early adult life were anything but. Most were like Ricky Blaine: ambitious, plastic, and deluded. I had no other frame of reference.

Besides, it never would have worked with Glen. He'd hated Edwin, my only "real person" friend. Glen thought Edwin was crude. Edwin's response was simple enough:

"He'd like me better if he saw my dick."

I told myself time and again that I wanted a normal life. I wanted to work and come home and have dinner and go to movies and sit in a recliner and share "game nights" with other couples and fix the garbage disposal and walk some fictional mutt around my neighborhood saying "Hey Frank, how're those tulip bulbs coming along?" and imagined adopting a couple of kids, so one day I'd have grandkids sitting on my lap asking me what life used to be like.

And what would grandpa say?

Well kids, when I wasn't too tweaked out on blow, I'd randomly fuck whatever I could get my hands on. Sometimes two or three or eight different people a night. I've been arrested for drunk and disorderly a few times, but never got snatched for possession, and I'm pretty proud of that. One time, grandpa made a complete ass of himself in front of Robert Plant, who was so disgusted, he called him a "Fucking wank." And did you know that grandpa once threw up backstage at the Grammy Awards? Now, how about that!

John Palmer had been right. Normal was not in the cards for me. I imagine that's why I craved it.

Thinking myself into a rather low place, I painted the door. I didn't bother with the sandpaper. It wasn't necessary. The primer covered the pink stain—*witch*—just fine. While it dried, I stood next to the railing and watched Sidney clearing shards of glass from the window frame, delicately placing them in a broad, wooden box. I lit a cigarette. Sidney turned quickly to the sound of the striking match.

"Could I have one of those?" he asked.

"You just quit, didn't you?" I said. I'd seen that look a dozen times, the vaguely desperate and shamed expression of a backsliding nicotine addict.

"Sort of."

"I shouldn't," I said, but Sidney knew I was teasing.

"Now, you're just being an asshole. Give me one."

We smoked together, both of us leaning on the rail. My nerves had settled some. I didn't feel quite so awkward.

"I imagine you're a Celebration native," I said.

"Yep. I grew up right over there," he said, pointing to the west. "About five blocks down."

"Is this the family business?"

"Pretty much."

"Do you like it?"

"Other jobs suck more."

"I can think of several," I said.

"Don't get me wrong. I don't lie in bed at night dreaming of being a doctor or lawyer somewhere in the big city. Most days go by smooth as a frog's butt and it doesn't even occur to me that I might be missing out on something. I'd like to travel, I guess."

Sidney stated all of this matter-of-factly. No drama. No romance. He simply spoke the words.

For the briefest of moments, I had the impulse to say something really stupid, something like, *I could show you the world*. Fortunately, I wasn't so exhausted, frazzled or infatuated that I let it slip out. Instead, in trying to be funny I said something equally stupid.

"Well, they do have these things called airports now."

"We can't all be rock stars," Sidney said. His voice sounded cooler. "Some of us have to worry about things like food and the mortgage."

"I'm sorry," I said. "That was a stupid thing to say."

"Nah," Sidney said, shaking his head. "You're right. The thing is, I keep talking myself out of going. There's no reason not to, really. But something will come up in the shop, or the town has some festival or someone's getting married or having a birthday, and I just get cold feet, figure it's best to stay put. Besides, I don't want to go alone. My friends are all married. They work and have families, so they can't just up and leave."

"Staying put isn't so bad. I've been doing it for a lot of years now."

"But you've already seen those things."

"Correction," I said. "I have been in a lot of places, but was generally too stupid or too wasted to actually see anything. It just wasn't the way things worked. But yeah, I lived in Paris for a few months, spent a lot of time in London and I used to go to Mykonos when I wanted a tan."

"Poor isolated baby." Sidney bumped me with his arm. A pleasant shiver ran from my elbow to the back of my neck.

"All I'm saying is that I don't do that anymore. The last five or six years, I've hardly left Denver."

"You probably have more responsibilities now."

"Less actually."

"No family?"

"No. Well, not in Denver."

"Noelle told me you were seeing some guy."

Sidney invoked Noelle's name casually, but it struck a chord. I felt tense. Uneasy.

"You knew Noelle?"

"Sure. My niece used to babysit for Isley all the time, besides it's a small ass place. Everybody doesn't know everybody, but we all know the same people. Is there a problem?"

"No, sorry." But something *was* bothering me. I just couldn't figure out what that something was. "As for having a partner, I did. Didn't quite get it right, and that's after two marriages."

"I know that tune," Sidney said. "Next week will by my two year anniversary. Well, the anniversary of my divorce. It's a very special day for me."

"Will there be cake?"

"Of course. Everybody likes cake. Why don't you come by and…" Sidney's face lit up. "I almost went to a very bad joke. I'd better get back to work."

I asked him to hold on a second. Conversational subtlety was never a strong point of mine, and most people took it for what it was: the residual trait of a crude upbringing, combined with little or no patience for games. I hated the mating dance shit–all of that coy and suggestive preamble, as if sex were some grand prize at the end of a trail of eggshells. Generally, I approached eggshells with the same delicacy I'd afford cockroaches, so while Sidney may have gotten his wires crossed (or I had) I wasn't about to tiptoe around the funda-mental issue: "Are you flirting?" I asked. "I mean are you gay, or am I totally off base here?"

"You're not off base," he said.

Relieved, and to a large degree thrilled, I smiled. But Sidney's admission invited a needling suspicion. Coincidences, even incredibly unlikely (and often awkward) ones happened. Fate was a trickster with a taste for human embarrassment, and it had thrown some fucking unbelievable twists my way, like the time I served jury duty with my second wife, eight years after our divorce in a different county and different state, and she didn't even know who I was, or pretended not to. Considering her access to an ample supply of undiluted bitch, I never thought to press the issue. But I'd been in Celebration for two days, and I'd managed to rent a cabin next to one–admittedly sporadic–gay couple and here I was facing another member of the brethren. The odds were against this kind of coincidence. They would have been against it anywhere but Key West, Palm Springs, or New Orleans, and yet it had happened. Suddenly, paranoia slid in to replace my thrill.

"And now you look upset," Sidney noted.

"What?" I asked. "No, it's nothing. I'm just a little surprised is all."

"You don't think Arkansas grows a sissy here and there?"

"Oh, I'm sure it does," I replied. "I just assumed they grew them for export."

Sidney barked a charming laugh and shook his head. "Mostly, you're right, especially out here in the sticks. I told you about my divorce, but I may have forgotten to mention the kids—two of 'em, to be specific. Angie, she's my youngest, is about to start the sixth grade and her older brother, Stephen, starts high school next week. So while Celebration isn't exactly a hotbed of action, just about nothing is going to pry me away from here until the kids head off to college."

"Makes sense to me," I said. "How are things with your ex-wife?"

"Did I mention we'd be serving cake?"

"That bad?"

"Baptist bad," Sidney said. "Rose, that's my ex, is pretty sure prayer can fix anything, and if it doesn't work out that way, it's because you aren't praying hard enough."

"And she thought God could cure your unwholesome urges?"

"To the best of my knowledge, she doesn't know a thing about my urges, she just knew I didn't have any left for her."

"So your family doesn't know?"

Sidney shook his head. "I won't let this spill out over my kids just yet. Rose already thinks I'm deep fried evil, so there'd be no loss there." He pointed at the still-wet primer on the door and nodded. "Tolerance isn't one of the early life lessons kids get around here. Me, I can move and not have to deal with it. The country is full of broken windows, so I could land just about anywhere, but Angie and Stephen, well, they'd have to stay with it, and I can't do that to them right now."

A hundred speeches about the value of coming out and being honest tangled up in my head, but I left them there. Sidney knew his environment better than I ever would, and from what I'd witnessed his assessment of community understanding was about dead on. Naturally, he took my silence as condemnation.

"You think that's bullshit right?"

"I think it's your business," I replied. "I've known you for about thirty minutes, so it seems a little premature to start telling you how to live your life, you know?"

"Then you sure as hell aren't Baptist."

"Sure as hell," I agreed.

"Any chance you'd like to grab some coffee after we finish up here?" Sidney asked. "My morning is relatively light."

"I have to meet Isley," I told him. I was grateful to have an excuse, but only because a lingering suspicion gnawed at me. Unlikelier things than meeting a few gay men in a small town had happened, and there wasn't a single thing about Sidney's character that made me doubt his sincerity, except perhaps for him being a little too friendly, but I felt that I teetered on the edge of a conspiracy, and any step I took had to be cautious. "I'll be in town for a few days, maybe longer. Rain check?"

"You bet," Sidney said, looking disappointed and even embarrassed. "You know where to find me," he said. Then he walked off the porch to toss his cigarette into the street before getting back to work.

15

The Wertimers lived in a plantation house on the east side of town. Even among the homes of Celebration's privileged, it made an impression. The house had been painted recently, and its white skin gleamed in the morning light. The reflected sun surrounded the house in a hazy glow, and though I'd never seen a house with an aura before, damn if the Wertimer place didn't look like the divine ghost of Tara.

I grasped the knocker, a ring clutched in the jaws of a brass lion that looked extremely pissed off. Knocked three times and waited.

When the door opened, I was greeted by a squat man with a bald head and wire framed spectacles. Though he wore khaki slacks and a white shirt, he made it instantly clear—by his manner and his posture—that he was the Wertimer's butler.

"Good morning," I said.

"Morning."

I tried to step inside but the crisp gentleman pushed his hand forward and jammed his palm at my chest. He locked his elbow and gave me a nudge backward. The hard disdain greeting me at the Wertimer's made it apparent I would have had a better time going out for coffee with Sidney when he'd suggested it.

"Can I help you?" the butler asked.

"I'm here to see Isley. She's expecting me."

"And yet, I doubt she has permission to be expecting you."

"Yeah," I said. "I guess she forgot to tell me about visiting hours."

"Wait," the butler said and closed the door. I looked over the neighborhood, noticed a kid on a bike riding in slow, tight circles down the street. Further down the block, someone was trying to start up a lawn mower.

The door opened about the time the lawnmower kicked into life. A woman with a plastic-looking helmet of black hair and a necklace with a chunk of gold dangling at its center the size of my pinkie finger stood with the butler in the foyer. Whereas he looked at me as if I'd just been caught vandalizing the property, she wore a sparkling grin. She fingered the necklace at her throat and looked at me with joyous wonderment.

This had to be Mrs. Wertimer, and Mrs. Wertimer was medicated to the gills. Aaron Dalfour had said she was a bit of a town eccentric, but about three seconds of looking at her convinced me Earth was just a rest area on a rather extended trip she was taking through space.

"Do we know you?" Mrs. Wertimer asked.

"I'm here to see Isley."

"Are you?"

"He doesn't have an…" the butler began, but Mrs. Wertimer's hand flapped like a wounded bird in his face to silence him.

"It's all right, Lance."

I heard his name and started to laugh. The guy looked like a polished thug, Cagney in a later role. I could see her calling him Dutch, Max or maybe even Seamus, but Lance? He didn't appreciate my amusement and let me know it with his glower.

"Are you one of her gentlemen from town?" Mrs. Wertimer asked brightly, taking some great pleasure in the question and what it implied.

"Is Isley in?"

"I imagine so. Lance, is Isley in?"

"Yes, Ma'am."

The news thrilled her. Her smile broadened, and she brought her hands together in a silent clap at her breast. "Wonderful. Isley is in. But we can't just let her run off with every man that comes to the door, now can we? We won't tolerate that behavior here."

Hatred at first sight was a rarity for me, but it was building up pretty fast with this prescription-addled hag.

"I am Mrs. Darrell David Wertimer," she said expansively, extending a vascular hand with pencil thin fingers and perfect, pointed nails.

I touched the hand. Tried to smile. Checked on Lance.

"And you are…?" she asked.

"Mick Harris," I said.

The name hit a nerve with both Lance and his employer. The butler went absolutely rigid. Mrs. Wertimer turned her head coyly to the side to peer at me through sweeping eyelashes.

"Are you?" she asked. "Well. Well. You're not quite what we pictured, are you? We expected someone more… oh, what's the word? Flamboyant."

It was Lance's turn to smile.

"Sorry to disappoint you."

"Well, you must come in. Lance, show our guest into the salon. We'll take coffee there. You go with Lance, Mr. Harris. We'll join you shortly."

I wasn't exactly clear on who this *we* the pill-popping loon was talking about, but I imagined I'd find out soon enough. In the meantime, I followed the blocky Lance into an opulent room that looked radioactive.

The place was awash in light. Gilt frames covered the walls. The first I noticed wrapped a six foot mirror over the sculpted white marble fireplace mantel; another, a ten-foot landscape painting of a field during harvest; and another, a portrait of an old woman with a bun of white hair. Across the room, a larger mirror, this one easily twelve feet tall and framed in mahogany clutched the wall behind something truly amazing—the Wertimer's piano.

A Boersendorfer concert grand jutted from the corner like a shimmering black pond. The instrument was exquisite, and it pulled at me, insisting that my fingers run along its keys, though my skill level as a pianist could never do it justice. I could bang out blues and jazz riffs and fake my way through some of the less complicated classical passages, but that instrument had been designed for virtuosos. And, of course, for people wealthy enough to simply have one sitting around.

The tables and couches were either Louis XIV or inspired by the design. I imagined some, if not all, of the furniture was authentic. The room was amazing. I mean, *Architectural Digest* hot, but someone needed to investigate the proper use of light.

The table lamps and the chandelier were all on, and cast off eye-burning radiance, coating the antique sofas and tables in a harsh, unflattering glare. The room was without shadows, even under the furniture. Lance's smooth head caught several rays from the chandelier and the twinkling shards of light bounced at me while he guided me to a sofa and pointed at the crimson cushions as if I couldn't figure out what to do with the thing.

After watching me sit, Lance took two steps away and folded his hands over his crotch and stared. His eyes were gray and not in the flecked color mix that could look grayish in the proper light. No, his eyes were absolutely smooth bits of concrete, flat and hard and unwavering. What amazed me most about this situation was the sheer volume of hostility pouring off the man. It was as bright and bathing as the room's lights.

Mrs. Wertimer returned a couple of minutes later. As she entered, Lance broke out of his stance and left through a white door in the corner.

"There we are," Mrs. Wertimer said as if explaining something. "Much better now, aren't we? You'll have to forgive Lance. He's very protective. Did you know, he once snapped a man's neck? Right here in this room? He really is a treasure. Thank God for Lance, don't you think?"

"Sure."

"And he protects Isley now, too."

"Does he?"

"Oh he's not fucking her if that's what you're thinking. He keeps his fingers out of that stink, I assure you."

Stunned by the remark, I almost laughed in nervous disgust, but saw enough insanity in Mrs. Wertimer's expression to keep silent. I just sat there under the baking lights, dull rage simmering in the pit of my stomach and feeling an intense need to get Isley away from these people. Even if she weren't my daughter, I could not, with any conscience, allow a child to remain in this house.

"No, Lance is just here for our safety," Mrs. Wertimer went on. "We feel safe with him."

"I'm glad," I said. "Now, can I see my daughter please?"

Having said the words, I felt a greater sense of control. As Isley's father, I had a right to see her. I had a responsibility. I wasn't just some guy requesting her time.

"Oh, now you want to be a father," Mrs. Wertimer said. "What a very nice idea. And how does that work exactly? You soil some innocent girl and leave her alone with child. And then what, Mr. Harris? After sixteen or seventeen years, you decide you might like to give fatherhood a whirl?"

"That's none of your business."

"But it is," she said. "We are Isley's legal guardians, Mr. Harris, and we take that responsibility very seriously. Do you understand that?"

Lance came back into the room, carrying a tray with a silver coffee service. He set it down on the table between myself and Mrs. Wertimer, stepped back two paces, crossed his hands again and stared. I gave him a more serious appraisal this time, and saw the hard blocks of muscle on his chest and his thick arms, and it became clear that he could easily snap a man's neck if he put his mind to it.

He was also big enough to beat the shit out of my cabin and put a serious scare into me.

I tried picturing Lance in the make-up and wig he would have needed to pull off the previous night's performance, but couldn't do it. Either the costume had been completely effective, or I was looking at a different man.

"Coffee?" Mrs. Wertimer asked. Lance stepped forward and in four quick motions prepared a cup for Mrs. Wertimer. She blinked, stroked her necklace and waited for me to answer.

"Please," I said. "Black will be fine."

Lance grudgingly poured me a cup, set it heavily on the table, then he returned to his sentinel position at Mrs. Wertimer's side. She kept staring at me. Her gaze probed, as if she held her finger over a button that would send electric current through me, and she searched my face for an excuse to press it. I rewound the conversation until I thought I knew what information she was looking for. Then, I lied.

"Noelle, Isley's mother, wanted to live in Celebration. My job wouldn't allow that, and so we agreed to go our separate ways."

"Really?" Mrs. Wertimer said. "That's not the story we heard at all, and I must say it's not nearly as interesting as the story Isley tells." Amused, Mrs. Wertimer lifted her coffee cup and chuckled.

I felt no need to argue out the story of my life with some highbrow dope horse. Besides, she was just messing with my head, playing a stupid game to amuse herself. I was a toy, a distraction, something to fiddle with until a new entertainment came along.

"I don't know what you've heard, and I don't really care. I'm here to see my daughter. Would you let her know I'm here?"

"We can't help but wonder, why after all of this time, you've come for her? Have you failed so terribly at making a life of your own? Do you actually think that after all of this time she's still a part of you? Odd. Over the years, I imagine you've flushed more significant bits and pieces of yourself down toilets. Do you want those pieces back too?"

"Fuck this," I stood up.

Before I knew exactly what was happening, Lance was in my face, his hands on my chest. Behind him Mrs. Wertimer glared with curiosity and contempt. She scowled and petted the necklace at her throat.

"Back off," I told the butler. His face remained blankly rigid.

"We've seen what she does to people, Mr. Harris. Mr. Wertimer is strong, but he's only human. Even he can't fight her stink. It's all over the house. Do you smell it? Can you smell the evil she leaves in her path? It's sickening."

"Isley!" I called. I stepped to the right to get around Lance, and he adjusted his position, keeping himself between his employer and me. "I'm getting her out of here."

"And we may call the police to arrest you for kidnapping. Personally, I can't think of anything I'd like more than to have the house rid of her stench, but Mr. Wertimer might not feel the same."

"Isley!"

I stepped forward into Lance's palms, twisted left and then bolted right. In the foyer, I peered up the stairs, called my daughter's name again. A thick arm went around my neck, another looped under my armpit, and with a flashing flex of the muscles, Lance had me immobile. Through our shirts, I could feel his heart beat against my back.

He once snapped a man's neck.

"Thank you so much for coming by," Mrs. Wertimer called from the salon. "We really must do this again."

The arm at my throat tightened. My head grew light, and then I was being dragged backward. Struggling and kicking, I nearly lost my balance, but Lance was more than strong enough to keep me upright. His restraint of my shoulder vanished, the door opened with a tickle of warm air. My chest heaved, trying to get oxygen past the bicep grinding into my throat, and the foyer grew fuzzy and blurred.

Then, I was falling. The concrete path stopped me, but it wasn't kind. My skull hit the poured rock, and I caught a glimpse of Lance walking back inside, closing the door as the scene dislocated into three topsy-turvy pictures before reforming into a single image of the front of the house.

Once I gained my footing, breathing deeply over a pained trachea, I stumbled away from the plantation house. The morning sun still blasted the structure; the Wertimer house still wore its aura, now made more pronounced by my rattled brain. On the sidewalk, I took in a few deep breaths, rested my hands on my knees until I felt a bit of the dizziness pass.

Then Isley said, "We'd better hurry. That crazy old bitch is probably calling the cops."

★   ★   ★

"*Where* are we going?" I asked, slamming the car door and jamming the key in the ignition.

"It doesn't matter."

"Are you okay?" I asked. I couldn't have been more serious. If Mrs. Wertimer and her guard dog, Lance, were Aaron's idea of "no problem," then Darrell Wertimer must have been a complete monster. "Have they hurt you?"

"No," she said, curling her legs under her in the passenger seat and staring out the window. I gunned the engine and raced away from the big white colonial. "I'd heard all about them growing up, so it's not like I was surprised or anything. Brenda seems to be getting most of Darrell's attention these days."

"There are other girls in there?" I asked, incredulous and near rage.

"Just one. But I think Brenda actually likes it there. She's about as stable as Chernobyl."

"Christ, how do people like that get custody of a dog, let alone children?"

"You don't know the worst of it."

"What do you mean?"

"Some of the kids at school say that Mr. Wertimer makes movies in the basement. Brenda might be involved in those, but she won't talk about it. Totally gross stuff. They say that a bunch of the old money men watch the movies, sometimes join in. I've never seen any of those old freaks in the house late at night, but that doesn't mean they aren't there."

"Did they ever… ?"

"No, but I know he's got a key to my bedroom. Luckily, the bathroom has a bolt lock, and he couldn't get through without making a major racket. I think the perv is too hung up on appearing proper to break the door down, so I sleep in the tub. He's made some comments about it, so I know he's been in my room at night. I figure he'll probably just have Lance take the lock off one of these days."

"And the police won't do anything about it?"

"Guess not," Isley said. "That, or no one has bothered to tell them. The judge is Darrell's cousin, so my guess is, even if someone called the cops and they actually cared, it wouldn't go very far."

"I don't want you going back there."

"Gee. Really? That's so human of you. But considering you have no control over the police or courts in this town, I probably *will* be going back there."

I wove through the streets of Celebration, working my way back to the freeway. Isley sat staring out the window, chewing on her thumbnail

and squirming every few minutes to get comfortable. Though I had
no clear plan, I knew we needed to be far out of the city limits for a
while, away from the local law enforcement, until I could figure out
how to proceed.

After thirty minutes a dense forest of pine rolled up on either side
of the rental car. I drove through the shadows. Long patches of silence
punctuated our trip, and I found myself unable to start a conversation.
For my part, there was just too damn much I didn't know. Who was
the girl in the seat next to me? I wanted to know about every birthday,
every Christmas, every boyfriend and school outing. Was she a good
student? What were her interests? What was her mother like, *really* like,
in the years after we'd met? Did Noelle ever marry? I wanted their
entire history in just a few moments, but I couldn't ask a single question.

Seeing me light a cigarette, Isley said, "I need one of those." Before
I could say anything, she had the pack in her hands and was fishing
for a Marlboro. She lit up quickly.

"You shouldn't smoke."

"Got a mirror?" The sarcasm was rich in her voice.

"Just because I do it… Christ, never mind. You have any brilliant
ideas about how to keep you out of that place. Mine all involve
firearms."

"You're rich, just keep driving. We can stay in hotels for a few
months until I'm eighteen."

The sarcasm remained, but I sensed she was also nearly serious about
the suggestion. "I'm not rich. Not that kind of rich."

"Blew it all on drugs and boys?"

"If that's what you want to think. Besides, I'm not thrilled about
the idea of having a federal warrant out on my head."

"You've been arrested before."

"Knock it off, okay?"

"Whatever. I'm hungry."

And there at least was a problem I could do something about.

★   ★   ★

Finding a restaurant wasn't as easy as I'd expected. I exited the freeway several times, only to find myself deeper in forest with no towns in sight, despite signs indicating otherwise. Finally, I pulled into the gravel lot of a small cottage that advertised French cuisine under the name *Maison Dupuis.*

We beat the lunch crowd, so Isley and I were escorted through a small empty dining room, with etchings of country homes framed on the walls and antique kerosene lanterns hanging from the rafters above. Dried flower arrangements poked out of tin holders fastened to the walls. The place smelled of smoke, old wood and garlic.

"I just wanted a grilled cheese," Isley said, looking uncomfortable.

"I'm sure they can make one for you here. The French are all about cheese."

Fortunately, the waiter agreed to instruct the chef on making the sandwich and took my order for coffee. Once the waiter left, I leaned across the table.

"Can you please tell me what's been going on here?" I asked.

"I don't know."

"Then at least tell me you had nothing to do with that Winchester kid and your mother." She gave me a look of wounded outrage, eyes slit, lips tight. "I can't help you if I don't know what happened."

"You can't help anyway. Mom's dead."

"Was she acting strangely before it happened?" I remembered what officer Richmond told me about Noelle wandering south of town, about her going into the river. Certainly Isley, having lived with the woman in the weeks leading up to her death, had noticed something.

"She barely spoke to me," Isley said. "After Sandy, she just kind of closed up and spent a lot of time in her room. I figured she blamed me for what happened to him."

"Do you know what happened?"

She shook her head and looked at the folded napkin on the table. "We went down the river to the Hollow for a picnic and had a really nice time. His mom made us chicken and salad. Sandy brought some wine he got from his parents' cellar. It was nice. You know? But that night, he died. His family wouldn't speak to me at all. Pretty soon, no one was speaking to me. Even my best friend, Gloria, froze me out. They all blamed me for what happened to Sandy. I think even mom blamed me."

Isley's sandwich arrived, and she pulled a piece of crust off the edge, twirled a string of melted cheese around it and popped it in her mouth. She chewed slowly, keeping her eyes on the plate.

"It's like she became someone else," Isley whispered finally. "I mean, sometimes she'd look at me like she didn't know who I was. She'd go out at night, sometimes all night and then show up in the morning covered in mud and needles, and she looked like she'd been crying. She just cried all the time, and I didn't know what to do."

"Did Noelle have a history of… Was she upset a lot?"

"God, listen much?" Isley asked angrily. "I told you, it was like she was someone else. Before Sandy died, she was fine. She was even pretty cool as far as parents go, but something happened, and I just sat there and watched it."

"Did you find her?"

Isley nodded her head slowly, then just stared at her plate for a moment. I told her I was sorry, and that I knew it was difficult for her, but I pressed for details. Understandably, she didn't want to relive that particular nightmare, but whatever had come to claim Sandy Winchester, and maybe even her mother, wasn't through yet.

"That night, I fixed dinner, because mom was in one of her moods. She sat in her room most of the day, staring out the window. I came in to check on her a lot, asked if she needed anything but she just shook her head and kept looking out the window. Around four, I went in and asked if there was anything special she wanted for dinner and she said no. But she asked me to sit on the bed, and we talked for the first time in over a week. We talked about Sandy, and she apologized for being such a 'ditz.' That's how she put it. She told me everything was going to be okay, and I was so happy to see her acting normal, I just started crying, because things were bad, but at least I had my mom back.

"That's when she told me about you," Isley said. "Whenever I asked about my dad before, she told me he was a businessman who traveled a lot. She said he wasn't the kind of man who would make a good father."

Isley looked up at me for my reaction to that. I have no idea if the extent of my heartbreak showed on my face. I felt it, but I can't imagine what my expression said at that moment.

"Sorry," Isley said. "That's just what she told me."

"It's okay. Go on."

"Then she pulled my birth certificate out of the drawer of her desk and showed me your name, Michael Harris. And she gave me one of your CDs, pointed to a picture of you on the back. She told me that it was her decision to raise me alone. She didn't blame you. She really didn't. But I was mad. I was mad at her for not telling me, and… mad about other stuff. But at least I knew. And it really seemed to help her, too. She apologized for lying to me, and she smiled then. I hadn't seen her smile in so long, I forgot about being angry for a while.

"Then she told me everything was going to be okay."

After saying that, Isley's eyes began to tear. She bit on her lower lip and looked down at her plate. I reached across the table and placed my hand on hers. Immediately, I felt her tense under my touch, but she didn't pull away.

"I had a lot of questions. I wanted to know where you guys met, and what happened, and why you never came to see me. She told me that you did once, when I was a little girl. She said you parked in front of the house, but she chased you away. She wouldn't tell me why. Mom said we'd talk all about it in the morning, and if I wanted to call you then, I could. She said it was all going to be okay again and again, like suddenly all of our problems were solved.

"Then she got that kind of weird look in her eyes, like she didn't know who I was. I left her alone and went to my room to listen to the CD and think. After a couple of hours, I went down to fix dinner. We barely said anything while we ate. She just kind of jabbed at her food. I tried to talk to her, but she just said, 'everything is going to be okay.' After dinner, I went back to my room, and I put the CD on again and listened to it for hours, wondering if I could hear your voice in the background somewhere, wondering if I'd know it, and I started writing you a letter. It was mean and angry, but I just kept writing it while the CD played. I fell asleep before it was done."

Tears were in her voice as she spoke. I kept it together as best I could, though my impulse was to pour out every detail of how I'd tried to be a part of her life. The letters I wrote. The phone calls that Noelle cut off with a terse, "Don't call again, Mick." The trust fund I established in Isley's name to help secure her future. But in thinking of all I had done, I couldn't help but see that it really didn't add up to much. Not for Isley. Noelle pushed me away, and I let her.

"And that was the night...?" I said, not certain how to finish the sentence.

"Yes," Isley said. Done with her sandwich, only half eaten, Isley pushed the plate away. "The next morning, I woke up and read the letter I wrote to you the night before. It was just ranty and stupid so I tore it up and threw it in the trash.

"Mom didn't come down to breakfast. We had so much to talk about that I decided to go to her room and wake her. I remember being afraid, standing outside her door. I remember thinking something was wrong because the house felt so quiet. I couldn't remember the house being that quiet before."

Isley sniffed back her tears. She wiped her eyes. Once she had herself together, as quickly as she could get the words out, she said, "Then I opened the door and found her."

That poor kid. She'd just learned the truth about her father, then her mother died, as if fate were forcing the trade off. *You have two parents, but you're only allowed to know them one at a time. You want a father? Then your mother has to go.* It didn't take me long to realize fate had nothing to do with it. Noelle forced this trade. She had made up her mind to give up on life—for whatever reason—and she didn't want to leave Isley alone. In a way, I was a consolation prize; a token Isley could take away so she didn't feel so bad about losing the game.

"I'm sorry you had to go through that," I said.

Isley wept quietly, dabbing her eyes with the napkin. "I just don't know what I'm going to do."

"Look, Isley, I know it's not the way you want things, but I'll do whatever I can."

"Right, like you're going to stick around!" Isley snapped, yanking her hand out from under mine. Her sudden change of temperament surprised me, and I pulled away. "This is all some vacation for you. You can see if you like the whole dad thing, and if it doesn't work out, you fly on back to wherever the hell. All you've lost is a couple of days, but this is the rest of my life, trapped here with a thousand people that hate me, and I didn't do anything."

"I know," I said. Already her aggression was turning my stomach cold. The familiar sensation of my emotional retreat unnerved me, which of course, just made it happen all the faster.

"Oh, you know?" Isley said. "You know what it's like to have everyone you ever trusted disappear? You know what it's like to have so-called friends turn on you? You know how much it hurts to be alone, and how fucking scary it is, because you think you'll be alone forever?"

"Yeah," I said. "I do."

"How?"

"Because I've felt that way most of my life."

16

Driving away from the spot Isley insisted I leave her, a street half a mile from the Wertimer place, a sense of loss tugged at me. It told me that she shouldn't be alone, not with those people. It told me I was a fool for letting her talk me into this abandonment. But there was little choice. Things between us were too strained for me to make demands. I gave her my personal card with my cell phone number and email address on it and told her to use them if she needed to.

It was early afternoon, not even two o'clock yet. There was no way I was going back to Faye's Inn on my own just then. Instead, I drove back to the interstate, thinking a nap in the motel might help clear my head. I needed to call my lawyer to get him rolling on the custody proceedings, so Isley could be removed from the Wertimer's elegant, brightly lit madhouse. And I would need to make a final visit to Faye's to pick up my belongings and settle the bill, to which I'm sure Faye would add the price of one cheap chair and a window.

Of course, the first thing that ran through my mind when I remembered the broken window was Sidney Tierney from Celebration Windows.

I saw an opportunity there. It was a coward's choice, I knew. Sidney would join me at Faye's Inn, fixing the window while I picked up my things. I wouldn't be alone out at the cabin by the river.

On the shoulder of the interstate, signs rose up for the Memorial Medical Center. Tony was there, likely, John too. Convinced that being alone was not in my best interests, I took the off ramp and drove to the hospital.

Adjacent to the medical center's lobby sat a nest of business kiosks with computers for Internet access and pay phones. From there, I called my lawyer: Bradley Bunny. Like everyone else, I about wrote the guy off the moment I heard his name, but Edwin gave Bunny his highest recommendation, and in the six years we'd known one another, he'd lived up to his reputation and exceeded it. He'd eased me through the whole Ricky Blaine fiasco without so much as a hearing.

Other than being overly serious, perhaps a learned defense from having grown up with a name that made him such an easy target for teasing, Brad was a good guy, and he always took my calls when he was in the office.

"What can I do for you, Mick?"

"Well, I'm hoping you can tell me," I said. Then, I launched into a brief rundown of the situation: Noelle was dead, leaving my daughter as a ward of the court; they'd seen fit to stick Isley in a house with a lunatic, a thug, and a pedophile.

"Does he have a record?"

"Not that I'm aware of."

"So he's a suspected pedophile. Go on."

The judge was a cousin to the *suspected* pedophile; Isley was in constant fear; she slept in a tub at night behind the bolted door of a bathroom; she was not allowed to come and go; I had not been allowed to see her. I went on to explain my encounter with Mrs. Wertimer and her butler, Lance, who had put me in a chokehold and threw me out of the house.

Brad grunted but let me finish with no further questions. When I was done telling him what I knew, he first made it clear that family law was not his specialty but he was not altogether unfamiliar with applicable statutes and precedents.

"But there are different procedures in every state, Mick," he said. "And the fact you haven't petitioned for custody before could play against you. What's your relationship with Isley like?"

Uncertain was the word that came to mind. She went back and forth between hostile and guarded. Granted, we were still getting to know one another, and there was a lot of pent up anger. I imagined she would come around, and I knew that she considered me a better alternative than the Wertimers.

"It's good," I told Brad.

Brad grunted. He kept me on the phone for the next thirty minutes, questioning me. He reminded me that Noelle took out a restraining order against me, and though it was ten years old, the Wertimers' counsel—should they decide to challenge—would certainly bring it up, along with a lot of other nasty information like my lifestyle on the road with Palace, my involvement in Ricky Blaine's suicide, and three arrests for drunk and disorderly. Further, I didn't even want to think what a judge in this part of the country would make of my proclivity for the man-on-man action, and though I realized this was another—perhaps unjustified—prejudice against the inhabitants of the area, I didn't know what the fuck to expect.

"A lot is going to depend on how far these Wertimers want to go. Let me make some calls and get one of the associates on the books. I'll try to get this in front of the judge ASAP, but until then, I suggest you don't do anything to compromise your position."

He spent three minutes listing the offenses that might constitute such a compromise, and then we said our goodbyes.

My next call was to Celebration Windows. I asked for Sidney, but he was out on a call. I gave my name, told the girl on the other end of the phone that it was something of an emergency. She told me that Sidney could meet me at Faye's Inn at four-thirty. Relieved, I thanked the young woman.

Then, I set off to find John.

17

When I found him, John was sitting with two women at a small, mauve table in the hospital's cafeteria. These places were obviously changing. The last time I'd been in an institutional restaurant, it had been a stark, cold place with a bar of hot food, a cooler with prepared salads and sandwiches, and a grill in the back for cooking small pucks of hamburger. The women with John, Mrs. Palmer and Mrs. Martin, were attractive, as John had told me. Both were slender with choppy, fashionable hairstyles, one bleached blonde the other dyed a subtle coppery red. The blonde dabbed at her eyes with a napkin, and the redhead leaned across, wrapped an arm around her shoulders. John lowered his head for a moment, shook it slowly. I could see these people, along with Tony, dressed for a night on the town, smiling and holding court at a church social, surrounded by their neighbors all of whom admired the perfect couples and hoped to ease themselves into their sphere. I know it's what I would have wanted.

I didn't want Tony to be dead.

John lifted his head, eyes red and swollen. He saw me, and his first expression was concern; it spread across his features like a rash. Wiping at his eyes, he whispered something to the two women and stood. The wives turned their heads in unison to look at me, and they didn't look away as John skirted another mauve table and walked over.

"Mick," he said, putting an arm across my shoulders to navigate me into a turn. John led me out of the cafeteria and into the hall.

"How is he?" I asked.

"Alive," John said. "That's something. They're monitoring him every second. They seem to know what they're doing."

"How are you holding up?"

"Shaky," he said. "Sometimes my legs get so weak, I think I'm going to drop, but Gretch and Molly aren't handling this well, so I've got to keep it together."

"I know this doesn't help, but this kind of thing happens every day. Doctors are prepared for it, and if he survived the initial attack, chances are good he'll pull through." I didn't know what I was talking about. I had no idea if I'd just lied to John or not, but it sounded like the right thing to say, and it appeared—and this may have been nothing more than my own hope—that his worry eased a little. Hoping to ease it further, I said, "And I got your room picked up. So, if you need to go back this afternoon... "

At first, John didn't know what I was talking about. Maybe his mind had already switched gears, back to the husband who paid bills and mowed the lawn and not the lover who traveled with nipple clamps and lube. When he remembered what he'd asked of me, he smiled lightly as if in pain and nodded his head.

"Thanks."

"Do they know what happened?" I asked. "I mean, was it his arteries? Was the muscle weak?"

The rash of concern returned to John's face, darkening it and filling his eyes with a gray caste. He looked back at the entrance to the restaurant and his expression hardened. "Someone was there," John whispered through a clenched jaw.

"You saw someone?" I asked.

"No. Not exactly. After we talked with you yesterday, and you went to see your daughter, we went on inside for a nap."

The way John said nap made it clear that this was code for an afternoon slam session. They'd gone inside to fuck and get the most out of their two-week vacation from married life. Then...

"After a while I got up for a shower. Tony was dozing on the bed. He was fine when I left him. He hadn't complained about any aches or pains all day, and he wouldn't keep that sort of thing quiet. Tony's very proud of his little miseries, and over the years, I'd heard about every one of them. But he didn't say a word about not feeling well."

I didn't interrupt, but I remembered the prescription for Viagra and the bottle of poppers. You didn't have to be a doctor to know what that combination could do to the heart, especially when coupled with exertion and more than a few miles on the tires.

"In the shower, I thought I heard him call for me, but he was always doing things like that. He'd carry on entire conversation with me, even if I couldn't hear him and respond. He'd just shout whatever came into his mind about the Cardinals, a story on the news, a model of car he liked, or our families. Whatever. After thirty years you get used to that kind of thing and just ignore it. It's as natural as air. But when I stepped out of the shower, while I was drying off, I got this feeling in my stomach. It felt like I'd just swallowed a block of ice, and I started shaking all over. I ran into the cabin and Tony was on the bed. He... there was... "

John tried to maintain the quiet in his voice. He bit on his lower lip. Ground his teeth. Ran a hand over the top of his head.

"He looked dead, Mick. In fact, I'm pretty sure he was. His arms were crossed over his chest, his fingers digging into his shoulders. His mouth was twisted and open wide like he wanted to scream. I ran to the bed, asked what had happened. What was wrong? He didn't respond. So, I performed CPR, what little of it I could remember how to do. When I thought I felt his breath on my cheek, I started looking for my cell phone to call 911.

"That's when I noticed that the door to the cabin was wide open."

"But no one was there?" I asked.

"Not anymore, but someone came in that room. There were footprints, Mick. I saw them when I went out to meet the paramedics. They were everywhere."

I'd seen those prints myself. I knew he wasn't imagining them. They ran along the muddy path. I also remembered that there hadn't been return tracks, nothing leading off into the woods, nothing leading back or forward. They ran to Cabin 3 and ended.

"I saw them."

"So I got to thinking about what you told me. You know, about someone leaving a note in your place that first night?"

The note. *The name.* Shit.

"I think he came back," John continued. "I think whoever left that note came back, and he tried to attack Tony. Maybe not attack. Maybe he just startled him. I don't know. But someone was there Mick."

"Did you tell the police?"

John shook his head. "I couldn't. At first, I didn't put it all together. I was too panicked, trying to keep Tony alive until the paramedics arrived. Then, I saw you in the lot and started thinking about all of the things in the cabin. By the time we got to the hospital, and I had a chance to think it through, to consider the open door, the footprints, I was also considering what the police would find if I sent them back. I couldn't do it. I was too scared. I can't explain it. "

I could. John was on the edge of losing his best friend, his partner of three decades, someone closer to him than his wife could ever be. If news got back to his family, his town, about just how close they were, he could lose everything else. I didn't even think of blaming him. Unlike me, he actually had a life that could be compromised.

"But you shouldn't stay there," John said. "You should just pick up your things and move into town. It's not safe there."

"I've already moved to the Quality Inn up the road." I retrieved a business card from my pocket and handed it to the distraught man. "Call me there or on my cell if you need anything."

One of the wives walked out of the cafeteria. She was a couple of inches shorter than John and her red hair turned the color of dried blood in the dim hallway. John introduced me to his wife: Gretchen Palmer.

"Nice to meet you," Gretchen said. She turned to her husband, put a hand on his shoulder. "We should go back up. They might have news."

John nodded and reached into his back pocket, from which he pulled a wallet. A moment later he was handing me a business card. "Be sure to stay in touch," he said. "Maybe when this all… " He let the sentence die off. "Just… uh… just give a call sometime."

Tony's wife, Molly, walked out of the cafeteria, looked at the three of us standing there and then cast her eyes at the floor.

"I will," I told him.

John surprised me then. He stepped forward and wrapped his arms around my neck and hugged tightly. "Thank you," he whispered. Before he released his grip he said, "You're a good guy."

"Yeah," I said. "Thanks."

He led the women away and disappeared around the corner.

I left the hospital, drove to my motel. My mind had reached a saturation point, absolutely flooded with real concerns as well as with fears that could only be put down to superstition and myth. When I closed my eyes, Ricky was waiting for me. The cruel son of a bitch wasn't going to let me enjoy the little rest I was allowed before meeting Sidney at the cabin.

18

Sidney was late. I sat in the parking lot until ten to five before his truck eased off the road to crunch over the gravel. Seeing him was still a pleasure. He climbed out of the truck with a curious look on his face.

"Twice in one day?" he asked.

"This actually happened last night."

"Oh, and here I was thinking you were smashing windows just so you could see me again."

I'd done more for less, that's for sure, but I didn't tell him that. Instead, I laughed and said, "You caught me. That was my plan all along."

"Such desperation isn't flattering," Sidney said, playing along with the joke. "Now, you want to show me your latest foray into vandalism?"

We walked along the trail. Sidney chatted about his day, but the woods kept my attention. The place needled me, like it was a haunted attraction, and I was waiting for something to jump out.

"May I ask how the hell you ended up out here?" Sidney said.

"Aaron suggested it when he called to tell me about Isley and Noelle."

"Aaron?" Sidney asked.

"Yeah, Aaron Dalfour. He was a friend of Noelle's."

"Really?" Sidney asked. His foot came down hard on a branch and it cracked. He looked down at the broken stick but kept walking. "*Were* they friends?"

"Apparently."

"Noelle never mentioned it," Sidney said. "But there's no reason she would, I guess. Not unless they were dating, and I seriously doubt she was snuggling up with that guy."

"You don't like him much do you?"

"Don't know him really, but no." Sidney laughed at this. "He's pulled a few things around town. Folks lost some money. Most of us know better than to leave our wallets out when he comes to call."

Though never comfortable with Aaron Dalfour I hadn't been suspicious of his motives until that moment. Who was this guy? He was
a schoolteacher. He lived in a good-sized house that was just about
stripped bare. His clothes were neat and tidy and far too expensive for
a guy living on a teacher's salary. Sidney seemed to be suggesting he
was a scam artist. He was involved in my daughter's life—and perhaps
had been involved in Noelle's—but they certainly had nothing in the
way of assets for him to swindle.

But Noelle killed herself, and Isley's boyfriend—perhaps the only
other person in town who could help her—was also dead. If Noelle
had at some point confided in Dalfour, revealing the name and history
of Isley's father, Aaron may have seen an opportunity to bring me to
Celebration with the intent of making me the target of a con.

All of this struck me as extremely paranoid, but in light of what I'd so
recently seen, I didn't discount it. Not outright. Hiring a couple of local
boys—the behemoth that attacked me and the little blond boy—would
be easy enough. That didn't answer all of the questions, though. How
would someone like Dalfour manage to scare a kid like Sandy Winchester to death? How do you make a woman like Noelle kill herself?

My mind was racing, and it suddenly shifted gears. I began to think
about the Wertimers, their assets and the lunacy permeating their home.
Weren't they even more likely suspects? After all, Old Man Wertimer
ended up with Isley. Maybe he wasn't just taking orphans in; maybe
he was creating them as well.

All of these speculations wound around in my head until they
became a knot. I was aware of Sidney staring at me, giving me an
are-you-okay? look. Instead of trying to untangle the knots, I simply
added to them.

"What else do you know about Dalfour?"

"Not much, really. He's from one of the old families," Sidney said.
"He married young, but his wife had a heart attack a couple years later.
Nothing suspicious in that. Heart problems ran in her family. After he
went through her money and the rest of his family's, he pulled some
strings and got himself a job teaching. Except for a few fund-raising

ventures which didn't pan out for anyone but Aaron, he's kept pretty much to himself. That's why I'm a little surprised to hear that he and Noelle were close. Unless she just felt sorry for him. She was kind of a pushover for the lost puppy-dog sorts."

We stepped onto the path running in front of the riverside cabins. I threw a cautious look at Cabin 3, found the door closed, the way Richmond and I had left it the night before. The trail was covered in tracks. Mine. Richmond's. Some made by big, thick-soled boots. And a set stamped into the ground by large bare feet.

At Cabin 4, I asked Sidney to wait while I unlocked the door. Inside I found the destruction from the night before, but no new signs of tampering. Still, I checked under the bed and in the bathroom to make sure the place was clear.

"What happened?" Sidney asked. He stood outside of the broken window at the side of the cabin, only the top of his head visible through the drawn curtains.

I walked up and leaned on the window frame, gazing down at the man who stood surrounded by foliage. "One of the locals thought I needed to be properly welcomed," I said.

"You're kidding?"

"Nope."

"How in the hell did you piss someone off this bad? You've only been in town for a couple of days."

"I'm that kind of charming, I guess."

"I'm surprised you came back," Sidney said, looking up at me.

"Just to get my things," I said. "I've relocated to the posh elegance of the Quality Inn."

Sidney shook his head and set off toward the porch. I met him there a few moments later.

"What does Dalfour do with his money?" I asked, taking Sidney off guard with the question.

"Beats me," he said. "A couple of bad investments and a lot of lousy nights at the casinos would probably drain the accounts pretty fast. Maybe he got himself mixed up with the wrong woman. It's hard to say. Some folks just can't hold on to their money."

"They have casinos around here?" I asked, knowing gamblers could go through money as fast as drug addicts. It wouldn't take long for a guy with bad card luck to go through a fortune or two.

"Down in Shreveport," he said. "They have gambling boats down there. It's a couple-hour drive. A lot of folks from town make the trip."

"And you don't think Aaron and Noelle were all that close?"

"I don't know, Mick. I spoke with Noelle a couple of times a month. We'd run into each other at the grocery store or down to Bump Carter's bakery and gab, get caught up. They were probably friendly. Noelle was friendly with most folks. After she died, I don't think Isley had a lot of people she could turn to. I suppose Aaron did what he could."

"This doesn't make any sense. Isley knew you, but she went to Aaron for help?"

"Well, I knew Noelle but it's not like Isley and I were close," Sidney said. "Look, we can chat about this all night if you want, but this is my last call of the day. It's about a thousand degrees out here, and I'd like to finish up, go home and have a shower and some lemonade."

"Yeah," I said. "Sorry."

"Not a worry. If you want to talk some more, let me take you to dinner and I can try and explain things… when we're sitting down… someplace with air conditioning."

At first, I wanted to accept the invitation. I genuinely enjoyed chatting with him, but the familiar suspicion arose, demanding my attention like a mirror reflecting sunlight in my eyes. The idea that meeting him could be completely random, especially after meeting John and Tony gnawed at me. I was a predominantly unwelcome visitor in this strange place, and it seemed flat out impossible that someone like Sidney would just appear in my life with no agenda.

I declined politely. "After last night, I just need to get some things done and crash."

"Okay," he said, sounding genuinely disappointed "I'd better get to work."

★ ★ ★

While Sidney worked on the window, I gathered my belongings and made three trips to the rental car to pack them inside. Once everything was stored, I walked into the office to settle up with Faye and drop off my key.

Her keen eyes, simmering with disapproval, landed on me the second I opened the door. She peered over the top of a pair of reading glasses with a transparent blue frame, nearly the same color as her hair.

"I saw what you done to my room," she said coolly. "I guess they don't have manners up where you're from. Treating somebody's property like that."

"There was a prowler," I explained, though I knew it would make little difference to the proprietor. "He broke the window. I was using the chair to defend myself."

"Dougy Richmond told me all about it. Said he didn't find nobody."

"The prowler was already gone by the time Officer Richmond arrived."

Faye made a sound like she was about to spit up a hairball and shook her head. "Found other things as well. Maybe next time you'll think twice about coming to my establishment."

Other things?

Then I remembered the paraphernalia I'd taken from John and Tony's room. When I left the night before, they were wrapped in a towel, pushed into the corner by the desk. I'd forgotten them during my packing and would need to retrieve the towel and its contents so I could dispose of the lot of it.

"Look, I'm having your window fixed, even though I didn't break it. I'll pay for the chair, just add it to my bill."

"Just because you pay for something, don't mean it ain't rude for breaking it in the first place."

That was about enough for me.

"I'm sorry I was attacked while staying at your lovely inn," I said, making sure the sarcasm was clear enough for the old hag. "Next time, I'll arrange to be murdered in a more appropriate location. For now, just overcharge my credit card and once your window is fixed, you'll never have to see me again."

Faye made that hairball clearing sound again. She ran my card. When she handed it back, she got in her last digs. Not much. The best she could do, I'm sure. "I charged you for tonight since check out was at eleven. And I added on the price of one of my towels."

I took my receipt. Made a conscious effort not to thank her out of reflex. In the parking lot, I looked at the bill.

She charged me twenty bucks for that fucking towel.

★   ★   ★

Sidney was just about to put the glass in the clean window frame when I got back to the cabin. I still had some time. I retrieved the twenty-dollar towel and its contents from the corner by the desk and walked out to the barbecue area where I saw a large tin drum with a plastic liner. I dumped the towel in, not caring if everyone in Arkansas saw the nipple clamps, the lube and the butt plug.

Screw 'em.

My mood was good and sour by then, and I didn't want to let that seep out onto Sidney, because a part of me wanted to believe he was as sincere as he seemed. I started walking down the trail. There was still plenty of light in the sky, and I heard voices shouting along the banks of the river.

At the place where I thought the outcropping of rock had been I paused, considered catching the view from the river's edge, but instead, kept walking along the path. I had no destination in mind. Just walking. Clearing my head. Footsteps on the path startled me, but it was just a couple of bearded fishermen walking downstream, carrying gear and the afternoon's catch. The two men were sausaged into canvas vests and wore khaki caps with flies hooked to the fabric; both smiled broadly. I caught them in mid-joke. We said hello. The two men continued on to the camp, leaving me alone on the path.

Further along, a wet snuffling sound drew my attention. Just off the path to my left, I saw a dog. It was a big animal, a black lab, I think. Its head was down and its tail was tucked between its legs as it worked over something on the ground. I called to it, and the dog looked, up, its snout covered in gray chunks, sticking to its muzzle on a smear of blood. The mongrel ran a tongue over its lips, collected the blood and the bits of gray. At its feet, I saw the opened body of a raccoon. My stomach turned, and I continued down the path.

A lot of the path was behind me when my stomach cramped. I don't know how long I had walked by then; it seemed like a good long ways. At first, I thought the sick feeling might have been a delayed reaction to seeing the opened belly of the raccoon and the mongrel that fed on its carcass, but this wasn't exactly nausea. It felt like panic. I checked the trees, believing that I would see the gray man (*His name is Jody, I thought... You said his name and he came for you*) racing towards me out of the woods. My ears grew keen. Frogs croaked and burped and the river shushed to my right, and though I saw nothing threatening, the panic continued to grow.

I looked up and down the path. The way I had come was empty. The path ahead was similarly vacant, but far less defined. Unlike the track up to this point, weeds and grasses had reclaimed much of the lane. Though a trail could still be seen, the foliage growing lower and sparser in a direct line ahead, fewer boots had trampled the greenery. Fewer people had continued down the trail.

Farther on, a pale blue glow pulsed beyond a wedge of trees. John had told me something curious when we'd viewed the mysterious light and the place it burned from downriver. He'd called it something. Freak Town? He told me that he'd tried to find it once, but got sick before reaching his destination. I took a step forward and my chest tightened. Sweat grew thicker on my brow and neck and the ill feeling rolled through me, but this wasn't a viral sickness. What I felt was dread. Plain. Simple. As thick as oil. The fear was tangible and nauseating. The further down the path I walked, the greater the feeling. And though I told myself to turn around half a dozen times, I was compelled to walk forward. My chest tightened like a cage in a vice and my heart fluttered—a bird sensing it would be crushed between the bars. Breath hitched in my throat, and I searched the pine trees and the dogwood and the drooping moss for whatever was waiting to spring at me. The panic attack took full hold after I stepped around the wedge of trees and into the glow of the blue flame.

By that time, going forward or back brought absolute terror. Everywhere I looked, the trees and shrubs and moss and rocks, they all seemed only moments from springing to life and coming for me. Jesus Christ, I'd only known this kind of fear once before: The night Ricky died for the first time. But then, it was brief, a few heartbeats before goading me to action. Now, it consumed me and grew until my legs went weak. What made it all the worse was that there was no identifiable source for this fear. No logic. It simply *was*.

I forced myself to step back, my hands clenched into painful fists, struggling against the panic that made my heart thunder in my chest. Desperation sent an uncomfortable rhythm into my ears. The blue flame burned around me, creating an odd, oscillating fence.

The fear I felt was old. I knew it. It had festered and fermented in these woods, trapped in this place. But why? What was this?

Freak Town, I thought.

What had happened here? What could have happened to so thoroughly permeate the atmosphere and the earth with such a deep and cloying fear?

I took another step back. Then another.

A tree limb reached down to touch my head, or so I imagined. Truth was I backed into it, and the needles tickled my neck, the branch jabbed, and I ran. My feet beat the path furiously. I knew that if I stepped wrong, came down on the rise of a stone or into a hole in the path, my ankle was likely to snap, but it didn't matter. Anything would be preferable to the palpable dread behind me.

Almost anything.

A black shape on the path ahead forced me to slow. The mongrel, having finished with his raccoon, now crouched in the dirt. His head was low, his teeth exposed.

I stopped and retreated a step. The dog barked three sharp cries before drawing his lips back in a ferocious snarl.

I searched the ground for a stick or a good-sized rock, anything the forest might offer up for protection. A knobby branch, about as big around as my arm, presented itself, and I crouched slowly toward it so as not to agitate the mongrel.

Apparently, the little fucker was disturbed enough. He pounced and charged forward as I knelt on the path. The branch felt good in my hand. I tightened my grip on it, but everything was happening too fast.

Next thing I knew the dog was airborne, flying at me like a missile, only this missile had fangs and spit and crazy black eyes. I fell back on my ass, and then lie supine on the path, holding the stick up like a flag of surrender, waiting for the dog to find a tasty place on my body to sink his teeth.

The black animal soared over me. His drooling muzzle glided by, gave way to filthy fore legs, which became a pronounced chest speck-led white, then his pinkish belly, his genitals and his hind legs. Thinking, he might have simply overshot his mark. I rolled quickly, got my legs under me and faced upriver, preparing myself to beat the animal's skull in with my club.

But the black dog was not interested in me. His fight was with someone else: a large man with black pants, gray skin, and no eyes.

Less than twenty feet away, the man I'd begun to think of as Jody Mayram whipped back and forth, trying to free his arm from the mongrel's jaws while beating at the animal's head with a fist. His face was twisted into a mask, equal parts rage and terror, and his long gray streaked hair swept his brow like a filthy mop. His rasping breath came at me like an electric saw. Around the man and the mongrel, a low cloud of dust rose, spreading from the fight like smoke.

Jody got free only when the dog tore away a chunk of skin and muscle. A ragged hole was left above his hand, skin rippled and dangled around the terrible wound. But there was no blood. From where I stood, striated lines of torn muscle, white bone, and the soft papery edges of his skin all showed. But the wound was dry as if the dog had ripped into an exsanguinated corpse.

Jody Mayram scurried back, his breath grinding now. On the path, the mongrel gagged and spat, hacking miserably to free his tongue of the blind man's skin. The animal's torso began to bellows, and I knew he was about to hurl up bits of arm and raccoon and whatever else he'd managed to scavenge that day.

I looked away. Stumbled back. I would have turned and run that moment, but a voice rose up and stopped me.

It was Jody Mayram's voice. Its tone was low but just as grating as his breath.

"Nollie Mayram," he croaked, holding his injured arm to his chest. "Durling Keel."

Was this some strange prayer? A curse?

It was neither of those things, and I knew it. He was reciting names. He was calling for help.

That's when I ran. I didn't want to see what kind of monsters would answer his call. I didn't want to meet Jody Mayram's people.

That would happen soon enough.

★   ★   ★

I ran. Despite years of inactivity and too many cigarettes, I ran faster and further than any other time in my life. Fear covered me like the sweat slathering my back and brow. It worked as an uncomfortable fuel, forcing me to push myself even harder. Momentary flashes of outright terror would set my skin alight. I'd get a picture in my head, an image of Jody Mayram stepping onto the path, arms wide and eager to ensnare me. Then the mental obstacle would pass, and I'd be alone on the trail, surrounded by trees and bushes, sucking in the pine and river scented air.

By the time I saw my cabin rise up on the left, a sharp spike of pain lodged in my side and forced me to slow down, catch my breath. I searched the trail behind me, and it was clear. How long it would stay that way was the question. Sidney must have thought I was nuts. He had just finished with the window and was coming around the porch when I stumbled to a halt. He made some joke about me picking a strange time to get some exercise, and I tried to smile, but was too involved with catching my breath. With no explanation, I herded him away from the cabin. I ran up onto the porch and closed the door for the last time. Sidney met me on the path, and I set a quick pace back to the parking lot. The whole time, my eyes kept flicking from his face, toward the woods and the trail running through them.

We paused at his truck, and Sidney replaced his toolbox. He turned to me.

"Can I tell you something?" he asked.

"Sure."

"I want to apologize if I came on too strong."

It took a moment for me to realize that Sidney had misinterpreted my haste to escape Faye's as an attempt to escape him, and though there was no doubt I had my suspicions about the glass man, I didn't see him as a threat—not exactly.

"It's not that," I said.

"Nice of you to say, but I think we both know it's not true. You look about as nervous as a lobster in a pot. And it's cool, Mick. I understand you have a lot on your plate right now with your daughter, and you don't need some local climbing all over you. It's just that there aren't a lot of people I can talk to here. So I may have gotten a little overzealous."

"Don't worry about it. Really."

"Well, I wanted to clear that up in case I don't see you again."

"Thanks, but there's nothing to apologize for. I'm glad we met. It was a happy coincidence."

"I wouldn't exactly call it a coincidence," Sidney said.

"What do you mean?"

"Maybe we should leave it at that," Sidney said.

"I'd rather you didn't," I told him. "What did you mean? You're telling me it wasn't a coincidence?"

"Look, I don't want you to think I'm a stalker or a freak or anything," Sidney said. "But the only real coincidence is that you needed a window fixed, and you called the office. Folks in town were buzzing about Isley's daddy, and from that buzz, I gathered you and I had something in common, so when I saw your name on a work order I made sure I took the gig, even though Karen had already assigned it to Kurl. So, it's not like we just happened to meet."

I thought about what Sidney had said and smiled broadly. This kind of coincidence I could accept. A gay man in a town like Celebration was bound to feel isolated, and it was perfectly natural for him to seek out a sympathetic ear. In light of his confession, I felt a tremendous relief.

"So you're a groupie?" I joked.

"Lord, I knew I should have kept my mouth shut."

"I'm glad you didn't," I told him. "And as for dinner, is there any chance the invite is still open?"

"I imagine so."

"Great."

"Really? Well then, I'm going to head out before you change your mind again," Sidney said. "I'll see you at eight."

★   ★   ★

Driving across town to Aaron Dalfour's house, the amusement over Sidney's "plot" to meet me faded quickly, leaving me trying to find reason behind what I had experienced in the woods. After all, I saw the large man, the one I was calling Jody, wounded badly. The dog had torn a chunk of the guy away, and it was like the mutt had bit into nothing more than a paper mache doll or a model made of clay. Jody felt the pain of the wound; reacted to it as any living man would, except he couldn't be living. I considered the possibility of an intricate costume, one that included a prosthetic arm, but that suggested knowledge of the mongrel, a staging of the entire scene. And that struck me as less possible than an explanation, which could only include the supernatural.

I didn't believe in the supernatural, though. Ghosts? Ghouls? Zombies? Bullshit. Human beings were dangerous enough. There was no need to create monsters.

The conflict of beliefs that followed made a crack in my mind, a tiny rift that was quickly torn open by complicated suspicions. They went from a trickle to a flood and covered nearly everyone I'd met in Celebration: the cast in a sordid plot of one kind or another.

This was one of the sour leftovers from my days in the music industry. Back then, I could count the people I actually trusted on one hand, and it went a good ways toward screwing up my interactions since. The two most obvious scenarios revolved around Dalfour and the Wertimers. In addition to my previous speculations–that Dalfour wanted my money and the Wertimers wanted my daughter–I wove in my encounter with John and Tony, making them accomplices. For all I knew, Tony faked the heart attack and wasn't even in the hospital when I met John and heard his story. They might have been a couple of local boys putting on a show to add credibility to the strange mythology of Jody Mayram and Freak Town. Hell, John was the one who first mentioned the place. Add that to his melodramatic insistence that someone had been in their cabin, and their talk about the Mud Witch and Bloody Mary, and I couldn't help but think they had been dropping crumbs to lead me deeper into a very dark forest. But such rationale suggested the hospital staff too were involved in the plot. Of course, Sidney was also a plant, one who'd guessed at my suspicion and countered it expertly with a harmless, deceitful confession. If Sidney had known Noelle and Isley so well, why hadn't Isley mentioned his name when I first insisted we get the window fixed? Right? Wouldn't that have made sense? As for Bump Carter and Faye LaMarche and the rest of Celebration, Arkansas' population, they were in on it too.

Why not? These country folks were known for sticking together. If a guy like Wertimer greased enough palms, offered the right incentives, every fucker in the town could have been a part of it. I even imagined the town meeting where everyone got their notes and laughed about the time they were going to have when the city-ot showed up.

As I drove and let the depth of my paranoia take hold, I noticed the houses lining the streets. They looked dark, despite the day's glare.

My head was a mess. I pulled over and screamed, "Fuck," emphasizing the word by pounding my palms on the steering wheel. Since that seemed to take a fraction of the tension away, I did it again and again. I leaned back in the seat and closed my eyes and tried some of the relaxation techniques my ex, Glen, had taught me. I pictured a calm ocean, a white beach, seagulls. I counted back from ten. Took deep breaths. All of this helped. My thoughts were no clearer, but my nerves were settling down.

Once I was breathing normally and the pinching grip of anxiety was off of my neck. I returned to my thoughts but took them one at a time.

This wasn't about me. It started before I came to Celebration.

It was about Isley. Her boyfriend... dead. Her mother... dead.

This wasn't a massive conspiracy. The townspeople, John and Tony, Sidney, even bitchy old Faye LaMarche were not in on some twisted game. People were dead and others, including myself, might die. I wasn't willing to believe in an entire community of psychos.

One person was behind this. Someone left me a note. Someone wanted me out of the picture. I needed to know who that was.

I pulled to the curb in front of his house behind a Lincoln SUV. The house was dark, and a man stood on Aaron's stoop. He was tall and broad shouldered, and from the back, he almost looked like my friend Edwin, except he wore a truly awful Hawaiian shirt painted in shades of lime and cobalt and ruby, over white slacks: a look Edwin would have never attempted to pull off.

When he saw me, the man's mouth turned down at the corners, and his eyes narrowed. I walked up the drive, and got a better look at him. His hair was shaved close to his head, so that he wore a shadow more than a hairstyle. His neck was thick and puffed out under his chin as if someone had inflated it with air. Black hairs curled up from the V of his shirt's lapel.

"Hey," I said.

"Howdy."

I stood in front of the guy for a second, not knowing what to say. So, I said the obvious, "You're looking for Aaron?"

"That's right."

"He's not home?"

"Seems that way." He looked me over like a boxer sizing up his opponent. Apparently, he was neither impressed nor concerned. "You got business with him?"

"Just visiting."

"You a friend of his?"

"*Friend* would be overstating the issue."

The guy in the Hawaiian shirt didn't quite know what to make of that. His brow knit, as if wondering whether I was worth further interrogation or perhaps a beating.

"What about you?" I asked. "You a friend of his?"

"Not even close. Right now, I'm about two steps from breaking his arms. I'm missing my son's birthday party for this shit."

"I can give him a message if you like," I said. "You really shouldn't miss your son's party."

"Damn straight, I shouldn't. A kid only turns ten once. His father ought to be there. He shouldn't have to tangle with some dickweed. He should be home, blowing up balloons and shit."

I didn't know what to make of this guy. He was obviously some kind of thug, probably muscle for a local bookie or loan shark (if Sidney's suppositions about Aaron's gambling problem were accurate). He dressed like a crook out of an Elmore Leonard novel with his tropical Technicolor shirt and white pants. He was certainly big enough to intimidate, and he looked like the sort who had taken more than one punch in his life. Still, I found myself comfortable with the guy.

"I can give him a message if you want."

"Nah," he said. "I have to talk to him myself. It's business."

"And it has to be today?"

"'fraid so. Just pisses me off. I went through hell finding R.J. the right present, and now, I'm not even going to be there when he opens it."

"Sorry to hear it," I said. "My name's Mick, by the way. Mick Harris."

"Good to know you, Mick. I'm Ryan."

Though he only offered the one name—and I didn't know if it was first or last—the fact he'd given a name at all was surprising. It struck me as kind of indiscreet for a thug. Maybe I'd pegged him wrong.

"Have you been waiting long?" I asked.

"Just got here. Dickhead probably knew I was coming. Did you guys have an appointment or something?"

"Nope. I just needed some information."

"Well," Ryan said, "my business with Dalfour is kind of private. Maybe you could swing back later."

It wasn't really a suggestion quite so much as a demand. I took the hint. I had more than enough trouble without adding Ryan to the list. "Cool."

"Thanks," Ryan said. "I didn't want to have to put on my hate-face."

"I appreciate that."

Ryan laughed and slapped my shoulder with a big hand. "You're a good guy there Mick Harris. Just remember, you never saw me."

I decided not to comment on how ridiculous Ryan's request sounded. He was an enormous guy in a shirt that all but blinked on and off, standing on Dalfour's porch at six pm in broad daylight. Half the block would be able to describe the hulk, but that wasn't my problem.

"Happy birthday to your son."

"Nice of you to say."

Leaving Ryan alone on Dalfour's porch, I returned to my rental car.

19

The restaurant Sidney chose was a steak house to the northeast of downtown Celebration. The place was called Jack's, and it was decorated in typical steak house fashion. A lot of paneling. Exposed beams overhead. A menagerie of mounted heads on the walls, staring out with glassy black eyes. Hung above our booth was a particularly confused looking buck, head slightly turned and lowered so I was given the full benefit of his final and eternal expression. In life, he'd been an impressive ten-pointer, but as ornamentation went he was no more interesting than the dozen other trophies lining the back wall. Sidney and I sat next to the window, with a view onto the narrow drive, leading to the parking lot in back and the woods beyond.

We were two of only six patrons left in the joint. Walking through the place, I noticed Bump Carter at a table with a slender young woman I had seen before. Though I couldn't place her, I knew I'd seen her face since my arrival in town. The baker looked up at Sidney and I, and his face grew bright with a smile. He lifted a fat hand to wave. Both Sidney and I waved back.

"Not a very busy place," I said.

"Two hours ago it would have been standing room only. This is a late dinner by Celebration standards. Bump and his wife are celebrating and the other table is being used by Jack and his wife to tally the night's receipts. This place is usually cold and dark before ten."

"Well, it's nice," I added, hoping Sidney didn't take my earlier comment as an insult.

"Best food in town," he said.

A waiter appeared. He was tall and slender with the face of a model and a scraggly black shag of hair. "Hey Sids," he said.

"Hey Jared. How's it going?"

"Cool and groovy," the waiter said. "You having a Heineken?"

"Sounds about right."

"What about your friend."

"He's having the same," I said.

"Don't even need to write that down," Jared said triumphantly and turned away from the table.

"So, how is Celebration treating you?" Sidney asked. "The last time I saw you, you looked like you'd just seen your dog run over by a semi."

How was Celebration treating me? I wanted to tell him it was similar to the way most folks treated their toilets, but decided a lighter approach would be more effective. This was Sidney's home.

"I feel like I've barged into a stranger's birthday party," I said, "and people just don't quite know what to do with me."

"That's understandable. Most folks are friendly though, aren't they?"

I thought about Faye LaMarche and the Wertimers. I thought about Isley. Not a lot of friendly from any of those people. But Bump Carter had been outgoing in his own way, and Officer Richmond seemed like a good guy, as cops went. John and Tony. And of course, there was Sidney. Overall, I guess I was batting five hundred.

"Sure," I said because he was looking at me expectantly. "I think I've just got a paranoid thing happening. You know, stranger in a strange land. Don't know what's really going on. Everything with Isley and Dalfour has me kind of thrown off balance."

"I know it's tough having Isley placed with the Wertimers. That old broad is as crazy as they come, but I don't think she'd hurt Isley."

"What about the husband? Darrell Wertimer? What do you know about him?"

"He owns about a quarter of this town, which means he's likely to get his way in most any situation. He travels a lot, though I don't really think it has much to do with business. More than anything, I just think he needs to get away from his wife and Lance."

"I can understand that."

"I've met Wertimer on a few occasions, and he strikes me as okay. I know he's very generous with local charities, and they do take in displaced kids. They've been doing that for as long as I can remember."

"Isley doesn't think Wertimer takes in kids out of the kindness of his heart."

"What do you mean?"

"You haven't heard anything?"

"No," Sidney said. "I mean, not really. Some folks think Darrell has a mistress in New Orleans, and that's why he travels so much, but that's about it on the scandal side of things."

I decided not to pursue the Wertimer issue just then. I didn't know who or what to believe. More than ever, I felt like an outsider, being led blindly through a maze. At every turn, someone new came along to grab the leash and jerk it in a different direction.

Jared returned with our beers and disappeared.

"You okay?" Sidney asked.

By that point, I was staring through my reflection on the window and into the dark woods outside of the restaurant. Was I okay?

"I don't know," I said. That was the only honest answer I had.

"What did you see today?" Sidney asked. "You've been acting odd since you came back from that walk. I thought it was me, but you cleared that up quick enough."

"You think you know me well enough to notice deviations in my character?"

"I take that as a fancy way of saying, 'None of your damn business.'"

Sidney's expression turned cold. He leaned back in the booth and frowned at me. It was the kind of look I usually got after using lines like "It's not you; it's me," or "It just isn't working out." I was shutting down. Pulling away. My life was filled with such moments. Any of my exes would testify to that.

"Look, sorry," I said, trying to muster a chuckle to lighten the moment. "This is all very complicated. Okay? Not for you, but for *me*. I know I'm being played, but I don't know by who, and I don't know what they want. But two people are dead, so I'm thinking it's pretty damn serious."

"Two people?" Sidney asked. "Oh, you mean Sandy."

"Right. and a guy I met out at Faye's also died, but his partner was there to bring him back. It might have just been an old guy having a heart attack. It happens, but I'm pretty far past believing in coincidences right now."

"What makes you think it's all connected?"

"Have you ever heard of a place called Freak Town?"

"Sure," Sidney replied. He reached for his beer bottle, then paused. His face lit up like he'd just realized the answer to a game show question. "Damn, that's where you went today."

"Yes."

"Did you see something?"

"Yes. I saw something, and I need to know what it was."

"Jesus," he said. Sidney shook his head and grabbed his beer, took a deep swallow. "Someone *is* playing you. How did you even know about that place?"

"That's the complicated part. Could you tell me what you know about it?"

"Just what everyone else knows. My paw-paw told me the story a lot when I went to stay at his house, and he probably embellished the hell out of it. I don't know how much I remember. It's really just a campfire tale."

"Would you mind telling it to me?"

Sidney shrugged. He looked at me with curiosity and then his mouth rose at the corners. He thought this whole thing was ridiculous, and I couldn't blame him. But I wanted to hear the story. Needed to hear it.

" Sometime in the late 1800's a man named Jefferson, who owned a paper mill upriver, came back from Europe with a new process for paper production. It included different chemicals and plant extracts and stuff. Naturally, all of the waste got washed into the river from the mill. About a year after he opened his mill, the children came.

"At first, no one took much notice. Birth defects weren't exactly common, but they did exist. Though no one can say for certain, the first of these children was born without eyes. His parents named him Damon, and while he was completely blind, he had an almost inhuman sense of hearing. They said he was enormous. Just built like an elephant."

A chill ran over my skin when I heard the description creep from Sidney's lips. The boy he described had been born, but Damon wasn't his name. Whether this was a calculated deceit implemented by a generation wanting to assure Jody Mayram's name was never spoken aloud or not made little difference.

"After a couple of years about a dozen children were born with deformities and a doctor from out of Memphis was hired and discovered the problem was with the mill. The city demanded that Jefferson quit using his chemical treatments or shut down the mill completely. Shocked and regretful, he immediately closed the mill and gave many of the afflicted families a considerable portion of his fortune for the care of their children.

"Over time, the children came together and formed a community away from Celebration. Upriver. About halfway out to the old mill. They formed their own families. Had their own children, also physically different.

"The blind boy, Damon, settled upriver with the other outcasts. He became their leader. But under his influence, the people became corrupted, so that they not only looked monstrous, they acted monstrous as well. Damon hated Jefferson, blamed him for his deformity. One day he attacked Jefferson's granddaughter. Raped her. Murdered her on Jefferson's property.

"When the sheriff and a posse of men from town went out there to arrest Damon, they were ambushed and nearly killed. A fire broke out. Freak Town was destroyed, and its inhabitants, the outcast children of Celebration, fled into the woods. According to paw-paw, they all committed suicide at Damon's order. But he cursed them and himself, so if anyone spoke his name, or one of theirs I imagine, they would come back for revenge."

Sidney leaned back and grabbed his beer again. "I remembered more than I thought I would."

"But it's just a folktale?" I asked. "No one actually believes it's real?"

"The mill is real enough. I've seen pictures of it in the town hall. It's nothing but a foundation at this point. As for Freak Town, who knows? More than likely, it's just a cautionary tale about progress or something." Sidney's face grew dark with concern. He leaned over the table. "What did you see out there, Mick?"

"I saw Damon," I told him.

An expression flew across his face like the shadow of a bird. Then he grew stern and leaned back. "Look man, you wanted to hear the story. You don't have to be an asshole and make fun of me for telling it."

"Sidney, I'm not. Christ. I'm having a tough enough time with this without you coming down on me too."

"Do you really think Noelle and Sandy Winchester's deaths are part of some plot?"

"Yes," I said.

"And you think it has something to do with that place?"

"Maybe. The night I got into town, I found a note in my cabin and…"

I laid it all out for him. The weight of my experiences since reaching Celebration was too much for me, and I had to unload it. It didn't matter if Sidney thought I was crazy, because I was getting the impression he already believed it. Maybe hearing the story from my own lips would expose an answer or at least a point of logic I had overlooked. So, I told him about the note, John and Tony, the blind guy that attacked me in my cabin and the blond kid I saw at Isley's. I recounted Dalfour's story about the Trash Boy and John's story of the Mud Witch, and I told him exactly what I saw on the trail upriver from Faye's earlier that afternoon.

"You really saw Damon?"

"I think so. Only his name's not Damon. I wanted to believe it was all a hoax, but the dog took half his arm off. I don't see how anyone could have faked that."

"Look, I don't mean to be rude, and it's totally your own business, but have you been on anything since you got to town?"

I should have expected that, but I didn't. "No."

"What about flashbacks. You know, from the wild days?"

"Sidney, my hallucinations couldn't give Tony a heart attack; they couldn't leave footprints in the mud; and they couldn't break the window of my cabin."

"My maw-maw believes in all this hoodoo hokum," Sidney said. "She never mentioned Freak Town, though. That almost makes me believe it. Paw-paw made it all out to be this big fairy tale–a warning to kids–but Maw-maw never played along. She had this thing about protecting me from the *real* badness of the world. When I'd ask her about hexes and castings, she told me the things I needed to do to protect myself from them, but never showed me how to actually work a spell on someone else. She said that kind of knowledge needed to die because it had no place in a modern world. Used to creep me out bad. And now you're telling me we have…what?… ghosts running through town?"

"No clue," I said. "I don't know shit about the occult. Obviously, he's not a ghost. I mean he's solid. So what does that leave? A zombie?" I choked out a laugh. "God, that sounds so messed up out loud. All of this does. But he isn't that either. He's something else. I don't suppose your paw-paw told you how to stop one of these things?"

"In his version, you didn't stop them. They came after you, and you died."

"Nice. Then I better find out who sent him after me and do some damage before it's my turn."

"What about Isley?" Sidney asked. "You've got your list of suspects, but she isn't on it. I'd think she'd be top of list."

"Yeah," I said. "Believe me, she's on the list, but she's so genuinely pissed off at me that I don't think she's hiding anything. Does that make sense?"

He tossed out a guess. "If she was hiding something, she'd be wearing her happy face?"

"Sort of," I said. "Truth is, I honestly believe she'd be happier if I left. She didn't want me here. She *doesn't* want me here, for that matter, and it has nothing to do with what's going on with Noelle or that Winchester kid. She's got plenty of reasons to hate me, and she's had a lot of years to look them over."

"Maybe you should leave. You could take Isley with you?"

"I'd love to," I said. "But I don't have custody. If I tried to take her back to Denver with me right now, I'd be looking at a federal rap. And

I can't leave myself because she could just as easily be a target as I am. I don't know what's behind this. Whatever the motivation, she's in the middle of it. If I left and something happened to her..."

"yeah," Sidney said. "So, what are you going to do?"

"I'm going to find out exactly what happened to Jody and his people. See if I can figure out what they are now and if there's any way to stop them before the rest of us end up dead. There has to be information somewhere."

"The library and the historical society would be good places to start," Sidney said. "Now, I think we'd better order. Oliver the chef just glared through the kitchen window at us. We're keeping him from his girlfriend."

★   ★   ★

Though the meal was fine, I barely touched the food. I cut the steak into small pieces and pushed them around on the plate, all the while conscious of Sidney's eyes on me. He was being remarkably understanding, considering the conversation we'd shared. He didn't know me from Adam, and I'd told him some truly unlikely shit, but he'd listened. He didn't run off or make accusations. I even convinced myself that he was excited by the prospect of having a childhood campfire tale come to life around him. Nothing else really explained why he would waste his evening with a man who was at best a target and at worst a lunatic.

"Not a big steak fan?" he asked.

"Just not particularly hungry. It's a great place though." To make my point, I looked around the room to take it all in again, ending with the trophy buck mounted above his head. "Thanks for suggesting it."

"You're welcome."

The conversation had hit another resounding lull, and Sidney looked away from me. It was my fault. I'd reached the point where I didn't want to talk about Freak Town or Jody Mayram. I didn't want to talk about Isley and Noelle. I didn't want to discuss Celebration,

Arkansas or the life I'd lived before arriving there. He appeared frustrated, his eyes half-closed as he gazed out the window.

I wanted to say something to bring him back. But I didn't have to.

His eyes grew wide and his mouth slowly opened as if he might be near voicing a question. He continued to stare at the window. So I turned my head to see what had caught his attention.

The boy had his face pressed against the glass with his hands cupped around his glaring eyes. Stringy blond hair draped the edges of his hands. He was shirtless and pale, and he didn't look happy. His mouth was drawn tight in an angry frown as he stared into the restaurant, right at me.

"Who the hell is that?" Sidney asked.

"I was hoping you could tell me," I replied. "I saw him at Isley's house this morning just before you showed up."

"He must be one of the Eastside kids. He looks kind of trashy."

Trash Boy, I thought.

Against the backdrop of nighttime wood, he looked even more ghostly. His skin, dull and gray, caught the restaurant light, while the forest at his back remained sketched in charcoal.

"I think we should go," I told Sidney, already reaching into my pocket to retrieve my wallet.

"What's wrong with his skin?" he asked.

Before I could reply, the Trash Boy pulled back from the window, leaving smears on the glass. He turned away, revealing his back.

Sidney gasped. I felt what little food I'd managed to get down attempt to come back up.

Ragged lips of skin ran from the base of the boy's neck to his waist. The knobs of his vertebrae jutted out, twisting and contracting with his movement. Trash Boy ran across the drive, his pale body still perfectly visible as he leapt through the tall grasses separating the drive from the forest. A moment later, he sprang upward, taking to the air. He flew from the ground and slammed into a thick tree trunk, clasping the bark with his hands and feet. He scurried around like a lizard until he was upside down, nearly ten feet up the tree.

A high-pitched squeak came from Sidney's throat. It met the curse rolling over my lips.

"Shit," I said, watching the boy scurry up and down the tree trunk with the agility of a gecko.

Though the spectacle of the Trash Boy amazed me, movement below him drew my gaze away. Shafts of moonlight cut deep into the wood. They seemed to pulsate and thicken in the dark places between the tree trunks. Slowly, they grew solid, taking on human shapes. The first of these, Jody Mayram, emerged from the shadows at the base of the tree to which Trash Boy clung. Others also pulled from the shadow like a family of corpses floating to the surface of a black lake. A woman on Jody's right was draped in long strands of moss. Her upper lip was ragged and split, but a simple harelip was the least of her imperfections. She had no lower jaw, just a pouch dangling from her cheeks to meet her neck. Her tongue, a slighty deeper shade of gray than her skin, lolled over the edge of the sack and the fence of crooked teeth above champed at the air. Two children stood next to her. Or rather, one stood, because the second had no legs. To Jody's left, on the other side of the tree Trash Boy clutched, stood a squat man whose skin hung in strips over his bones. Tassels of flesh dangled from his brow and his ears, draped beneath his arms like thick fringe. A slender woman with no nose, just slits to accept and release breath. A girl of maybe ten years, bald with an egg-shaped head and small fleshy claws, like those of a shelled lobster, dangling at her wrists. And more. Many more.

"Lord ah-mighty," Bump Carter cried from his table across the room. His wife wasn't quite as eloquent. She screamed, a sound so high and piercing it drew every staff member of Jack's Steak House into our wing of the dining room.

Sidney and I left the table and crossed to meet Bump Carter and three members of the wait staff, one of which, a big man with white hair, clutched a meat cleaver in his ample hand. Closer now, Jody's people were easier to see but no easier to look at. Further anatomical tragedies–missing limbs, exposed organs, twisted facial features–became apparent but they all bled together in my racing mind.

The leader of this terrible aggregation, Jody, reached out to grasp the tree at his side; his eyeless face swept from one side to the other searching for a scent or a sound. He appeared to be trembling as if trying to hold the tree up with nothing but his palm.

"Who the ever-loving fuck are they?" our waiter Jared asked.

Jody's head stopped swaying. It cocked to the side.

"He heard ya," Bump whispered. He clutched his wife closer and pulled her with him away from the window. The scared woman pushed in tight as if trying to camouflage herself with his bulk.

"I'm calling the authorities," Jack the owner said, backing away from the glass. "I'm not having some crystal meth freaks run off my clientele."

"Mick," Sidney said, "I really want to go now."

"Yeah," I whispered. "Okay."

Jody Mayram's head whipped around before I completed the words. His eyeless face went rigid and his posture straightened. He stepped forward breaking through the tall grass with broad strides that propelled him toward the restaurant. His damaged people followed.

The realization that it was my voice drawing him hit hard. I had spoken his name to resurrect him, and he was using the voice that called him as a beacon to find me.

As Jody and his people approached the window, each step bringing their perverted anatomy into finer definition, those of us inside the restaurant had a variety of reactions. Some fight. Most flight. Bump and his wife were in a full run. The big man sent a table toppling when his hip slammed into it, but he didn't pause to survey the damage. Dragging his wife by the arm, he fled the restaurant. Our waiter, the owner Jack and his wife, escaped into the kitchen leaving Sidney and I in the center of the dining room. The only one of us who hadn't moved was Oliver, the chef, who stood straight backed, facing the glass, arm up with the meat cleaver cocked and ready for action. He barked curses at the window, ready to defend his place of business as he might a home and family.

I was less in the fighting mood. I'd seen what having his arm torn away did to Jody Mayram: very little. I imagined the cleaver would make some holes but do no real injury to the residents of Freak Town.

With Sidney at my side, I walked through the dining room and into the reception area. Pushing on the first of two glass doors and looking through the second, I skidded to a stop. Sidney ran into my back, his hands going around my waist either by reflex or to keep himself from toppling over.

Bump Carter knelt on the walk in front of the door. His wife lay face down on the concrete at his feet. The big man was grappling with her weight. He screamed and tears rolled down his cheeks as he rolled the woman into his arms. Bump's eyes grew wide then. He snapped his head up and skittered back on the walk, letting his wife drop to the poured stone. It didn't really matter. She was already dead. I could tell by the contortion of her face, the wideness of her eyes, the paleness of her skin. She had seen something terrifying, and it had stopped her heart.

As for Bump, he only made it a couple of feet back before a blur of gray appeared through the window. It was one of the children of Freak Town, a little boy with crooked legs and a texture on his skin like scales. He hopped up and down twice, then leapt at Bump Carter.

The boy hit the big man in the chest, his bent legs clamping onto either side of Bump's belly. The boy's hands shot up and clasped the sides of Bump's face and pulled it close as if they might kiss, but Bump fell backward, taking the boy with him. He hit the pavement like a side of beef. Bump's body rocked and bucked but he was not fighting with the kid (though he certainly should have been able to best the kid's strength). Instead, he seemed to be caught in some kind of seizure. His body convulsed. His eyes grew wide, and a steady stream of tears poured down the side of his head.

"Oh hell, Bump," Sidney whispered.

I was already out the first door. Before it swung closed, I had the second door open and the night air fell around me like a hot blanket.

On the ground, Bump's legs kicked and scrambled as if slipping on a muddy hillside in a dream. His voice, locked deep in his throat, was a high, sustained squeak like someone being choked. Bump squeezed his eyes closed as if preparing for a blow, sending another wash of tears over his face. The boy didn't change his position in the least. Whatever he was doing to Bump, he did by touching him.

I reached down with the intent of yanking the kid off of the baker. Grasping tight, my head grew light and the boy, his victim and the sidewalk were gone.

The world flipped, and I was on my back, staring up at the blade of an axe, arcing through a nighttime sky toward my head. The hallucination hit me so hard, I barely registered its happening. Suddenly, I was not just *someplace* else, but I was *someone* else. All around me, I heard screaming. A fire burned nearby. Men's voices laughed and called, cursed and cried. And the blade came straight for my face, leading a trail of bloody drops. I opened my mouth to scream but the blade...

Then I was back on my feet, my hands falling through the boy's shoulders. In fact, the shoulders and the boy vanished beneath my touch. Nothing hovered over Bump Carter, but a thin gray cloud that blew away with the motion of my arms. Eyes still tightly closed, Bump Carter lay motionless on the concrete. Dead.

Sidney stood behind me, jabbing my shoulder with his hand. I turned quickly and saw half a dozen of the things standing at the corner of the restaurant.

But some residue of the hallucination must have remained behind my eyes. Disoriented, I looked at the residents of Freak Town and was momentarily pleased to see them as if they were lost friends. A loved family. The woman with no jaw was named Mama Leche, and the girl with the bald head and the claw-like hands was named Nollie.

"Mick," Sidney said, hauling off and cracking his palm across my face. "Come on."

I let him lead me away, toward the parking lot. Not exactly struggling, but confused at his haste to be away. Inside the car, I looked at the wheel for a moment, absolutely dumbfounded by the machine and its workings. Had I ever seen anything so strange and interesting before? Sidney busied himself making sure the doors were locked, but I marveled at the odd box we had climbed into.

Sidney punched my shoulder like he was picking a fight. "Mick! For God's sake, drive!"

And the confusion passed. I jammed the key in the ignition and threw the car into reverse. I flipped on the headlights. Their bath fell over Jody and his people congregating at the side of the restaurant, watching us.

★   ★   ★

"That did not just happen," Sidney said, pressing deep into the passenger seat.

"It got into me," I replied.

"It's just a damn fairy tale. It can't be real."

"For a second, I was him. I was that little boy."

We could have continued having two completely separate conversations all night; Sidney was experiencing a mild shock. I was distracted by thoughts of my own. I could not shake a disturbing certainty: touching that boy had taken me out of myself and dropped me into him, into his veins and muscle and mind. I was him for a time, a time in the past, sharing the moments leading to his death. The boy carried no animosity. I felt his innocence and goodness as clearly as I felt the cold air blowing through the rental car's vents. The tale Sidney had told was wrong, just as it had been wrong about Jody's name. Jody's followers did not commit suicide at his command like some small scale Guyana in the woods of Arkansas. They had been murdered, likely by Jody himself. The son of a bitch had cursed his followers, and he killed them to act out his revenge over and over. Throughout decades. Eternally connected to the world of the living by their names and the magic their leader forced on them.

The cruelty of it worked into my skin like a swarm of feeding mosquitoes. I physically itched with discomfort, felt things crawling on me. The people of Freak Town were victims. Maybe not all of them. I had heard men laughing nearby, calling out good-naturedly to one another before the axe fell. Apparently, Jody had sergeants amid the population, men who shared his violent vision. One night at Jody's command, they must have turned on the innocent and struck them down.

These poor estranged people followed Jody from the city, creating their own community where they could feel safe and welcomed, away from the fear and misguided disgust of their parents and siblings. No pointing. No jeering. No blatant stares of distaste as they went about their business. Then the man they'd looked up to ripped safety and comfort from them, the man they had trusted more than any other.

Sidney shook my shoulder, chasing away my thoughts. "Where are we going?" he asked.

I wasn't thinking about that. My goal was to get away from Jody and his people. I looked at the streets, the homes and the yards. We were still on the north side of town.

"I'm taking you home," I said. "They aren't after you. You'll be safe at home."

"What about you?"

"I'll be fine at the motel." I hoped that was true. I didn't really have anywhere else to go. "If I have to leave town suddenly, I'll call."

"If you had a brain in your head, you'd be leaving town right now."

"You may be right. Now, tell me how to get back to your place."

Sidney wore a frown of concern as he gave me the directions. I followed them silently, my head still working through what I knew about the disaffected followers of Jody Mayram. When I dropped him off, he all but jumped out of the rental car. Then sensing he was being rude, he leaned back in and said, "Be careful, Mick."

"Thanks."

It was difficult to say anything else. Sidney must have felt the same way because he closed the car door and turned away.

So, I drove. I knew I was a target. I knew that what pursued me was not from my realm of belief, at least not the realm I'd operated in prior to coming to Celebration. Jody and his people were dead, long dead. But they were alive and coming after me. I had done nothing to them, but that obviously made no difference to the disfigured mob. They were designed for one thing only, and that was revenge. I was convinced of that.

Turns out—as in many things—I was completely wrong.

20

It snowed on the night Ricky Blaine died that first time. It was the last snow of the year. Early in the evening, I returned from a mind numbing date. I can't remember the guy's name, but he was a producer with one of the local news programs. Very pretty. About a ten on the self-obsession scale. The few words he allowed me to speak had to be phrased in the form of a question. Any offhand reference I made to my own life was immediately acquired and adapted to reflect something "important" in his history. So, I could say "I used to be a musician," and it would become, "Really? You know what's *really* interesting? I used to make it a rule not to date actors or musicians," and then the next ten minutes were tied up in his personal philosophy and how it impacted his development as a person.

Needless to say, I came home alone that night. That was probably for the best.

At about two in the morning, I woke to the sound of someone stumbling around my living room. Concerned, I grabbed the phone and the baseball bat that I kept propped behind the door in anticipation of these very occasions.

I found Ricky Blaine, hunched and shivering, by the cabinet where I kept my liquor.

God, he was a mess. The world he'd once ruled had turned on him. Like Mussolini, he was battered and torn by traitorous followers but left on public display to complete his humiliation.

The easiest way to explain it is: Ricky was the front man of Palace, and that's all he was. When the band dissolved, he lost himself, not in a temporary tempest like the one that had thrown my life around for awhile, but in a deep and enveloping maelstrom, culling him to its center and pulling him down and down. Even before that, when the grunge movement rose up out of Seattle to spray the glittering music scene with earth-toned angst, you could see Ricky clawing and scraping to remain relevant, to keep the spotlight burning on his face. He pulled one outrageous stunt after another but no one cared. MTV wouldn't touch him (or us) with a ten-foot boom mic. Always the party beast, drugs and weeklong festivals of debauchery, lawsuits and ridiculous investments left him broke only a year after Palace's last record. Clyde Markham, our drummer, went on to be an executive with Crunch Records, our old label, and Rudy Trevino, our guitarist made a good living doing studio work, but Ricky was the tree in the forest that no one heard. He tried a couple of solo projects. They tanked. He tried his hand at band management and ended up a quarter of a mil in debt. Ricky was a celebrity; he was born for it. But Ricky was at best a good singer, not great, and he wasn't a musician, a songwriter or a businessman. He was the throat and the face of Palace, and he meant absolutely nothing else to the world.

It was a tough thing to watch. Ricky and I had worked together for a lot of years. We were very much family in a way my blood relatives could never have been. No, we didn't get along. Most of the time I flat out hated the guy. But time weaves you together with people. If those threads get worn or pulled loose, you feel it.

So, at two in the morning when I walked in and saw him pouring himself a drink, I felt enough sympathy to let the intrusion slide, even though I saw the window he'd broken to gain entrance. His hands shook, his body twitched. He'd been out in the snowstorm in only a t-shirt and jeans, but that was only part of his palsy. He was coked up. Nose bleeding. He looked bad with eyes the varied colors of ground meat. What was left of his hair—once a proud mane of platinum—jutted from his head like long tendrils of plucked cotton. His pink scalp flaked. His teeth were the color of urine and framed by trickles of blood from his rotten nose.

"We gotta get back on the road," he said.

"Christ, man, you're bleeding all over the place."

Ricky gulped at his whiskey. A tremor ran through him. He sighed. "I was at a meeting earlier. Business meeting, right? And these poseurs were telling me they needed someone more like David Draiman or some shit, like they didn't even realize that nu-metal died at birth, right?

And it was right there, man. Right fucking there I realized: We have to get back on the road and show these fuckers what real music sounds like."

I told Ricky to sit down, but he was too wired. He paced back and forth, the bottle of whiskey never more than three feet away from him. Telling him to hold on a second, I went into the kitchen, ran a towel under the tap and went back to the living room to clean him up.

While I wiped his nose and lips with the towel, he kept talking and every third sentence was, "We gotta get back on the road."

That was his mantra, his rosary. In his twisted state, he honestly believed that we were a legendary band that was ripe for a comeback. He couldn't understand that we were irrevocably fused to a time, like Donna Summer and disco or Chuck Berry and the infancy of rock and roll. Out of the context of nostalgia, we were nothing but a joke. But he wasn't hearing me. His raw meat eyes were wild and when he reached out to grab my shoulders, I saw the comet-shaped wounds in the crook of his elbow.

He'd kicked a few years before, but apparently he'd jumped back on the horse and was bare backing his way into the sunset. Sweat poured over the tight ridge of his brow and traced the ditches on either side of his mouth. It was like being grabbed by a corpse, boney fingers digging into my shoulders. I dropped the bloodstained towel and tried to ease out of his grip, but he wouldn't let me go. The whole time he tried to convince me that getting back on the road would save my life. He told me that I wouldn't be killing myself, that I wouldn't be humiliating myself if I just got back on the road and played the tunes and felt the crowd.

Of course, he wasn't talking about me. Ricky was *all*, and when Ricky suffered, it was expected that everyone shared his pain.

I played along for a while, knowing that any logical refutation of his dream would be pointless. He pulled out a vial. Did a bump. I assumed it was just coke and thought little of it. I hadn't touched the stuff in years, and it held no interest for me but like his fantasy of getting Palace back on the road, his devotion to chemicals would not be shaken.

He mellowed some. I guess I should have known that it wasn't just coke in there.

Ricky asked how I was doing. Commented on the house, calling it a "soccer mom paradise." I laughed, gritted my teeth and asked about his business meeting, which I knew was nothing more than a failed audition. Considering the audition was being held in Colorado, not L.A. or New York, I had to assume it was a second rate act.

Ricky did another bump. Then another. His raw meat eyes went darker, dreamier. "Poseurs, man. Fucking poseurs. They keep talking about being relevant and making music that matters. Well, what the fuck did they think we were doing for twenty years?"

Palace had been together for a little over fifteen years, actually. We were only popular for about ten of those. I didn't correct him.

"You can do better," I suggested.

"Fuck man, we were the best. How can I do better than that? We gotta get back on the road."

Looking at Ricky was beginning to mess with my head. Only a few minor adjustments to my life, and the bleeding, doped-up zombie on the sofa could have been me. I didn't want to look at him anymore. Couldn't. I offered him the guest room, told him he could chill out in there for a few days until he was feeling better.

He wasn't ready to stop talking, yet, but I couldn't bear to hear anymore. I said that we'd talk about Palace in the morning, once he'd had a chance to straighten up.

Ricky started laughing: a sharp, raspy witch's laugh that got under my skin like frozen needles. "You think you've got it all together," he said. "You got your soccer mom palace and your two cars."

"You should really just go to bed now, Ricky. You're dosed too high."

"You weren't shit until we found you," Ricky said. He did another bump. Another. A third. "Couldn't even fucking play until we showed you how. Even then, you never were very good."

I agreed with him. It wasn't true, but I agreed with him to shut the dope-babble down.

"That's why the hose beasts loved Rickyland. They could smell a poseur from three counties away. They could smell *you*."

"Yeah, man. I stunk. I couldn't play. Couldn't write. Couldn't fuck. Let's discuss it in the morning."

"Couldn't fuck," Ricky said with a snort. A fresh torrent of blood oozed out of his nose, spread over his lip, painted his teeth. "That's what the Arkansas bitch used to say. Of course she didn't know you were homo."

I was out of my chair and across the room in two heartbeats. Yeah, he was doped up and a fucking loser that the world had shit on a few times too often, but I was having my own problems with logic at that moment. My punch caught him on the chin. One of my knuckles broke from the impact. So did Ricky's jaw, but that was the least of either of our problems. Ricky recoiled from the blow and slid off the sofa to the floor. He lay on his back, convulsing. Vomit erupted from his throat; it filled his mouth, bubbled over his bloody lips to drool onto the floor. His eyes, open and staring, were glazed. His hands and feet slapped at the floor and the flood of foaming puke kept flowing. I knew he'd drowned in it if I didn't do something, so I rolled him off his back.

Once I had Ricky on his side and the contents of his belly seeped freely over the tiles, I stepped away and tried to figure out my next move. The fact that Ricky had been snorting a good amount of chemicals didn't occur to me then. I thought his seizure was a result of the blow I'd landed on the side of his face. If he died… Jesus. If he died.

I tried to snap him out of it. I called his name. I slapped his hand because I'd seen people do it movies; his palm was ice cold.

Finally, I called an ambulance. It was likely I'd end up in jail on an assault rap, possibly manslaughter if Ricky died, but I couldn't just leave the guy flopping around my floor like a landed trout. After I made the call, I waited with him, holding his hand, checking his pulse.

As the paramedics drove into my drive, their lights blasting across the front of the house, Ricky's heart stopped beating.

21

I looked through the curtain and saw Officer Richmond standing on the second story landing outside my room. Dawn had barely opened its eyes and a pale glow radiated to the East, cutting a soft line across the horizon.

I'd been expecting him sooner, and I told him so after I opened the door.

"Jack was a basket case. He ranted for an hour before I could get anything useful out of him."

"And what did he say?"

"His exact words? A pack of sideshow freaks attacked his restaurant and killed two of his customers."

"And what do you think?"

"Bump and Charlotte looked like they saw the devil dragging 'em down to hell before they left this world. These were two healthy adults that just keeled over within minutes of one another. Sure Bump had him a gut, but I dragged Doc Taurisano out of bed and got enough out of him to know that Bump and Charlotte were in damn good shape. We got no indication that any kind of drug was being used, though we're having the labs in the city fine-tooth comb it. So, what does that leave us?"

"Do you believe in ghosts?" I asked.

Richmond glared at me. He'd been up all night, and while that may not have been uncommon for him, I'm sure the level of stress that came with following up on a double homicide went a long way toward draining him. I was probably his last stop before going home to bed, and the last thing he wanted to hear was some city-ot's ghost story.

"No," Richmond said.

"Then I don't think anything I could add would be helpful to you."

"Okay," Richmond said with suspicion. He struck me as just too exhausted to run this particular obstacle course, so he went around it.

"But I assume you can confirm Jack's story? Sounds like what happened to you the other night."

"It is what happened to me," I said. "But it's a lot worse now."

Richmond nodded his head and rubbed his eyes dramatically. He wanted me to know that his patience was just about tapped.

"Look," I said, "I didn't believe in any of this until I saw it."

"I thought all you musician guys were into the occult and Satan and shit," Richmond said.

"I was into music," I told him, "There is little else I found spiritual."

"Fair enough," he said. "I imagine you'll understand if I don't put any of this Freak Town business in my report, though?"

"Do what you need to do," I said. "But keep in mind that whatever these things are, they didn't start this. Someone alive and real left that note for me. They probably did the exact same thing with Sandy and Noelle."

"So what do you suggest I do?"

"Keep an eye on Aaron Dalfour," I said. "He's the one that got me involved in all of this."

"Fine, I'll keep an eye on him. If I see him swinging a dead chicken at midnight, I'll slap a fine on him."

"Thanks for the support."

"You're welcome," Richmond said. "Look, Mick, I like you, and there aren't too many folks in town who wouldn't be happy as a pig in shit to see Dalfour knocked down a few pegs, but I can only operate within the confines of the law. You get that, right?"

"Sure."

"Now, I'm going to do everything I can to protect Isley, and you for that matter. It's my job, but I'm not going to spend my time or energy looking into local legends or hexes, because they aren't going to help anyone in a court of law."

"I understand that." Honestly, I didn't understand that. People were dying, people he knew most, if not all, of his life. The idea that he would let this continue just because it didn't have a code number in his little police book was ridiculous. I barely knew any of the victims, and their deaths bothered me more than they appeared to bother Officer Richmond. I didn't know what to make of that.

"As for you," he said, "I'd suggest you leave this alone. It might even be a good idea if you left town for a while until this is squared away."

"You're the second person in twelve hours that has suggested I leave."

"Then maybe it's a good idea."

"I can't go anywhere until this business with Isley is straightened out. I'm not leaving her here."

"Fair enough," Richmond said. "Then I'm going to suggest you don't tell too many people about your theories."

"Who the hell would I even talk to about it?"

"No one," he said. "But if there is hoodoo behind this, the worst thing you can do is get people talking about it. Places like Freak Town are best left buried and forgotten."

I couldn't agree more, but I wasn't the one digging it up and giving it life.

22

In my room, I prepared for a second drive out to the Wertimer house, and my cell phone rang.

It was Isley. I was very glad to hear her voice. She told me that things were "Okay" at the Wertimer's. The day before, Mrs. Wertimer had dosed up on medication after my departure to take the edge off of the excitement and spent the day in bed. Lance was in town running errands. Isley was in her room, with the door locked. I told her about my conversation with Brad Bunny and made it clear that the decision was hers. If she wanted me to proceed, just say the word.

"Yeah, great choices. A perv, a loon, and a psycho... or the Wertimers."

That actually struck me as funny. It was good to see the kid had a sense of humor after all she'd been through. Still, I wondered if she had heard anything about the events at Jack's Steakhouse the night before. I didn't bring it up just then. I didn't want to dampen what I felt was a relatively good moment between us, but I had a whole bag of crazy to spill to her, and the more information she brought into the conversation, the better.

"I was just going to come see you," I said.

"Better not," she said. "The Wicked Old Wertimer is on her broom and causing trouble. Darrell gets home today, and she's acting like the president is coming for a visit, which means nothing is where it should be and nothing is clean enough. I'm about to get out of here."

"Where are you going?" I asked.

"Doesn't matter. Anywhere but here."

"Why don't I pick you up? We'll get some breakfast or something."

"I'll meet you," Isley said.

"Wouldn't it be easier if I drove?"

"I can drive myself."

That came as news. In my head, I imagined she was relegated to walking or public transportation on those odd occasions when she was allowed out of the house. It never occurred to me that she might be allowed to use one of the Wertimer's cars. As it turns out, she wasn't.

"Mom's car is here," Isley said.

"Can you drive it?"

"I've had my license for over a year. Christ, I'm not a total dysfunction."

"I meant, are you *allowed* to drive it?" I was thinking about Brad Bunny's warning not to cause any trouble until after progress was made with the courts. I didn't want to blow the whole deal before it even got started.

"Yes," Isley said as if for the hundredth time. "Stop freaking out. I don't need it today."

"Sorry," I said. "Where do you want to meet?"

"I'll be at my house."

★   ★   ★

This time when I visited the house on Amaryllis Street, Isley let me inside. Walking up the porch stairs, I felt a moment of pride, looking at the clean, white door. I rang the bell and followed the lines of the jamb, checking to make sure I'd done a clean job with the paint. Satisfied, I stepped back and peeked through the living room window Sidney had repaired. It still had the putty film framing the glass. I told myself to give it another day to cure, and then I'd come out to rub it off.

Isley opened the door but didn't wait for me to return to the stoop before disappearing back into the house. Inside, I found her standing in the kitchen. Leaning on the counter. Holding a folded scrap of paper.

"Did you leave this for me?" she asked, waving the note in the air.

The sight of the notepaper, exactly the kind that was left for me on my arrival in Celebration, sent a bolt of fear to my neck. "Put that down!" I shouted, rushing across the kitchen.

My outburst startled her, and her face flashed with momentary surprise, but was quickly replaced by a hard glare. Isley shot a look of ferocious contempt in my direction. I reached for the note, but she spun away, clutching the paper close to her chest.

"Give me that," I said. "Isley, please. Just fold that back up and hand it to me. Don't look at it again."

"What is it?" she asked.

"It doesn't matter," I said, knowing I could never get the whole story out in time. "Please, just put the note down and don't say anything."

"Oh, daddy's got a secret," Isley said bitterly. "Big surprise."

I eased closer, forcing her to the corner where the counter made a sharp L. She looked at me like I was a stranger, a rapist, or a murderer. I knew how my outburst must have looked to her, knew how I must have sounded, but I couldn't let her say those words, would not allow her to speak whatever name was written on that paper. "Please," I said again. "Just don't say anything until I can explain. This is *very* important."

"When I gave you the keys, you promised you wouldn't come inside except to let the window repairman in."

"I didn't write that," I said. Close enough, now, I shot out my hand and grabbed the edge of the note.

Isley yelped, and pulled back, tearing the sheet in two.

"What in the hell is wrong with you?" Isley cried. "Christ, you're as crazy as old lady Wertimer. Crazier."

"Just give me a chance to explain."

"I trusted you," Isley said. "You promised you wouldn't come inside, but you just had to sneak around. Did you go into my room, too?"

"Isley, I did not write that note. Now, please give me the other half, and I'll explain."

Isley looked at the torn sheet of paper in her hands. Looked at me. Even before she spoke, I knew what she was going to say. To spite me, she screwed herself.

"So, is Jody Mayram some guy you were trying to pick up? Next time you might want to get a phone number to go with the name."

Desolation crashed over me. It started as rage, and I felt a brief urge to lunge forward and shake Isley, scream in her face for being a stupid vindictive brat. But the feeling passed. The damage was done.

I dropped my half of the note and turned away, walked out of the kitchen, dejected. It felt like someone had just hollowed me out from the back and dropped a four hundred pound boulder into the hole. The weight crushed my ribs, ground against my stooping shoulders.

"You *are* crazy," Isley said at my back.

"Yeah," I whispered. "I am."

I kept walking into the living room where I dropped down on the sofa, felt a spring jab me in the ass, but didn't bother to shift on the cushion to find a better spot. I wasn't going to be comfortable, and right then didn't believe comfort was my right. I'd been a fool. I let her say the name. There, on the sofa, with my hands clasped and my head lowered, I felt like my daughter's killer.

"Well, who is Jody?" Isley insisted.

"Quit saying that name," I shouted.

"I'm not going to stand here and have you yelling at me. This is *my* house."

"Oh, shut up," I said. "Just shut the fuck up."

"Get out."

"I'm not going anywhere," I said. The cold dark empty that always unlocked in me in times of conflict burst open. I stood from the couch, faced off on my bitter-faced daughter and grabbed her arm. "Sit down."

"I'm not…"

"Sit down," I said with so much ice in my voice, it froze her. Fear crept over her features, and I figured it was about damn time. I shoved her toward the sofa. She made a play to resist, but Isley saw I wasn't fooling around. She sat, still holding her half of the note.

"I know what killed Sandy Winchester," I said. "It was probably the same thing that drove your mother to kill herself. Last night, two more people died. I'm telling you this so you know how serious it is. I'm telling you this so you'll be afraid. That's the only thing that's likely to keep you alive."

"What are you talking about?" Isley asked. Her body trembled. Tears spilled over her lashes. She looked at the front door, like she was going to bolt, then gazed down at the note in her hand.

"There's a place by the river," I began. "A place some people call Freak Town…"

★   ★   ★

Throughout my story, Isley reacted with predictable expressions: disdain for a deluded jerk who pretended to be her father; angry amusement, that I might actually believe such nonsense; incredulity, realizing that I did, in fact, believe every word of it; and finally fear when I described what happened to Bump and Charlotte Carter at Jack's Steakhouse. By the time I was through, the fear remained and had a good solid hold on her. She didn't question the story or launch accusations at me. She took me for my word.

"Who would do something like this?"

"I don't know," I said. "Exactly how well do you know Aaron Dalfour?"

"You think Aaron's doing this?" Isley asked. She looked at the sheet of paper still clutched in her hand and recoiled. She wadded the note up and dropped it on the coffee table.

"He brought me into this," I said. "He was involved in you and your mother's lives."

"But why?"

"Money," I said.

"We don't have any money. Mom barely had any insurance."

"I know, but I do have some. Maybe Aaron thinks I have a fortune lying around."

Isley thought about this. Then she shook her head rapidly. "No. I mean, he didn't even know about you until after mom died. I know, because I told him."

"Your mother might have told him."

"But why kill Sandy? He didn't do anything."

"Because he might have tried to help you. If you had Sandy's help, you wouldn't need me. His family is well off. They probably would have looked after you if Sandy hadn't died. But you have no legal claim to their estate."

"Well, it's not like I have a legal claim to yours either," she said.

"That's not exactly true," I said. "Technically, you're my next of kin, so even if I had nothing formal written into my will, you could challenge it. As it happens, I do have provisions made for both you and your mother. Aaron couldn't know that, but he might have suspected."

"You made provisions for us?" Isley asked. Her expression softened.

"Yes. I have a trust set up in your name. You'll get that on your eighteenth birthday regardless of what happens to me. Your mother knew all about it. It's more than enough to cover college and get you set up with a life of your own. There are also insurance policies, and like I said, as my next of kin, you certainly have a case if you wanted to challenge my will. Now, you may not even consider something like that, but Aaron would."

Isley said nothing. She nodded her head and looked at the floor, absorbing what I'd said.

"How he expected to get the money from you, I couldn't say. You're young, so he might have figured it would be easy to trick you. I don't know. I'm not even sure it's him, but he's the most likely suspect right now, unless you know of anyone else?"

"Like who?" Isley asked.

"What about the Wertimers? God knows, they aren't the Brady Bunch. Have you noticed anything around their house to indicate Darrell or his wife are into this stuff?"

"What stuff?" Isley asked, so overwhelmed by the conversation, she didn't seem to remember where it had begun.

"Magic," I said. "Sidney Tierney calls it hoodoo. Have you seen anything at all to suggest those whack jobs are into the occult?"

Isley puzzled over the question. She brought her thumbnail to her lips and began to chew. She shook her head twice and then stopped. "Lance!" she said, her voice sharp and loud like the winner of a Bingo game.

"What about him?"

"His room is in the basement, but I sometimes hear things through the vent. A couple of times, I heard him chanting, and there was this weird smell like dead flowers burning. Like incense."

That could have meant nothing more than Lance practiced Buddhism or some new age religion. Hell, he might have studied yoga to keep his temper under control, though this last theory held no more water than a net, mostly because he didn't strike me as the sort looking for inner peace.

"Anyone else?" I asked. "You've lived here your whole life, any rumors about people who dabble in magic or witchcraft?"

"No," she said.

"Okay. We'll go with what we know."

"What are we going to do?"

"Find out what we can," I said. "Then see if we can stop it."

★   ★   ★

The Celebration Public Library was an impressive structure with its stone construction, its towering columns capped with intricately sculpted vines, and its pair of concrete lions, guarding the double doors opening onto the library's lobby. Large brass plaques ran on either side of the entrance. Etched into the metal sheets were the names of the men, the women and the family's who had donated money to the facility. I noticed the Wertimer name on at least four of these signs.

Inside was also a surprise. Expecting to find a chamber lined with densely crowded bookcases, I wasn't prepared for the modern fixtures filling the library. Tall anti-theft detectors rose on either side of the door. To the right, a long polished desk ran to the room's center. Behind the desk, tall bookcases held hundreds of volumes of reference materials. In the corner beneath a frosted-glass window, half a dozen return carts were corralled. But these were the only souvenirs of the libraries I remembered from my youth. To the left of the entrance and running all the way to a broad staircase at the back of the lobby, computer stations had been installed. About a dozen people sat in front of glowing screens; the rest of the monitors were dark and sleeping. I assumed the stacks were on the second and third floors of the place, because with the exception of reference titles behind the counter, no other space had been allocated to books.

Sun poured through the frosted windows, soft yellowish light that formed pools for swimming dust. The air was cold and scented with the rich odors of old paper, ancient leather, and floor polish.

At the long counter, a small blonde woman with high cheekbones and almost no chin greeted Isley and me. The dramatic slope her face took beneath the nose gave her the general appearance of a trout.

"Help you?" she asked, eyeing Isley with suspicion and doing little to hide it.

"If I wanted to research town history, what would be the best way to go about that?"

"What town?" the chin-challenged woman asked.

"This one."

"Oh sure," she said. "What you want to do is search the library database. That's where the local stuff is. Well, that's where everything is, except all of the other crap from the internet. I mean, you could search the internet but then you'd get all kinds of stuff you don't need."

"Thank you."

Apparently the librarian wasn't finished speaking yet, because she said, "This one time, I typed in 'Celebration mayor' because I was doing a report for school and I got about two million pages back." She smiled. "I went on the internet instead of the library database. Gotta be careful of that."

"I'll do my best."

The blonde flashed a strange look at Isley. When she smiled it pulled her lips so tight, I thought they might tear open.

We walked away from the counter and found a computer station near the front of the lobby. Most of the other terminals that were occupied sat near the back—probably locals looking to get their fix of internet porn.

"Are we safe here?" Isley asked, looking over my shoulder at the expanse of the lobby.

"As safe as anywhere else, I guess. Just keep an eye on things while I search the database. You'll know these guys if you see one of them."

"And what if I do see one of them?"

"We run like hell."

Though not thrilled with my response, Isley stood watch at my shoulder while I got to work.

I typed the name Jody Mayram into the search box and hit return. The screen filled with the results of the search, though only two of the articles carried any relevance for me. The first was a newspaper article. It read:

> *From the Celebration Gazette, October 8, 1924:*
> Manville's Miracles a Lot of Hooey
> When times are hard, and times don't get much harder than these, people put aside their reason and Christian knowledge. They look for magic and mysticism at every turn, and Trevor Manville is more than happy to give it to them, at a quarter a pop. Instead of putting a loaf of bread on the table or buying warm socks, people spend their good money on freak shows and sleight of hand acts.
>
> If this were simply a means of distraction, this reporter would not be concerned, but after attending Manville's Miracle Show this past weekend, and listening to our poor citizens finding omen and prophecy in the petty tricks of freaks and sham artists, I felt the need, nay the responsibility, to reveal these hucksters for what they are.
>
> I trust that even the dimmest of us saw right through the "magik" of Bertolucci the Brilliant. If he could actually pull a rabbit out of thin air, I doubt he'd look as if he were starving. With rabbits that plentiful, he'd always have a stew on the stove, but neither Bertolucci nor his hare seemed to have had a good meal in ages.

Similarly, if the "witch"Verna Ellyn were truly the "Mistress of the Occult," she might be able to conjure up a decent gown, instead of the threadbare skid row frock that all but fell from her shoulders during her lewd performance. Indeed, were she truly gifted with unprecedented powers as she so vehemently claimed, I'd imagine more than one savvy businessman would have hired her away from Manville's dreadful troupe to turn his straw into gold.

Manville, knowing the world's taste for the grotesque, travels with an extensive cadre of deformed and twisted outcasts. Under more genteel circumstances, I might look upon Manville's freaks as pitiable, but when they proudly and shamelessly exhibit and parade their deformities for pennies and nickels, hard-won by the citizens of this county, I feel only disgust.

Manville's featured act is the greatest sham of all. Anyone from Celebration surely knows the name of Jody Mayram. I am not without heart, and readily admit that seeing that blind child wandering the streets of our great township during my own boyhood filled me with sad dread.

Now, he has taken to using his hideous affliction as a means to steal money from his neighbors, and for this, I cannot just stand by. Barely thirty years of age, Mayram looks weathered and worldly, adding, I imagine, to the credibility his audiences give him. His hair has gone white in great strands, salting the tangle of long brown hair that nearly covers his monstrous face.

"Your mother has pneumonia," Mayram tells a fragile looking woman in a brown coat. "Though your father is a good man and trying to help, he should not be giving her whiskey for her malady. She needs warm blankets and hot tea. With your care, she will become well."

The woman who received this information began sobbing and thanking the blind man. When she took her seat,

she quickly told everyone within ear shot that there was no
way he could have known about her mother or her illness.

But in reality, there was a way. You see I was in the park
on the periphery of the Manville's tents before Mayram's
show began. At that time, I was very near the woman in
the brown coat and heard her confiding in a friend about
her mother's condition, even stating the measures her father
was taking to speed the woman's recovery.

Had I walked up to her at that point and told her exactly
what Mayram told her, she would have found no magic
in it. She might have even scolded me for eavesdropping,
but because she had heard the news from a man with no
eyes, sitting in the middle of a ring of torches, she took it
as miraculous.

Now, I do not admit to having seen Mayram in our
periphery before the show. Likely, he had a fellow huckster
wandering through the waiting crowd gathering this information. Many vaudeville acts used this same device and the
assistant feeds the "seer" clues. Though Mayram had no such
prompts, his methods are perfectly transparent.

None of us who knew Mayram as a boy could forget
the sensitivity of his ears. Perhaps age has further honed his
ability. For all I know, he could hear the woman from across
the midway. This is irrelevant. What is relevant is that this
woman threw an additional dime into the ring of torches
at Mayram's feet when he completed his drivel.

In these difficult times we can't afford such reckless
expenditure. Manville and Mayram and their ilk exploit
our sorrows and the miseries of others. If you must pay for
such grotesqueries, take them for what they are: terrible
distractions. Imbuing them with your hope and faith loses
you far more than coins.

After finishing the article, I fell back into the chair, incredulous and unnerved. Jody was real. Though I knew he *existed*, he had been an abstract, part of the mythology surrounding Freak Town. I was now looking at proof he'd once walked the streets of Celebration. He was not merely a local boogeyman. Jody Mayram had lived in this town, had been a performer with Manville's Miracle Show.

Another important piece of information hid in this article, though I didn't know it until my search led me to the second mention of Mayram. Most of the pages my search called up referenced the name "Jody" but were about other citizens of the county with that first name. On the fourth search page, the word "Mayram" was highlighted in black. Opening this, I came across an excerpt from a book, a novel by Charles Harold Hopkins.

The author's name wasn't familiar, but a brief biography ran above the excerpt:

Charles Harold Hopkins was a writer who emerged mid-Twentieth Century. Though he never achieved the notoriety of many of the writers to follow him, he was a master of what became known as the Southern Gothic. What really kept him from becoming much more well known was his style, which was stripped down, unromantic and not nearly as florid as say Faulkner or McCullers, and he leaned toward very dark subject matter, considered far too coarse by literary critics and the public. He had a regional following in his home state of Arkansas, and the French revered his novels, but by US literary standards he was a minor author.

Beneath the biographical information was a short, hardly a thumbnail, excerpt from a novel written in 1934 called *Dust in the Palms of Our Fathers*:

Just like the men who went down to that damnable place, that Mayram Ellyn Glen, with their loaded guns and their harvest blades and their torches for the burning, Old Harper saw the Devil ahead and charged forth regardless, carrying the possibility of destruction upon his back like a scorpion, all but weightless.

"Well?" Isley asked. She stood next to me, gently bouncing on the balls of her feet. Frightened. Anxious. "Did you find anything?"

"A couple of things."

"And?"

"I'm not sure yet," I said. "I have to check something out."

I typed the words "Mayram Ellyn Glen," into the search box, and found ten references, all of them from Charles Harold Hopkins's novel. Most of the mentions were merely slams against the place used for description: "…as foul as Mayram Ellyn;" and "…suffused with evil like the dirt beneath Mayram Ellyn Glen;" and "… with distortions akin to the monstrous population of Mayram Ellyn." Hopkins spoke of the place like it was iconic, a touchstone of depravity and malevolence. Sodom. Gomorrah. Auschwitz. But he was the only one invoking the name of the place, as if it were a fiction he'd created.

I knew this wasn't the case. In the first article, the reporter mentioned a woman by the name of Verna Ellyn. She was part of the same traveling show as Jody Mayram. It seemed clear, though I could have been finding connections where they didn't exist, that at some point these two had formed a union, perhaps romantic, and they left Manville's Miracle Show. They returned to Celebration. They became the Lord and Lady of a place that would come to be known as Freak Town.

Hopkins confirmed my deduction with the passage:

Such was the perverse nature of Mayram Ellyn Glen. Nothing good can grow in earth walked by witch and monster. Their spawn, like locusts, devour and desiccate all in their paths. As to their home, it is a pit, a hollow, a rut in decency and Christian morality. Evil flows through this glen as thick and as deep as the river at its border, and were Hell confined to our imperfect earth, it surely would be found there.

At my side, Isley gasped. I looked up quickly and saw her facing the door. Two kids, barely ten years old, walked into the library, through the anti-theft detectors and made a line toward the computers at the back of the lobby.

"Sorry," she said.

"It's cool. I'm about done, but I need to print some of these pages out. I also have to see if they have a certain book here. I'll work as fast as I can, but try to relax. If nothing else, we're in a public place with plenty of people around. We should be okay."

But I could tell by her expression that she was thinking about the events I related regarding Jack's Steakhouse. It too was a public place; it too had people around, and now two of those people were dead.

The chin-challenged librarian guided me through the process of printing out the few pages, spat from a printer behind the counter. When I'd printed out everything I needed, I returned to the counter and paid for the low stack of sheets and requested information about the title, *Dust in the Palms of Our Fathers* by Charles Harold Hopkins.

"You know," the librarian said, sounding extremely put out, "you can check a book's location on one of those terminals over there. We're not busy, so I'll do it. But for future reference…"

"Thank you," I said.

She worked over her keyboard for a few seconds and leaned in close to the screen. "We have the 1972 edition with a forward by some guy named Gibney. The first edition is considered rare and is no longer in circulation. Must be in the basement someplace."

"The 1972 will be fine."

"Sorry," she said. "The book is checked out right now."

I took this information as good news. It was unlikely that such an obscure book would be taken out at random. The only references to Mayram Ellyn Glen were between its covers, so it made sense that someone would want to keep the information out of my hands or the hands of anyone else curious about its content. Obviously the tack failed since the computer brought up specific references, but perhaps the clue to ending this nightmare was held within the book's pages. Whoever had that book was likely Jody Mayram's living accomplice.

"This is very important," I said. "Can you tell me who checked the book out?"

"No," the blonde said in a crisp chirp.

Never having been the subtle type, I asked, "Can I buy the name from you?"

I figured she'd put on a show of mortification at the suggestion or insult that I should even ask it. Instead, she thought it over for a couple of seconds and said, "Twenty bucks."

I produced my wallet and a twenty a dollar bill. She took the bill quickly, looked around to make sure no one witnessed the transaction and returned her attention to the computer screen.

"It was checked out on the fifth of this month," she said. "Hmm. It's overdue. Oh yeah, now I see why."

"What do you mean? Who checked it out?"

"Noelle Vale," the librarian said. "I guess we won't be getting the late fee."

23

The drive back to the house on Amaryllis Street was quiet and uncomfortable. The sensation of being watched fell over me again. Stronger now. The information gathered from the library fluttered in my head. I imagined that it was in some way responsible for the feeling that someone was near, observing and waiting. From the corners of my eyes, flashes of movement drew my attention, as I checked for Jody Mayram or one of his followers on the quiet, brightly lit streets of Celebration. In the seat next to me, Isley sat with her legs curled under her, a thumbnail captured between her teeth.

At least one mystery was solved, or so I believed. A so-called witch named Verna Ellyn had involved herself with Jody Mayram. Together they'd created Mayram Ellyn Glen, where the disturbed and damaged gathered to form a community of their own. When their monstrous acts were revealed, and the townspeople retaliated against Jody for the murder of a child, it was Verna, likely at Jody's urging, who cast the spell, laying the curse on the heads of her people. Manville's Miracle Show billed her as the "Mistress of the Occult," and in light of all that had happened, I was willing to believe she'd earned the title.

Coming to a stop outside of Noelle Vale's house, where we were hoping to find a copy of Charles Harold Hopkins's book, I suddenly thought that what we really needed to find was a witch of our own. Someone who would understand and be able to reverse the curse cast on the citizens of Freak Town. It stood to reason that if one person knew the magic to create this horror, another would know how to end it.

Isley climbed out of the car and trudged toward the porch. She climbed the stairs slowly, in the labored fashion of a very old woman. She seemed beaten and resigned.

In the house, I kept following her, up the stairs, down the corridor to the last of four doors. Her bedroom was uncluttered save for the walls, which wore posters and banners and a collage she'd apparently made in the last couple of years. The triangular banner for the Celebration High Rockets hung over her bed, pointed like an arrow to the collage, which was a compilation of letters and faces. The letters spelled *friends are forever*. Pictures of young, happy kids filled a poster board. Beyond that, her walls were adorned with posters for Rob Zombie, Trivium, and Marilyn Manson. Despite my anxiety, I was proud to see my kid leaned toward the heavy stuff.

To the left of the room was a bookcase, jammed full of books and music CDs, and a simple white lacquered desk on which sat an old computer, a cup of pens and a low stack of papers. Isley fell on the bed to the right and drew her knees to her chest. She curled up in a fetal position, facing away from me.

"We should really find that book," I said.

"Go ahead," she whispered. "I don't want to think about this anymore."

"I'm sorry but you have to."

She rolled over, her eyes moist with tears. "Is everyone on the planet an asshole? I mean does everyone just lie and screw you over and then disappear?"

Yes, I wanted to say. I knew it wasn't true. I understood that my feelings were formed by spending much of my life with exactly the kinds of people Isley was describing, but I *felt* it was true. I empathized with her frustration and anger. I also knew supporting her feelings of betrayal would get us nowhere. We didn't have the luxury of bitching about the world's population.

"Not everyone," I said.

"Mom knew this was happening, and she didn't say anything."

"She was trying to protect you. I'm sure of that."

"How can you know anything? You didn't even know her!"

"That's true," I said, agreeing yet stung by the comment. "But I didn't tell you for the same reason. None of this is logical or easy to believe. If Noelle had that book, she was trying to find proof, trying to stop what was happening, like we are."

"I just want to get away," Isley said. "I hate this place. Why can't we just leave?"

"You know why. I'm not your legal guardian. Not yet."

"So what?" she asked. "God, something's trying to kill us, and you're worried about getting busted? What kind of brilliant logic is that?"

She had a good point. Not many years ago I wouldn't have thought twice about the consequences of such a disappearing act. Standing in her room though, my thoughts were filled with holding cells and excruciatingly long court sessions, not to mention Bradley Bunny's warnings to play by the rules. Strange how much power these concerns had over me. Ricky Blaine would have said I'd totally pussyed out.

Instead of trying to defend my position to Isley, I offered a compromise.

"Let's just find that book. I'll call Wertimer and try to convince him to let me have temporary custody until the court date. If he refuses, I'm going to have you get in your mother's car and drive way the hell out of town. Go out of the state if you'll feel safer. I'll meet you when I can."

"You're going to leave me alone?"

"Isley, whatever these things are, they have limitations. They can't just teleport from place to place and appear. If they could, they'd have been all over us half dozen times by now. Fuck, I'd be dead already if they could that. I think that once they have a solid form, they're stuck in it, which means that unless they decide to hitchhike, you'll be safe as long as you're far enough away. I'll give you money to last a few days. By then, this will either be finished or... "

I will be dead and you'll inherit enough to keep you comfortable for the next ten years.

"Yeah... or," Isley said miserably.

I walked to the window and leaned over to check the street. In talking about the limitations of Jody and his people, I realized hours had passed, and I hadn't seen any sign of them. Maybe they had more limitations that I'd imagined. Surely, they could have made it to my motel at some point the night before, but they didn't appear. Were they unable to find me? Or confined to a limited radius around the city? Even if I knew what to call these things, I still wouldn't have known what to expect from them. At any rate, the street was clear.

"Come on," I said. "One thing at a time. Let's find that book."

"Fine," she said, sliding off the bed. "But I don't know where the hell it could be. The police went through her room about fifty times after she died."

"Nobody was looking for it though. The police wouldn't think anything about an old book... would you?"

"No."

So we started the search in Noelle's room. It wasn't what I'd expected. The bed was unmade, just a bare mattress and naked pillows thrown at the head. Stacks of papers climbed the top of the dresser and covered a small desk by the window. The closet doors were open and Noelle's clothes were shoved to one side, leaving a broad blank slab of white wall. Shoes spilled over the closet floor. Boxes and various garments littered the shelves above the rod.

"Boy, they did a number on this place," I said.

"Tell me about it," Isley said. "I should have straightened it up. I meant to, but I didn't want to come in here, not after the morning I found her."

"I can understand that," I said.

"In fact, I don't want to be here, now," she said. "I'm going to look around downstairs."

Before I replied, she was already in the corridor, nothing but a shadow growing smaller against the wall, and I was left in her mother's room, wondering where I should begin to search.

When we met, Noelle was a beautiful young girl wearing acid washed jeans and a crisp white blouse. Her hair was pulled back and her eyes sparkled with a genuine love of life, no stain of drug or drink in them. Noelle was something solid and good when she came into my life—a life decorated with lascivious Barbie dolls, looking for bragging rights and bumps of coke. She wasn't pure—because nothing really is—but she was untainted by the hedonistic demons boogieing through my life, a wallflower at the *deca-dance*. At least she'd started that way. Standing among her things, strewn here and there around the room, I felt close to her again.

My throat closed tight and my eyes grew moist. I lifted a picture off of the nightstand. In it, Noelle and Isley hugged casually and smiled for the camera. From the way Isley looked, the picture had been taken recently. Noelle had changed so little the photograph might have passed for that of two sisters rather than mother and daughter. Her voice came back to me then, and its message dealt me some misery:

I can't do this anymore, Mick. I don't like what I'm becoming.

So become something else.

Can we just discuss this like adults?

Is that what he did? Did he talk to you like an adult? Did he make you feel like a real grown up?

Mick, don't.

You know… fuck this. Plenty of fish in the sea, right?

Would you just wait a minute?

I don't think so.

Well, where are you going?

I'm going fishing. See ya.

I put the picture back on the nightstand, wiped my eyes and looked around the room. This was all that remained of her. This sad little room, picked through by the police looking for clues.

And there's nothing

Left of the sidewalks,

Nothing left but tears.

But that wasn't right. There was our daughter; there was Isley. She was left behind, and I had to do everything in my power to keep her safe.

★   ★   ★

The search of Noelle's room took longer than it should have. Distracted by memories of her, I found myself pausing when I opened a drawer, pushed aside a pile of shoes, or touched one of the summer dresses shoved against the closet wall. I rummaged through her desk and her dresser, but found no book, just souvenirs of Noelle, bits and pieces of her life.

I checked behind the other doors upstairs, a bathroom, a large linen closet. Nothing. So I met Isley downstairs, in the kitchen, where she was methodically going through the cupboards.

"I don't think it's here," she said quietly, lifting a stack of muffin tins so she could see the back of a cabinet. "The cellar is empty, except for some dust."

"Where should I look next?"

"The living room, I guess."

So I lifted sofa cushions, crawled on the floor peeking below the furniture, checked every title on the small bookcase in the corner twice. During my search, I came across a large photo album, resting on the bottom shelf. I lifted the volume out and opened to a random page, found myself staring at several pictures of Noelle holding an infant in the crook of her elbow. Some gut feeling told me Isley would disapprove of this trespass, but I couldn't help myself. I leafed through the book, saw my daughter growing up one image at a time, going from baby to young woman too quickly. Though my inclination was to linger with these images—study every dress she wore, every toy she held, every birthday cake—Isley's likely upset at finding me forced me to move quickly through the album. I replaced it on the shelf and went to the window.

Through the new pane of glass, the neighborhood looked idyllic, though some of the shadow I'd attributed to Celebration's streets still clung to the roofs and siding of the houses. My gaze roamed over lawns and porches and driveways, looking for signs of Jody, the Trash Boy, or any other denizen of Freak Town.

"Are they out there?" Isley asked. She had come into the living room so quietly, the sound of her voice made me jump.

"No," I said, turning away from the window.

"Did you find anything?"

Again, no.

"What are we going to do now?"

★   ★   ★

I sat on an excruciatingly uncomfortable wooden bench at the periphery of a food court. Radiating out from the court were dozens of low
buildings, forming the sprawl of a rural outlet mall. I smoked a cigarette and drank a cup of coffee while Isley continued to shop. Before
leaving Celebration that morning, I'd called the Wertimer house to
speak with Darrell Wertimer about temporary custody. Lance made
it quite clear that even if Wertimer were home—*he won't be back until
late afternoon*—he wasn't likely to speak to me. Not wanting to spend
hours in Celebration, constantly looking over our shoulders to see
what new horror might appear, we left town. My thinking was simple
enough: if Wertimer refused to remand custody to me, Isley would have
to escape on her own; she'd need clothes and toiletries, enough for a
few days anyway. Many of her belongings were still in the Wertimer
house under Lance and Frances Wertimer's guard.

At first, Isley looked through the clothing racks sheepishly, not really
committing herself to the shopping (not comfortable spending the
money of a guy she didn't particularly care for). But this passed soon
enough, about the time she found a pair of black Italian boots she
desperately wanted. From that point forward, she threw herself into
the task with the energy of any kid given a blank check.

About halfway through the Armani Xchange, my steam ran out. I
liked watching her shop, enjoyed doing this for her, despite the solemn
circumstance demanding it. I'd missed seventeen birthdays and sixteen
Christmases and dozens of other gift-worthy events in her life. This
little spree could hardly make up for so much absence, but it was
something. Still, several restless nights with minimal sleep and days of
exhausting stress caught up with me in front of a rack of sheer white
blouses. I gave Isley some cash so she could continue shopping and
excused myself to the food court.

After the cigarette, once the coffee was gone, I dozed off. Several
times I shook myself awake, embarrassed, wondering if I'd been snoring
like some old man on a park bench. But the sleep kept coming for me,
and finally, I let it take me away.

★   ★   ★

The vibration of my cell phone surprised me. I woke absolutely confused by my surroundings. In front of me, an overweight little boy
with a melting ice cream cone had his face only a couple of feet from
mine. His head was cocked to the side.

"You died," he said before licking a blob of melted cream from
between his fingers. "I saw you. You died."

"Not yet," I said. Again the cell phone rattled in my pocket, and I
pulled it free.

Bradley Bunny had good news. Not great news, but it was good
enough.

"I've got a buddy in Dallas who has a buddy in Little Rock. He
went to school with this guy that lives in the county. To make a long
story short, you have an appearance in front of the judge on Tuesday.
If all goes well, you'll walk out of the hearing with custody, as long as
Darrell Wertimer doesn't want a fight."

"And if he does want a fight?" I asked.

"We'll give him one."

"So are you flying out to handle this, or will your friend be doing it?"

"You don't really need me there, and considering the nature of this
case, you'll be fine with Dub."

"Dub?"

"Dub Skillings. Don't let the name fool you. My buddy in Dallas
tells me Dub is sharp as a tack. I was on the phone with him for
about an hour before I called you, and I have to agree. He's got your
cell phone number, and once he puts some things together, he'll give
you a call to get rolling. With any luck, you can have this whole thing
straightened out in under a week."

"Thanks, Brad. That's great news."

What I didn't know was that we would never get to that hearing.
By the time Tuesday came, my world had already crumbled. I was back
in Denver, and the bulk of this story had come to an end.

24

Something incredibly strange happened in the parking lot of the outlet mall. Something I could never have expected. Isley hugged me.

We were loading up the rental car with bags of clothes, cosmetics, whatever else she'd decided she needed. I was still groggy from my brief nap, and the murderous sun made my sweating face feel tight, like wet leather. We still had the long drive back to Celebration. Then I needed to speak with Darrell Wertimer, whether on the phone (as I was hoping) or face to face. It would have been generous to call myself grumpy, but the truth was, I was incredibly uncomfortable, frustrated, scared, and ready for a fight.

But Isley smiled. She said, "Thank you." She hugged me.

Holding her then, feeling my daughter's body against mine, the only pure embrace, the only one free of calculation or expectation that I'd had in as long as I could remember, something inside me shattered. That's the only way to explain it.

There are moments in life, moments when it seems that you've finally reached a point of happiness, and you think every other moment from that point on will be colored with it. You convince yourself that sacrifice and pain were worth the cost, because they are forever behind you, washed away by a single act, a momentary joy. Of course, it doesn't work that way. My life up to that point had several such moments: first gig, first record deal, first time I heard one of my songs on the radio, first gold record, first platinum, first marriage, second marriage, Glen moving in, the very number of such moments refuted the ridiculous magic I imbued in them. And yet, here was another. I convinced myself that everything was going to be okay, everything was finally in sync. Standing in the vast parking lot, baked by midday sun, I felt happy. My daughter and I were together, though not exactly the way I'd imagined it. In that short, short, far too short time, hope broke me down as if exploding a skeletal shell I didn't know existed beneath my skin.

Then it was over. Isley pulled away, still smiling. She asked if she could drive, and I said yes. I was experiencing such deeply confusing feelings, long buried and no longer familiar, that I probably would have agreed to anything she asked at that point.

During the drive back to Celebration, she talked about the afternoon, what she bought, showing real pleasure in the time we'd spent together. *Oh and that old woman with the bad teeth, she said with a laugh. What a bitch! I couldn't believe she actually thought I'd fight her for that nasty blouse. And what about that kid at the Nike store, acting like he's just so cool? He was like fourteen, and he was trying to play me. Did you see that? And I just love those boots. Oh, and that blue dress. God, I hate all of my clothes.* She went on and on, in one thrilling stream of dialogue, and I did all that I could to encourage it, fearing it might end. Now and then, the cold shell within me tried to reform, but the sound of Isley's voice quickly dismantled it.

About ten miles out of Celebration, I cracked the window, lit a cigarette.

"When this is over," I said, "do you think you'd consider moving to Denver?"

"With you?" Isley asked seemingly startled by the question. "I never thought about it. I mean I just didn't think... "

"Look, if I get custody, you'll have to live with me, and I suppose I could arrange to live here for a while, but a fresh start might be what you need. Honestly, I don't think it's a good idea for you to stay here. Even without all of this hoodoo bullshit going on, I don't like the idea of you being here."

"Do you *want* me to live with you or is it just your legal obligation?"

"It's not the obligation. You're going to have your own life soon enough, but for a while I want to be a part of it. You'll have plenty of room at the house. We can bring your mother's car up, or I can get you a new one. Whatever you want to do."

"I don't know," she said, but she was smiling from ear to ear.

I took that as a good sign. "It really is up to you." But in my head, I was already picturing her in the large Spanish style house, lounging on the sofa, playing video games or watching sitcoms, talking with new friends on the phone, introducing me to a boyfriend and telling me not to wait up. I saw her filling out college applications, imagined myself at her high school graduation. A hundred tiny moments ran through my head in a wonderful flickering parade.

"Can I have a dog?" she asked. "Mom was allergic."

"You can have a dog."

"Then I'll definitely think about it," she said. I could tell by the tone of her voice, she'd already made up her mind, and it thrilled me. "But I can't make this decision on my own. We need to go somewhere first."

★   ★   ★

"I wanted us all to be together."

We stood in a cemetery beneath the shade of a willow tree. A light breeze blew over the expanse of grass, whispering across the granite and marble tombstones. Nestled in the shallow valley at our backs, the town of Celebration spread like a doll's village. A stand of willows rose in a wall ahead. Behind these, a higher wall of pine reached toward the sky. Clouds rolled in, a gray foam oozing over the sheet of blue above. At my feet was a simple marker, neither granite nor marble, just a metal plaque fitted into the ground.

Noelle Catherine Vale.

It was a sad marker. Alone I would have wandered through the tiny cemetery for hours and never noticed it. Isley found it easily of course. I had no idea how many times she'd come out here on her own in the last few weeks, seeking the company of the only person who really knew her. The sight of the small rectangle saddened me, brought me very close to tears.

Isley knelt down and brushed stray grass clippings from the marker. She kissed her fingers and placed them against the metal.

Despite finding this visit touching, I didn't know what was expected of me. Was I meant to talk to the plaque, to the ground where Noelle's body rested? Or was my presence enough? Further, the waving branches of the willows–those in the distance and the one sheltering us–kept drawing my attention. I felt threat all around me. It worked over my skin like long pointed nails, scratching and jabbing. This wholly uncomfortable sensation was made no better by the darkening sky. Night was still some time off. It was summer, after all, but the encroaching clouds promised storm and darkness. I didn't like the idea of being outside once the sun was covered. We were back in the city limits. We were back in Jody's realm.

"She's okay, now," Isley said, wiping a single tear from her cheek.

Feeling certain I had heard her wrong, I said, "What?"

"Mom," Isley said. "She's okay now that you're here. She can rest. She knows you'll take care of me."

"Oh," I said, as if it were the most obvious answer in the world. The first thing through my mind after responding was the word, *witch*. A small voice said it, a thin voice. The squeaking spider-voice of Ricky Blaine from my dream. It was unkind, but it just leaped into my head and sent a chill over my shoulders. Certainly Isley didn't mean she was actually holding a telepathic conversation with Noelle's spirit. Did she?

"Weird, right?" Isley asked.

"Not at all. But I'm getting a little uncomfortable out here, you know? We really should get back to the house. If I can't get Wertimer on the phone, you'll have to head out. I don't want you in town once it gets dark."

"It doesn't really matter, does it? They aren't like vampires. I mean, you said you saw Jody in broad daylight."

"I'll just feel better if you're away from this place. With any luck, I'll be going with you." I scanned the graveyard, remembering the opening scene of *Night of the Living Dead*, and fully expecting to see our own undead creature shambling toward us. The wind continued to blow. The clouds kept oozing across the sky like spilled mop water. But we were alone in the cemetery.

"Maybe you should call Darrell now, before we get back home."

"I don't want to give him any warning," I said. "I want you in your mom's car and ready to go when I make that call. You can be on the Interstate before he has a chance to call out the dogs."

Isley stood up and brushed the knees of her jeans. "You know, if we were thinking, we would have taken both cars, and I wouldn't have had to come back."

"Yeah," I said.

If only we'd been thinking.

25

On Amaryllis Street, at ten past seven, we transferred Isley's shopping bags from the rental car to the trunk of her mother's old Ford Escort. The car appeared to be in pretty good shape—hardly a ping in its white paint. No dents. No rust. If the engine was as well maintained as the exterior, Isley could drive the thing cross-country if she had to.

The storm had settled over Celebration in earnest with black clouds above and the scent of impending rain in the air. Inside the house, I gave Isley another wad of cash I'd withdrawn from an ATM at the outlet mall.

"This should cover a motel and food for a few days," I said. "Let's just hope you don't need to use it."

"Are you going to call Darrell now?"

"Yeah. I'll do it from the kitchen, just in case things get ugly."

Isley nodded her head. "I'll be upstairs. I want to see if I left anything here I want."

"Good idea. Keep an eye on the street and the front of the house, though. I'll be checking things in back."

In the kitchen, I lifted the plastic phone from the wall mount and dialed the Wertimer's number. Once it began to ring, I walked across the kitchen, looked out the window, searched the neatly mown lawn and the low fence. Another house backed onto the property and beyond that a street and another row of houses. A typical suburban grid with enough open space to see anyone trying to approach. Between two houses I noticed a couple of boys playing catch with a football under the spray of a sprinkler. They laughed and slid on the grass, tackled one another.

"Darrell Wertimer," a thick, mellow voice drawled into my ear, interrupting the pleasant scene.

"Mr. Wertimer, my name is Mick Harris."

"Oh, yes," he said as if we were dear old friends. "You're Isley's father. I heard you were in town. How are you, Mr. Harris?"

His response wasn't what I'd expected. His tone held none of the disdain both his wife and butler exhibited. In fact, he sounded welcoming and cool and completely comfortable speaking with me.

"Doing good," I said. "Look, I want to discuss something with you. It has to do with Isley."

"Of course," Wertimer replied. "Tell me Mr. Harris, is Isley with you now?"

"No." The question struck me as odd, even conspiratorial in its delivery. It brought my suspicion of Wertimer into focus again. "I assumed she was home by now," I lied.

"Well, we haven't seen hide nor hair, but she may have stopped somewhere on the way back. Now, what can I do for you?"

"It's about Isley's guardianship. With her mother dead, I think I should assume responsibility for her."

A long pause followed, and I prepared myself for the bluster and good-natured refusal I felt certain Wertimer was about to lay on me. "Well, you are her father," he said. "Are you quite certain you can manage?"

"Of course," I said, trying to ignore the fact it was the kind of question you asked a child. "And I've spoken with Isley, and I think she'd agree that it's what we both want."

"Then I don't see any problem." A clenching at my chest eased, but Wertimer wasn't finished speaking. "However, I really feel we should speak, you and I. Would it be possible for you to come by the house this evening? I promise not to take up much of your time, but there are things we need to discuss. If you'd rather, we could meet in town."

"Your house will be fine," I said. Again, I gazed out at the two boys playing in the yard, burning off their suppers, slipping and laughing under the arc of a sprinkler. From the look of the sky, nature would be providing more than enough water shortly, but that didn't seem to bother them in the least.

"We'll be sitting down to supper now, so about an hour?"

"I'll see you then."

"Oh, and Mr. Harris."

"Yes."

"Thank you."

The statement baffled me, sent my mind to wondering. Before I could ask for clarification, Wertimer broke the connection

After hanging up the phone, I wandered back into the living and was surprised to find Isley standing on the threshold of the front door; it stood open. I hadn't heard the bell or a knock, but she stood in the doorway, hands on her hips, facing off on a familiar law enforcement officer.

"I'm not going," she told Doug Richmond.

He eyed me when I came into the living room, nodded and returned his attention to Isley, his face serious. "The court says you have to, Isley."

"Forget it."

Walking up behind Isley, I asked what was going on, even though it was obvious enough.

"I need to get her back over to the Wertimer's, Mr. Harris. Frances Wertimer has been calling for the last hour. I understand you've got an appointment with the judge next week, and you all can get this settled then. In the meantime, I need to get Miss Vale back there."

"Look, Doug. I just got off the phone with Darrell. He's already agreed to give me custody." Isley looked at me sharply, a glint of hope in her eyes. "I'm supposed to go over there in an hour and talk it out with him. I'll take Isley with me then."

"It doesn't work that way, Mr. Harris."

Richmond's formal address annoyed the shit out of me. That and his starched posturing. He was playing by the book.

"Let's go, Miss Vale."

"He's a fucking perv," Isley said angrily.

The words brought a cloud to Doug's brow, and his eyes went cold and glassy. He straightened himself further, squared his shoulders. "By the order of the court," he said, his voice sharp with authority, "I will be escorting you back to the residence of Darrell David Wertimer at Rose Street."

I tried to reason with him. He'd seemed more than decent enough in the aftermath of Tony Martin's heart attack and at the motel that morning.

"Please step back, Mr. Harris."

Isley freaked. She started shouting at the cop, her hands flying up around her head to emphasize her words, which were mostly obscene. She was scared now. Darrell Wertimer had returned from Little Rock, and she knew what that meant. Maybe they'd removed the bolt from the bathroom door. Lance had probably done it after expelling me from the house the previous day. I felt helpless and foolish. I tried to calm her, put my hand on her writhing shoulder, and she about clocked me with her elbow.

Neighbors began to gather in the yards across the road. Richmond had left his bubble lights on, so red and blue strobes flashed over the street, the lawns, and the curious faces of men and women whose television viewing had been interrupted by something far more interesting.

"If I have to subdue you..." Doug said.

"Look," I shouted. "Everyone just calm down. Isley, stop it. Okay. There has to be something we can work out. Like I said, I was just on the phone with Wertimer..."

Still hard-faced and rigid, Doug said, "By the order of the courts..."

Great.

Isley turned to flee and ran into me. Her eyes, only inches from mine were drowning in tears and panic. I tried to calm her, but Richmond stepped in, locked his hands on her arms and pulled her back to the threshold.

"Mick," Isley cried. "Don't let him. Mick."

I didn't know what the hell to do. I couldn't bust the guy in the head without going to jail, and then Isley would still end up back in Wertimer's house of lunatics, and I'd probably lose any chance of gaining custody. So, I stood there, failure weaving into the misery on my face. Isley saw it, broke into sobs and was guided across the porch by Officer Richmond. Her face was at turns red and blue in the flashing lights, but through it all, disappointment in her father remained.

On the porch, I watched Richmond take her down the stairs, onto
the path. What could I say? My heart ached and my stomach clenched
with sickness. I said nothing. Did nothing. Nothing heroic sparked
in me, and as Richmond helped Isley into the car, resolution made
me stop on the cement walk. Her pleading eyes found me once more.
They grew cold, and her jaw tensed. She turned her head and didn't
look at me again.

With Isley in the back seat, Richmond drove away, trailed by the
aurora of his emergency lights.

Among the curious neighbors on the sidewalk, I noticed a familiar
face. Beatrice, the teller from Arkansas First Trust stood next to a tall
bald man with two days' growth of beard. She had changed out of
her proper business wear and had traded it for frayed denim shorts
and a pink blouse. Like the rest of Isley's neighbors, they spoke to one
another in hushed tones and pointed.

Their hunger for scandal made me sick, furious. I wanted to scream
at every one of them. If they weren't such superstitious and vindictive fools, blaming an unfortunate girl for crimes she couldn't have
committed, things would never have gone this far. But Isley had been
an easy target, an outcast among people she'd known her entire life.

I felt grateful when the rain started to fall. Blankets of water dropped,
scratching the scene before me with little warning. The neighbors
scurried back to their homes like frightened cats.

Pleased that the weather had done me a service, I returned to the
house and locked the front door. In the rental car, I took a moment
to cool down, watching the wipers clear away one sheet of water
after another. Then I started the ignition and headed out, early for my
meeting with Darrell Wertimer.

$$\star \qquad \star \qquad \star$$

The Wertimer place was lit up for evening in a bath of illumination
from a dozen ground-mounted floodlights. Rain blurred the scene,
feathering the edges of the lights and the house. I slowed and pulled

to the curb behind Richmond's cruiser. At the front door, I used the brass knocker and bounced nervously on my toes.

Lance greeted me, looking annoyed. Over his shoulder, I noticed Officer Richmond, standing in the foyer next to a sideboard with a lace doily runner. He had his hat in his hands, water dripped from its brim. He spun it around, gripping the bill in worried fingers. From the salon, Isley screamed, demanding to be set free of the Wertimer's.

"Oh now," a thick syrup voice said. "Now, calm on down, Isley."

I took a step forward, and Lance's familiar palm found its place against my chest. "It's not your turn yet," he said.

"I have an appointment with Darrell," I told him.

"Indeed, but he's not expecting you for another thirty minutes."

"Lighten up, Terminator. This is none of your business."

"Give it a minute," Doug Richmond said. "Mick, seriously, give it a minute."

I turned to the officer barely able to contain my frustration. The whole scene was insane. Darrell had agreed to speak to me. He'd approved of my taking custody of Isley. All of this drama could be avoided if these bit players would get the hell out of my way and let me talk to the man. Instead, they blocked my path as my daughter–confused, hurt, and furious–begged to be released from the house. Couldn't they hear her desperation? Were they that stupid or just that cruel?

"He's my father," she cried. "I want to go with him. I don't want to be here. I don't!"

"Isley," that rich voice said, "we're not keeping you against your will, and we certainly don't want to keep you from your father. Mrs. Wertimer was concerned and phoned Officer Richmond. If you'll just settle down for a moment and let me speak to…"Wertimer's sentence ended abruptly.

In fact, all sounds seemed to vanish as if someone had put the scene on mute. I suddenly felt like I stood in the center of a vacuum, completely removed from all sensation but sight. Even the sound of the rain had retreated. The long banister of the staircase snaked up before me, curling around at the peak to run along the second floor.

The chandelier in the foyer, brilliant with too-bright lights, appeared to breathe, expanding and contracting. In the salon, I saw Isley, with her hand over her mouth, eyes wide. Behind her Mrs. Wertimer fondled the golden necklace around her neck and looked bored. Lance stepped back. He turned toward the salon.

I heard the footsteps then, or perhaps I imagined I did. Each tread brought thunder to my ears. Lance bolted through the archway, into the salon, taking up a position in the center of the room. Richmond followed, already pulling his gun free of its holster, and I followed. Voices. Everyone talked at once, except for Mrs. Wertimer who was too sedated to react. In the salon, I saw a broad shouldered man with a child's face wrapped in slick white hair; he wore a blue seersucker suit, a powder blue tie draping from either side of his collar. He had one hand on the Boesendorfer piano and the other was at his neck. Like his servant and the police officer, Darrell Wertimer scanned the salon as if hearing sounds from all sides. The footsteps halted just beyond the door. Isley turned to the window. Screamed.

Looking that way, I saw a flash of a pale head disappear from the rain-spattered glass.

The door from the dining room creaked open and the eyeless Jody Mayram stepped into the room, walking with measured steps and swinging his arms in gentle waves, feeling the air on either side of him.

Richmond was already calling for the man to "Halt. Freeze. Don't come any closer," but his demands were ignored. Mr. Wertimer waffled protests that could barely be heard above Richmond's stern voice. Lance squared off in the middle of the room, inflating his chest and taking a fighting stance. Richmond waved his gun to emphasize his gravity, but seemed ignorant of the fact the intruder couldn't see the weapon.

"He doesn't have any shoes on," Mrs. Wertimer mused. "My. My. My."

"Oh God," Isley whispered from her place behind Lance in the center of the room, and all hell broke loose.

Jody's head ticked up at the sound of Isley's voice. Determined, he waded into the room, his graying tangle of hair whipping back and forth over his eyeless face. His arms swung wide, nearly touched

Wertimer who was trembling next to the piano. Wertimer stepped back, clipped the bench and fell backwards. He hit the ground hard, cracking his head on the wood. Richmond fired his weapon. In the high-ceilinged room, it sounded like dynamite had gone off. He fired a second and a third time, but Jody moved ahead unmarred. With a rocking of his body, Jody threw a vicious backhand that caught Richmond under the chin, sending the cop flying into the immaculately painted wall. His eyes flashed wide and then dimmed before he dropped to the floor.

A girl screamed from behind me. I turned and saw a pretty blonde on the staircase, clutching herself and trembling. Isley had mentioned another girl in the Wertimer's care: Brenda was her name. She wasn't looking at me at or the destruction coming through the living room, but rather, up the stairs at the approach of a broken little boy who descended toward her, crawling on all fours. Stumbling, crying, Brenda bolted down the steps and ran through the front door.

"Not in my house," Mrs. Wertimer cried. "How incredibly rude. Lance."

The servant pivoted on his heels to look at the doped up mistress of the estate. When he turned back to Jody, he wore a determined face, though the resolution defining his features was drenched with fear. Still, he had been hired to protect the Wertimer family.

I motioned for Isley to join me in the foyer, waving my hand frantically to get her out from the melee. She made a sound deep in her throat and shook her head. She was too frightened to move. Instead, she crouched down into a ball near the window, covering her head with her hands. I made a move to reach her, but never had the chance. Jody's head snapped around, following the whimpering sounds coming from my daughter. He moved for her. She had spoken his name; she was his target. Two steps in Lance blocked the giant's path. Put up the halting palm—his trademark move. He landed a punch to Jody's throat and his hand sank into the flesh. A puff of dust rose from the wound, and Lance grunted, yanking his fist free. The butler tried another punch, but before it could land, Mayram had him by the throat. The powerful intruder drew his arm back, taking Lance with it. The monster stepped forward and flung Lance at the window.

The butler's body whipped through the air. He hit the window frame, his back and the wood snapping with equal volume. His legs shattered the glass, and the momentum of his lower body pulled his broken torso around, whipping it through the window. A shard from the pane sliced off a chunk of the butler's face. The bloody meat clung to the glass, slid and fell to the sill.

Isley knelt on the floor, screaming and trembling. Glass glittered in her hair and on her shoulders. Above her, Jody hovered, his arms wide, his face tilted down to observe her. In the monster's shadow, my daughter drew into a tighter ball.

Jody leaned down, reaching for Isley.

And I did the only thing I could think to do.

"Jody Mayram," I said.

★   ★   ★

Jody froze in place, hovering over Isley's body. I stepped back and repeated his name. The syllables hit him like bullets jerking his form back in quick succession until he stood upright, facing me. "Over here," I said.

When he lunged forward I ran toward the back of the house, his footsteps pounding on the floor behind me. At the end of the hall, I'd intended to go through the door into whatever room was beyond and work my way back to Isley through a different route, but the door was locked.

I turned in time to dodge Jody's charge. He hit the door, seemed to flatten against it for a moment, and then pulled back. He shook his head as if dazed and then cocked it to the side, again listening. Certainly he could hear my heart beating, some other tiny sound I made, but it was the voice, he was waiting for. When he was alive he'd used his gift to fool carnival goers into believing that he could read their minds, now he used it to hunt.

I took a cautious step to the side, waited for him to sweep his massive arms at me, and when that didn't happen, I ran back down the hall. Isley met me in the foyer.

"Jesus, who is he?" she cried.

I grabbed her arm and said, "Shut up until we get out of here."

She obeyed the command for approximately four seconds, enough time for us to get outside and see what waited for us there. Then she said, "Shit," in a tearful, trembling whisper.

Jody Mayram's people had gathered in the Wertimer's front yard, a collection of damaged humanity that would have shamed the sideshow denizens of Manville's Miracle Show. More than twenty of them stood, knelt, or crawled on the front lawn. The bright floodlights fell harshly over distorted anatomies and twisted faces, all wearing expressions of eager hatred.

We'd never get passed them to my car. So, I grabbed Isely's hand tightly and yanked her back into the house, across the foyer and the salon and through the dining room. Jody Mayram was somewhere behind us, but we didn't turn to find him.

Seeing him would change nothing. All we could do was run.

26

We raced across the vast lawn at the back of the Wertimer's house. The heavy black accumulation scabbed over the sky, making it midnight dark. A wall of trees rose ahead cutting a jagged ridge against the furious sky. I checked over my shoulder and saw Jody's people moving in and around the lights at the back of the big house, scurrying randomly back and forth. A pale shape shot off to our left, and I turned back toward the trees, the horizon, the moon. I gripped Isley's hand even more tightly to drag her toward the cover of the woods. A high note from my daughter told me I had gripped too hard, and a flash of panic ignited behind my ribs, knowing any sound she uttered would be the equivalent of a whistle calling a pack of dogs.

As we ran, I attempted to make sense of the situation. I'd spoken Jody Mayram's name, and so had Isley. We'd called him from whatever hell he'd made home, and he was determined to make us pay. But Jody had called these followers himself, and instead of targeting the blind man, they'd made the journey from death to once again follow his leadership. It seemed discordant. Shouldn't he have become their target or did the rules differ for the living and the dead?

Once we gained the cover of the trees, I stopped. Rain hissed through the heavy foliage, and the bits of illuminated trunk nearby only served to accent the absolute blackness of the forest. I turned to Isley who was barely visible through the gloom. She searched the woods over my shoulder and spun back to the yard to see if Jody's people were in pursuit. I looked that way myself, and saw no one on the lawn. Even the people who had been dashing about madly at the back of the Wertimer house were no longer visible, but amid the downpour and darkness that didn't mean they'd given up.

"They're gone," Isley whispered.

I quickly threw a finger to my lips and shook my head, hoping she could see the gesture. She did but it didn't silence her.

"What?" she asked, sounding annoyed as if I'd been harping on her for hours about her behavior.

Obviously, she wasn't going to shut up until I started talking, but doing so took what minor amount of courage I had. Jody wasn't gone. Neither were his people. They'd taken to the woods at the sides of the lawn, avoiding the clear field of grass, so we couldn't track their progress as they stalked their way through the tree cover to converge on our location. We could wander through the woods for hours, lost until one of them found us, or we could make a break across the back yard toward the house, which would be like running a futile gauntlet. Isley couldn't see how completely fucked up our situation was, so I had to tell her.

"Don't say another word," I said. "They're in the woods. They're hunting us. The big one, the leader, Jody, he does it by the sounds of our voices. Right now, Jody is probably homing in on us, so I'm going to make this quick. We have to work our way back to the front of the house, quietly. Once we're in the car we're gone. I'll drive you back to Denver with me and worry about the legal shit later, but first we have to get to the car." I handed her the keys to the rental. Despite the hissing rain, I could tell by the jangling sound they made that she'd fumbled the ring and nearly dropped it to the ground. When I felt certain she had them, I said. "Keep hold of my hand. If you can't, and we get separated, run. Don't call for me. Don't answer if I call for you. I'll keep them focused on me for as long as I can. If you get lost in the woods, text me, and if you get to the car first, don't wait. Just drive and keep driving until you're way the hell away from here. I'll get to you if I can. Okay?"

"Okay," she said with a trembling breathless voice.

"Good," I told her. "Now, stay quiet, take my hand and let's go."

There is no way to move silently through a wooded area. No matter how carefully you step, a leaf will crunch or a twig will snap. I must have held my breath a hundred times in the first five minutes alone. Every footfall brought another noise that rang in my ears like a cymbal crash, echoing endlessly through the forest, certain to draw the revenant spirits of Freak Town down on us. I'd hoped the clatter of rainfall would help mask our sounds, and maybe it did to a degree, but even when we would stop walking, I heard the rhythm of my heart thundering in my chest, and I imagined that Isley's accompanied it, added to its volume because no single heart could produce such deafening noise. All through the woods, I heard the crisp pop of limbs tread under foot and the softer, even more disturbing rustle of brush.

My eyes grew as accustomed to the darkness as they were going to, which is to say the ink-black sea of atmosphere engulfing us softened, revealing shadows upon shadows, rather than a single sheet of night. Isley's face moved palely next to mine, but no details of our surroundings came clear.

I led us to the south, making a broad arc away from the house in an attempt to circumvent Jody's people, but I needed to keep my bearings and in order to do that, I couldn't stray too far from the Wertimer's. It would have been far too easy to get lost amid the black columns of tree trunk with no landmark to guide us.

We heard the first tromping of feet just as we completed what I believed was half the distance back. From that point we would head north to the Wertimer's and the car I had parked in the drive.

At first, the steps blended into the other forest sounds–the racket of raindrops ticking through the treetops. Then the footfalls took on a heft and a rhythm that clearly indicated the animal making them walked on two feet not four. Isley and I halted simultaneously, and her pale face turned to mine. Again, I held my finger up to my lips and then pointed downward, indicating that we should crouch and take advantage of whatever cover the woods offered. She took my cue, and we knelt quietly. Isley pushed close and I continued to hold her hand with mine as I put my arm around her shoulders.

The footsteps grew louder, crunching and snapping the deadfall, indifferent to the warning clatter–perhaps confident that the prey had no genuine chance for escape. I wiped the worst of the water from my forehead and eyes. Looking around but unable to find the stomping hunter in the gloom, a new level of panic froze my chest and sent bolts of dread through me, like lightning conducting through ice. He or she was close, sounded as if they were only a few steps away, but I couldn't see so much as a new shadow among the other shadows surrounding us. And even if I could see this thing, this resident of Freak Town, what in the hell was I supposed to do against it? No convenient stray was going to come leaping out of the woods to save my neck a second time. I had no weapon and could barely see well enough to navigate the woods at a walking pace. Trying to run through the forest would have been like trying to cross a busy highway.

Then a second set of footsteps echoed the first. This tread was lighter, but no less threatening. It pushed through the woods, not twenty feet ahead, as the first hunter passed us and tromped to the east.

When we'd first hunkered down and I'd put my arm around my daughter, I'd felt the tremors coming off of her skin through her wet blouse, but those had given way to a terrible shaking. It felt like Isley was attached to a paint mixer, and I knew she wouldn't be able to contain her fear much longer. I rubbed her back lightly with my hand and held my breath again as the second hunter came alongside of us.

She walked so close to where we knelt, I could feel the air move in her passing. That's when I looked up at a woman standing in profile whose barely visible face seemed to be made of clustered lumps, like bunches of cauliflower affixed to her cheek, her chin and her brow. Tendrils of long brown hair ran over her face and neck like eels, clamped to her skin. She gazed off to the south, and my heart pounded as I prayed for her to keep moving. To gaze anywhere else but down.

She did look down, though. I noted the cocking of her head, the dipping of her chin. The little game of hide and seek was over, and Isley and I had lost.

"Run," I said, releasing Isley's hand and springing to my feet.

The woman with the lumpen face whispered a curse. She was as surprised as we were terrified, and I took what small advantage that gave us.

I lunged forward and planted my hands on the woman's chest, sending her crashing over a sapling. In the second my palms touched her, a flash of memory ran through my head. Shouting. Torches. Sharp blades like the reaper's scythe rising into the air. I could smell blood and shit and the stink of unwashed bodies so strongly that I gagged and stumbled back, covering my mouth with a palm. A cry rose up from the forest. The first hunter had heard the racket and was sending up the alarm. Footsteps crashed toward me, seeming to surround me in the woods. I turned to grab Isley so we could make our escape, but she was gone.

At first her absence confused me. Yes, I'd told her to run, but it seemed she'd disappeared completely. I mean, I couldn't have had my back to her for more than a handful of seconds, and yet there was no sign of her, not even the sounds of her racing through the forest. All of those kinds of noises were coming from my back.

The other residents of Freak Town were answering the call of the first hunter and the fallen woman, who worked her way to her feet, screaming at the top of her lungs behind me.

That was good though, I thought. They were behind us, and Isley had a good head start. The commotion in the woods would help cover her retreat. She'd make it to the car even if I didn't.

But I wasn't going to give up. If anything I could buy my daughter a few more minutes, so I started to run with instinct driving me again to the south, away from the Wertimer place and deeper into the dark woods. I didn't give a thought to the amount of noise I made then. I wanted Jody Mayram and his followers to hear me; wanted the pack to chase me down; and though I didn't want to die, I wanted Isley to live, and the two things were beginning to seem mutually exclusive. Still there was a chance. If I could get enough distance between the hunters and myself, I could try to make a stealthy retreat or find an adequate place to hide until they gave up for the night—if they would ever give up.

The ground proved remarkably flat and easy to navigate. Even at my top running speed, I managed to weave in and around the tree trunks with a dexterity that surprised me. After ten minutes of blind sprinting through the forest, the trees suddenly pulled away, and I found myself standing at the edge of a road.

A tall street light cast a cone of light on the highway, its illumination made static by the pelting rain. It gave the pavement a pale gray

appearance like a band of contained mist running to a slight rise on
my left. Across the road was another forest, and though I seriously
considered following the highway–staying close to the only sign of
modern life available to me–I instead hurried across to the next stand
of forest, forsaking the road for the same reason I'd not taken a chance
on the Wertimer's yard once I'd crossed it. I would be exposed on the
pavement, and the chance of a well-intentioned motorist appearing
to aid in my escape seemed unlikely in the extreme.

Once I'd crossed the street, I again set off in a run, but it only lasted
six steps. Suddenly my leg was out from under me, and I was tumbling.
I landed on my back with a *splat*, a rock digging into my kidneys and
my breath flying from me like my soul. My eyes had still been drinking
in the light of the street lamp, and I hadn't seen the jutting branch that
tore into my thigh and sent me sprawling ass over hat into a thatch
of wet brush. I'd barely felt the puncture and the ripping of my skin.
Allowing myself no more than a few moments to indulge the pain, I
sat up and peered over my shoulder at the way I'd come.

The jagged blade of wood stuck across the path I'd taken; its terrible point showing in silhouette against the pale road beyond. Blood
ran over my thigh in warm rivulets, ushered away by the cold rain to
pool on the dirt beneath. Then the pain came, in a blinding wave that
rolled up my leg and through my body, gathering in my throat where
it tried to escape as a scream, but I bit down on the hurt and refused
to vent the suffering. Instead, I gasped for air, rapid inhalations that
helped to expel the worst of the ache.

The first of Jody's followers emerged from the forest then. She
was the woman with the cauliflower complexion, now made all the
more horrible under a bath of moonlight. She crept from the wood
and looked up and down the highway as if checking for traffic, and
then she ran with a gliding grace across the pavement and entered the
woods on my side of the road only forty feet from where I lay, panting
through my misery. Next, the girl with arms like flippers appeared. Her
gait was nowhere near as graceful as the woman's, but it was equally
rapid. She entered my side of the wood and promptly vanished amid

the shadows. Another followed and another. I counted six in all, but those were only the ones that crossed my field of vision. Others may have entered the woods further to the east or the west. There was no way for me to know, but I feared that the party had again separated, with many of the misshapen hunters pursuing Isley as well.

But no, I told myself. A good portion of them had been on the far side of the Wertimer's property, stalking through the brush. They may have heard the alarm their brethren had called up, but they wouldn't have been able to catch up to them, not considering how quickly they'd attained the road, so soon after me.

Isley was safe, I told myself. She had to be safe.

★   ★   ★

I waited for thirty agonizing minutes. The constant rain chilled me and my ass sank deeper into the growing swamp of the forest floor. In that time, I removed my shirt and tied it around the gash in my thigh, having no clue if the makeshift bandage would do me a fuck bit of good. The tromping and cracking in the woods faded and then vanished altogether. I wasn't foolish enough to believe they'd given up on me. If anything, their search had simply drawn them deeper into the forest—far enough away that the rain covered the sounds of their pursuit. They would be back, I knew, and I couldn't wait around for them.

When I climbed to my feet, the ache in my right leg sang out. The knee had grown stiff and unwieldy, and I felt lightheaded. Maybe I'd lost too much blood. Maybe the damn branch had cut through an artery, and I'd bleed out here in the forest, just another snack for Mother Nature's bestiary. Or worse, I'd collapse and Jody Mayram would finally punish me for daring to speak his name.

I worked my way along the edge of the wood, keeping the highway in my sights, making my way west. After ten minutes fear and exhaustion and pain wrapped around me with a paralyzing grip. Suddenly, dread burned in my chest, and I looked over my shoulder and around the forest for the source of this panic. It only took me a second to pinpoint it.

Up ahead and far to my left, a dull blue glow radiated through the tree trunks. Freak Town. The terrible feelings the place engendered seeped into my head and my torso like a virus, feeding on what little hope I'd mustered. My hunters had probably gathered there, and I'd all but delivered myself to their doorstep.

I began to see my escape attempt as hopeless. More than likely, Isley had already been killed. If not—if she'd somehow managed to reach the car and get out of town—then my duty to my daughter was done. She'd be okay as long as she kept driving. My lawyer, Brad, would see to the rest.

Resolved, soaked to the bone, and exhausted, I walked out of the woods and onto the highway. The clenching fear of Freak Town tickled at my neck, but could no longer hold me. I limped out there in the open, expecting one of Jody Mayram's clan, or Jody himself, to leap out, lay their hands on my body, and bring my life to an end.

27

The highway led me to Faye's Inn, a place I'd hoped to never see again. When I reached the edge of the parking lot, I pulled the cell phone from my pocket and called Sidney. With the tear on my leg I wouldn't be able to walk another block, let alone the distance back to the Wertimer's. I'd hoped to find a voice mail or text notice from Isley when the screen came on but there were no messages, and my hopes sank a little further.

"Mick?" Sidney asked.

"Yeah, Sid," I said. "I need some help."

"You sound like shit."

"That's nothing compared to how I look. Can you meet me at Faye's Inn… like now?"

"I thought you weren't going back to that dump?"

"Long story. Sad ending. Please, Sid, just get out here."

"I'm already holding the car keys."

"Thanks, man."

Faye's office was closed but lights burned in several of the cabins. Knocking on the door of the cabin closest to the road, I propped myself against the jamb and waited for someone to open up. When no one did, I tried the knob and since it wasn't locked, I walked in and sat on the edge of the bed. The second my ass hit the mattress what remained of my strength drained out as if escaping through the hole in my thigh. I slumped forward and stared at the bloodstained shirt. Mud covered my shins and shoes.

I wanted to call Isley or send her a message, but a vivid image of her crouching in the woods, surrounded by Jody's people filled my head and cancelled the urge. That would be the ultimate fuck you from fate, if the ringtone that announced my call got my daughter killed. I tried to convince myself that Isley had gotten away. She hadn't tried to reach me for the same reason I hadn't tried to reach her, but

I'd never been good at wishful thinking. I figured you threw a dime in a wishing well and you got nothing from it but a ten-cent deficit.

Beat to shit and sitting on a stranger's bed in a cabin at Faye's Inn, I felt empty. Worthless.

As I soaked deep in self-pity, the tenants of the cabin returned. They were a young couple, drunk and unattractive, with wet hair and bare feet. Likely, they'd just returned from a bit of summer storm skinny-dipping, which had culminated the way a lot of scenes involving two naked people ended. They had that freshly fucked glow to them, which went out about the time they saw me dirty, bleeding and disheveled on their bed.

The young woman, who had bleached her hair to death, gasped. The guy reared back, startled. He was a pudgy, bland looking guy with a dense beard adding further animal characteristic to his already porcine features. After the initial shock wore off, he put on his tough-guy face and stepped into the room between me and his girlfriend in a protective stance.

"What the fuck do you fucking think you're doing?" he demanded.

I asked him to give me a minute. I was polite enough and had intended to explain that I needed to catch my breath, maybe dry off, and that it wasn't safe outside, but decided it best to not expand on it.

"You got two seconds, asshole," the kid said. He looked around the room, eyes flashing from me to either wall, probably looking for a weapon. He struck me as the sort who'd keep a shotgun handy. "Either move your ass or I'm going to kick your fucking ass."

"Give me a minute," I yelled. It was a deep, resonant booming sound. Full throat and from the diaphragm the way Palace's vocal coach had taught us. The power behind the command came as a surprise. I didn't think I had it in me. Apparently, neither did the kids because they backed up a step. "I've had a supremely fucked up evening," I told them. "A buddy is coming to pick me up. He'll be here in a few minutes. Until then, I need a place to sit and some quiet."

"Well, you're not staying here," the kid with the porky features said. "I'll kick your ass."

"Yeah, you mentioned that," I replied. "But the thing is... you won't. If you were going to start shit, we'd be in the middle of it by now. So I'd suggest you call the cops and have them forcibly remove me, but the thing is, they're all probably identifying bodies out at the Wertimer place. When you call, be sure to mention that Officer Richmond is probably dead."

"Dougy?" the homely girl asked.

"Yes, Dougy," I said. "He died a hero, I guess. Whatever the fuck that means."

It was apparent that both of these young people had known Doug Richmond to some degree. Hell, the girl may have dated him, I didn't know, but the suggestion that he might be dead affected them both. The girl looked like she might cry, and the boy regarded me with apprehension as if he thought I had killed Officer Richmond myself.

"Did you get shot?" the girl asked, pointing at my leg.

"No," I said.

"But you're running from the cops," the boy insisted.

"Why would I tell you to call the cops if I was running from them?" I asked.

Fortunately, Sidney pulled into the lot as the two kids attempted to puzzle that one out. I forced myself to my feet, enduring flashes of white-hot pain as I did so. Then I limped across the room and onto the porch into the applause of the downpour. The couple gave me a wide berth as if I was contagious, and I continued down the stairs toward Sidney's truck.

At my back I heard the pig-faced boy say, "I could'a kicked his fucking ass."

Charming.

★   ★   ★

Sidney made a commotion about the way I looked and insisted on taking me to the emergency room to get my leg stitched up, but I told him to drive to the Wertimer house, and the tone in my voice made it clear that the argument ended there. I needed to see if the rental car was still in the Wertimer's driveway, and a sick feeling in my belly told me it was.

"You're not going to do her any good if you bleed to death," Sidney said.

"If I was going to bleed to death it would have happened by now," I said.

"Oh, you're a doctor now?"

"Can this wait?" I asked. "I'm not quite used to being scolded by people I haven't fucked. God knows, it's happening more and more often, especially in this town, but I'm not quite coping yet. So give it a rest."

"So if I fucked you, I could point out exactly how stupid you're acting?"

"Yes, absolutely. It's actually something of a comfort zone for me."

"You're messed up," Sidney said, and he meant it.

There was no point in arguing the issue. I couldn't agree with him more.

I saw the rental car bathed in the flashing bubblelights of three police cars and an ambulance when Sidney's truck crested the low rise in the road leading to the Wertimer's house. "Shit," I hissed under my breath, feeling an emotional collapse in my chest.

"Don't freak," Sidney said. "She's probably inside with the police."

No, she wasn't. I knew it. If Isley had made it out of the woods, she wouldn't have gone back into that house, and she certainly wouldn't have waited around for the police to show. She'd have done exactly what I told her to do and drive out of town. Not because I'd told her to do it, but because she wanted to get away from this place, and the sight of that rental in the driveway was all the proof I needed that she hadn't gotten away at all.

I was wrong about one thing: Doug Richmond had survived the attack. He sat out of the rain just inside an ambulance with an ice pack on the back of his head and a dazed expression on his face.

"What the hell did you do?" he asked me, his words slurring wildly.

He should have been lying down or on his way to the emergency room. Did the paramedics really think an ice pack would be a fine fix for the cop's concussion?

"Is Isley inside?" I asked.

"What did you bring to my town?" Doug persisted.

"Nothing. It was waiting for me when I got here."

Sidney and I left Richmond on the back of the ambulance. A long black bag lay in the middle of the lawn outside of the shattered picture window. A body bag. Lance. Water pooled and ran off the rubber sack, giving it the glistening appearance of a giant slug. I moved as fast as my torn leg would allow, but after stepping into the house, the leg gave out, and I fell against the wall in the foyer, balancing as best I could on the good leg as Sidney wrapped an arm around my back for support. From my position, I could see the living room. Darrell Wertimer stood in the corner by the amazing grand piano, trying to console his wife who shrieked obscenities like a sailor who'd lost a bet. Frances Wertimer clutched at her throat and shook her head furiously, slapping at her husband's hands as if his touch brought agony.

"It was her fucking stink," Mrs. Wertimer screamed. "That's what they came for. The stench drew them. The whore scent. Those cocksucking motherfuckers wanted her stink."

The officers combing the living room for evidence uniformly winced with each foul epitaph, though one was trying very hard not to laugh. I probably would have done the same thing in his position. In a scene this crazy, laughter was as good a response as any. But I wasn't in his position. I needed to find my daughter, even if it was simply to identify her body.

"Hey," I asked of a young policeman who knelt just inside the living room, reaching for something under a table with a pair of tweezers. He paused and looked up. "My daughter…" I began, but lost my train of thought. What was the right question to ask? "Have you found anyone else?"

"What are you doing here? This is a crime scene."

"I was here earlier, visiting my daughter when the attack happened. We ran outside and were separated in the woods. Have you…?"

"An officer will take your statement if you'll wait."

"I'm not interested in giving a statement. I want to know if you've seen my daughter?"

"If she's not in this room or on that lawn, I haven't seen her," the prick replied.

Gearing up for a tirade, I was surprised to find myself moving. Sidney dragged me away from the wall.

"Mick," he said. "Let's go."

"What the hell are you doing?"

"I'll explain in the truck," Sidney said.

"I'm not going anywhere until I get some answers."

Suddenly, the supporting arm vanished, and I fell to the floor, cracking my elbow painfully on the tile. "Fuck," I said, rolling onto my back and looking up at Sidney.

"These are your choices," he said. "You can crawl around in here, pissing off the local authorities or you can come with me to the truck."

I chose the truck, but as soon as I was standing again, allowing Sidney to guide me outside, I called him an asshole. It made him laugh.

"Look over there," Sidney said, pointing to the woods south of the Wertimer place.

The storm was diminishing, but the steel wool atmosphere remained thick. Still amid the trees and gloom, I saw flashlight beams cut the night. "And why am I looking at that?"

"I'll tell you when we get to the truck."

Once situated in the cab, my leg grateful to be effectively out of use, I asked Sidney to explain why he was so insistent on getting me away from the house.

"Because, those boys are distracted right now," he said. "Once they get themselves un-distracted, they're going to want answers, and you're going to spend the rest of the night at the police station while your leg slowly rots off. They've already started searching the woods, and you aren't going to be any help in that regard, so the best plan is to get you to the emergency room and get that leg taken care of while they do their jobs, because there's not a thing you can do to help them. After the doctors get you patched up, you can call the police and see what they found."

"I need to know what happened to Isley," I said. How could Sidney not understand how important that was?

"And you may get answers here and you may not," he told me. "You don't know she's anywhere near here. She might not have been able to make it to the car. She could have seen a chance to bolt down the road and taken it. You just don't know. What *I* know is that every cop Celebration has is currently on the Wertimer property, which means there are a whole lot of places not being searched. Whatever happened here is done, and you can't change a bit of it, but if you think you feel bad pulling away from this place, just imagine the level of shitty you'll be feeling if you find out there was a chance to help Isley and you used it twiddling your thumbs."

He was right, but the idea of driving away felt wrong. For all of the strength of Sidney's logic, it made a weak opponent for a father's desperation. But one thing he said got through all of my hard-edged protests: *There are a lot of places not being searched.* Isley could still be fleeing Jody's people. She could be in the middle of town screaming for help. There might still be a chance. Sidney had planted a sick hope in my head, and it grew fast.

"Okay, drive," I said. "But we're not going to the hospital yet. Take me to Amaryllis Street. If Isley went anywhere it would be to her mother's house."

28

The rain stopped as we crossed town. The house on Amaryllis was dark when we pulled up. I saw Isley's Escort, her mother's car, and my heart skipped for a moment only to realize it had been there all afternoon. Officer Richmond had driven her to the Wertimer's in his cruiser. I pounded on the door of the house and waited. I called Isley's name and finally got up the nerve to use my cell phone. She didn't answer and the emptiness inside of me hardened like flint, turning my sorrow into a kind of anger that was more powerful and overwhelming than any I'd felt in my life.

Isley was dead. End of story. If she'd escaped, she would have come to this house; she would have answered her phone; she would have gotten a message to me. Denial played its little games, and I entertained hope futilely like some loser betting his last buck on a long shot, but the shiny bits of possibility lasted only seconds. I shut down optimism with plain concrete logic.

"Let's go," I said.

"Maybe we should check inside," Sidney suggested.

"She isn't here. We're not going to find her."

Sidney looked worried. He wanted to say something, but fumbled the words. I didn't give him the chance to try making me feel any better.

"Let's go back to the truck," I said. "My leg hurts."

★   ★   ★

Over the years I'd learned to expect the bare minimum from people; it made leaving them easier. I think early on, when I was a kid, I expected too much and the repetition of disappointments eroded those expectations, leaving me comfortable with the distance I kept from most of the human race. People had moved in and out of my life and I'd moved in and out of theirs. I never fought to be with a person, didn't even ask Glen why he was leaving. The *why* never mattered. Someone wanted to be with me or they didn't. A guy I used to date once called me "emotionally transient," and it sounded a lot better than "dead inside," but it came down to the same thing. Whatever. This isn't a fucking psychology test.

But that was the sort of thing that went through my head as I sat on an examination table in the niche of a hospital corridor. The doctor swabbed out my thigh with a long Q-tip and then set about sewing the two lips of wound together. He'd given me a couple ibuprofen tablets and used a local anesthetic on my leg to deaden the pain. I wish he'd knocked me out.

Isley was gone. On some level I'd always known she would never be a part of my life, not a real part at any rate, but there was a profound difference between understanding the limitations of a relationship and having any chance for that relationship to develop stolen. As I've noted, I expected little from people, but somewhere in my head there was that kid, still wanting to be needed and important to somebody else, and he waited in there, hoping that one day I'd get beyond cynicism and let it happen again. In the meantime, he tossed out bits of glittering possibilities like bait. I'd eluded the little bastard's hook until Isley came along. For a moment I'd felt connected to someone else. And somehow I'd worked Sidney into this fantasy. I don't know what I expected to happen there—we weren't even romantically involved—but Isley had been the emotional inch, and the kid in my head had taken the mile.

Fucking brat.

The doctor finished my leg and gave me an aluminum crutch. Slapped a bandage over the mess and told me to have the stitches removed in a week. Stay off your feet. Slowly flex your knee. He told me to take as much time as I needed on the examination table, then he promptly disappeared. A few minutes later a nurse appeared with more papers for me to sign, and then Sidney walked into the niche and took a seat in the molded plastic chair.

"The police didn't find any trace of Isley at the Wertimer's," he said.

I'm sure he meant this as good news, but it didn't mean much to me. Acres of woodland bordered the plantation house; a few cops with flashlights weren't likely to cover even a meaningful fraction of the area. I nodded and looked at my feet.

"Your leg feeling any better?" he asked.

"I want to hurt them, Sidney," I said. "I've never wanted to hurt anything so badly in my life. But how do you stop something if you don't even know what it is?"

"I don't know," he said. "Maybe it's just something you have to let go. If Isley is dead, you might want to think really hard about leaving town. You're still in danger from what I can tell."

"Yeah but the thing is someone set this up. A flesh and blood moth-erfucker put that note in my cabin and put another one in Isley's house. They killed Sandy Winchester and Noelle, and it doesn't look like anybody gives a shit."

"And you don't want him to get away with it?"

"No. I don't."

"You already know who's doing this, don't you?"

Aaron Dalfour, I thought. Who else? "I have a good idea, but I don't want to confront the son of a bitch until I know how to stop Jody and the others."

"Then there's someone you're going to want to talk to. It's too late tonight, but first thing in the morning we'll go talk to her. For now, it'd probably be best for us to get out of town."

29

In the motel room, I dropped on the bed and stared at the ceiling. My leg throbbed and ached. It hardly competed with the pain gnawing at my brain and chest. Sidney said all the right things, but his voice came to me through a muddy filter, the words muffled and too flat. I couldn't respond. Instead, I kept my eyes on the ceiling and wished I could cry, imagining that it might relieve some of the pressure at my temples and ribs.

But I hadn't cried in years, maybe not since the aftermath of seeing my daughter for the first time. I tried to remember when I'd last allowed tears, and it proved a momentary distraction.

Sidney sat on the edge of the bed and put his hand on my shoulder. "Should I go?" he asked.

"No," I told him. Amid so many uncertainties, the one thing I could say with absolute authority was that I didn't want to be alone.

He leaned down and kissed me. It wasn't a hungry kiss, fueled by lust and expectation. It was warm and comforting, and when it ended, I rolled onto my side and stared at the wall. I didn't want sex. That familiar and powerful amusement never even occurred to me. More than anything, I needed somebody to be there, to know someone had chosen to stay with me, even though they weren't likely to get a damn thing out of it. Sidney wrapped his arm across my chest and snuggled in tight, spooning me, the warmth of his body radiating through our clothes.

Eventually we fell asleep. Then the nightmares came.

★　　　★　　　★

From Sidney's description of his grandmother, I'd expected him to lead me through a swamp to a tattered old shack lit with kerosene lanterns and candles. I expected chickens hung by their feet dangling over a slanted porch; their heads removed with the whack of a machete. At that point, I didn't care. He could have taken me to a cave that smelled of bat shit and carbon monoxide, and I'd have charged in without a second thought if I believed the crone within could give me answers. Those settings wouldn't have surprised me in the least; they were, after all, where witches dwelled. What did surprise me was the neat two-story square house, painted powder blue with white trim and a neatly manicured front lawn.

"This is it," Sidney said.

I opened the car door and stepped onto the drive. My thigh flared pain and it threatened to drop out from under me. I clutched the car door for support and ground my teeth against the ache.

Sidney came around the front of the car and wrapped an arm around my back. Once he had a firm grip he led me along the walk and up the stairs. A strong voice, made jagged with age, called "Y'all come in. Ain't locked," before Sidney's finger made it to the doorbell.

Inside we were greeted by the aroma of a freshly baked apple pie, the tingling chemical scent of furniture polish and another odor, like that of clean sheets. A small table behind the door held a cut crystal vase brimming with a single magnolia blossom, some letters and what looked like the bone of a chicken leg. Sidney helped me through the entryway and into the living room, where his grand-mother waited for us.

She sat on a wooden rocker, next to the fireplace. The room was exactly what I would have expected from a woman of advanced years: two dozen photographs of varied sizes in gold plate frames, sitting on any available surface; a floral print sofa with thick rounded arms, bright throw pillows in the crooks and a crimson knit blanket over the back; knick-knacks gathered over the decades of her life, some perhaps heirlooms of her mother's next to her pictures on the shelves and the table. Even the woman herself was approximately what I expected. Sidney's grandmother was old, and I mean rotten apple shrunken-headed old, but she wore a cloud of beautiful white hair, neither thinned nor made brittle by time. In her pink woolen robe and matching house slippers she seemed wholly normal, yet at the same time, not. The guitar she clutched in her vascular hands certainly didn't strike me as normal. What did surprise me about the woman was the fact that Sidney's grandmother was Caucasian.

"About time you two got over to see me," she said, doing a remarkably fast run down the fret board, filling the room with a snappy blues progression.

"Sorry, Maw-maw," Sidney said. He led me to the sofa, eased me onto the cushion and then crossed to give his grandmother a kiss on the cheek.

"A lot of folks is sorry now," she said. "Ain't a bother. Nothing to be done for them." She made another quick run over the guitar neck, this one less precise than the first. Then she hoisted it from her lap and rested the instrument against the fireplace stones. She looked at me, her eyes like clear bits of gray glass, too young for the wrinkled skin that surrounded them. "You shouldn't have given up on your song," she said to me. "Music is the magic god gave you. Won't help you here though. Not against them."

I opened my mouth to ask a simple question—*What are they?*—but the woman was already answering the question.

"They got a dozen-za names, and most of 'em are just empty-headed wrongness. The revenant souls been called everything from spooks and ha'nts to beasts and Beelzebub himself, but they ain't so different from you and me."

"Where do they come from?" Sidney asked.

"From The Glen of course. Mayram Ellyn Glen where this was done to them, and before you ask me what was done to them, I'll tell you. They was hexed. A hateful and nasty curse. Keeps 'em trapped... neither here nor there. You and me and most folks get to walk on through when we go to meet our judge, just like passing through the foyer of a house to get outside, but they're trapped in the foyer, and it's a terrible place, just full of anger and need and confusion. Whoever put the hex on them must have wanted those souls to suffer good and long."

I didn't understand what the withered woman told us. She either read it on my face or in my mind.

"Think of this room as the life you're living and the whole out-doors as the life that comes next. You got that in your head? Well fine then. In between the two, there's a place that's neither here nor there, like I said about the foyer. It's a limbo that they can't get beyond, and they're locked in there with what they was feeling at the end, so if they was scared or angry or hurt when they died, then that's what they keep on feeling. It's all they can feel in that place. All they want is to pass on through, because coming back into this room, this life don't change the pain."

"Why do they kill?" I asked.

"They're looking for a way out of this painful world. They figure they can be escorted through the door by someone else. They do get escorted a bit of the way, but the hex holds them back. So, they find themselves in the foyer again, til they're invited back into the room… or get set free."

"How do we set them free?" I asked, impatient to put an end to Jody Mayram, wondering if I was already too late to save Isley.

"Sidney," the woman said, "You're being a poor host in your Maw-maw's house. You haven't offered your young friend a cup of coffee. Now, I know your maw and paw taught you better'n that."

Sidney lowered his head. "Sorry, Ma'am."

"Don't waste the apology on me. I got a pot on the stove, be a happy cricket and fiddle 'em up for your friend."

"Yes, Ma'am."

Once alone with the aged woman, I felt the atmosphere of the room turn thick. It was the strangest thing I'd ever felt. The air actually had weight and it hit my lungs like fog. I looked into Granny Tierney's eyes, and they were soft and caring.

"You already lost that girl," she said. The news hit me like a steel bar, first to the head, then the belly, then the throat. I couldn't speak. It wasn't true. "I feel nothing but sorry for you, and I mean that. You've got a fine soul. But she's beyond your help now. She'll live for a little bit longer. It'll be a misery for her, but that's not your doing. You done right by her. All along, you done right. And that counts for a lot, no matter what you're likely to tell yourself."

"No," I croaked, barely able to force air through my strained windpipe. "You're wrong. You can't know that."

"True enough," Granny Tierney said, her warm eyes fixed on mine. "I can only feel things, and that sure ain't knowing them. I get a heat in my bones and it climbs on up to my noggin', and it settles in like a coal, just burns, it does. But it ain't knowledge. No sir. You are right about that. Don't know what I was thinking."

But her backpedaling only made me feel worse, like she wanted to be free of the burden of informing me of Isley's death. "Where is she?" I asked.

"Couldn't say."

"You have to help me stop this," I said, not even trying to hide the desperation in my voice.

"I intend to," said the woman.

"You can't read the future. You can't know what's going to happen."

"No, I can't. True enough."

"Then we can stop them. I can still save my daughter."

Something I said affected the old woman. Her face pinched, making the creases covering it all the deeper. She put a hand to her throat and looked at the floor. "How many are there?" she asked.

"I'm not sure. A couple of dozen, I think."

"Surely not," she whispered. "Who would summon so many?"

"Jody. I said his name and he came. Then, he called the others."

"*He* did?" she asked, the hand at her throat trembling visibly. "You sure you got that right?"

"Yes. I saw him do it."

"Oh my. I wouldn't have thought of that."

"What do you mean?"

"Best wait for Sidney. This isn't right. None of this is right."

Again that feeling of the atmosphere growing heavy came on, only this time it was three times worse. I felt as if I was drowning in Granny Tierney's living room, as if I could reach out and scoop the air in my hands, comb it with my fingers. So intense was this horrible feeling, I wanted to flee the quaint room with its menagerie of precious gold frames and its lace curtains.

Sidney returned, holding two cups of coffee.

I thanked him and turned back to Granny Tierney. "You said something wasn't right? What did you mean?"

"None of this is right, is what I'm saying. You tell me Jody made the hex, but he's a revenant soul himself. That can't be."

"Wait," I said. "Maybe I explained this wrong. According to what I found out, Jody married a woman. She was supposed to be a witch. I think she's the one who made the curse."

"But she'd be dead too," said the old woman. "The holder of souls must be living and breathing. He can't be in their world or the next. Someone must keep the vessels."

"Vessels?" Sidney asked.

"Whoever cast the hex needed material from Jody's people. He needed flesh or blood or bone, and it had to be taken from a living body and kept somewhere. A jar or urn. The magic is done to the material and it's held there. If the vessel is opened or broken the revenant is freed."

"Then we have to find those jars," I said.

"The first thing you have to do is listen to what I'm sayin'," Granny Tierney said, her voice terse and upset. "When I was a little girl, barely old enough to hold a doll of my own, my mama told me about the hexes, started learning me in the ways of divination because I had the gift. What we understood about the revenants was their need... their only need. If they were called, they raced to the one that brought 'em, shared death with them, and rode their spirits over the threshold because the pain in this world is worse than it is in their limbo. They are compelled to cross back over, to try to get through the foyer and into the world beyond. That's all they want, like a dope fiend wanting more dope. There's no thought or calculation beyond that."

"But that didn't happen this time," I said. I put my cup down on the coffee table, and prepared myself for the pain of standing up. "Is there anything else you can tell me? Are there any charms or chants that will drive these things away until I find those jars you were talking about?"

"I don't imagine anyone's ever lived long enough to figure out a spell to protect themselves."

"That's... not very comforting."

"Wish it weren't the case."

"You and me both. Look, thank you for your help. If Isley is still out there, I have to find her." I looked at Sidney and asked if he was coming with me.

"Sidney can't go," Granny Tierney said. "I need him to do a few things for me."

"Maw-maw, this is important."

"So are the things I need you to do."

I searched the old woman's wrinkled face. I saw concern there, carved as if by razors in the lines on her skin. She knew something, held a bit of knowledge she wasn't willing to reveal. She was protecting her grandson.

"Stay here with me," Granny Richmond said, her voice no longer powerful. In truth, it was hardly a whisper. "Terrible things are happening out there."

"And I should help stop them," Sidney replied.

I heard the tremor in his voice. He knew as well as I did the implication of his grandmother's protest: If he followed me out the door, Sidney could die.

30

The first place we needed to look for the vessels was Aaron Dalfour's house. At first neither of us said anything. The sun burned in the sky. The neighborhoods were quiet. The only other person I saw during the drive was a little boy, riding a fancy silver bike and wearing a Razorbacks cap, completely oblivious to what had come to his home-town. Finally, the silence got the best of me, allowed me too much time to think, about Isley, about Jody, about a peaceful future that was far less likely to happen.

"Is she always right?" I asked. "I mean when she says that crazy shit, does it always happen?"

"About fifty-fifty," Sidney said. "When I was twenty-six, she told me that I needed to be real good to mama and tell her I loved her every day. Two weeks later, mama was diagnosed with breast cancer. She was gone less than two months later. Maw-maw told me the same thing about my daddy the following year, and I drove myself crazy with it. Turns out he was just fine, lived another ten years. Her divinations are iffy, but she knows the hoodoo, so if she thinks the revenants are planning something, I imagine she's right."

"Well, what could they be planning?" I wanted to know.

"Maybe they want to punish all of us. The whole town."

That didn't seem likely, if only because they hadn't done it yet. All Jody had to do was command his followers to attack and kill. By now, dozens of people would have carried the revenants to death. Then, Jody could simply call them back to rebuild his crew. It didn't make sense, and I told Sidney why.

"You're probably right," he said. "Next time we see him, why don't you ask?"

I chuckled at that, and it turned into a cackle of laughter. The question wasn't even remotely funny, but it triggered a need for laughter. Soon, Sidney was laughing right along with me.

When we reached Dalfour's house, Sidney parked at the curb. At the door, I pressed the bell, and he leaned to the side to look through the window.

"Aaron's got a light on in the back of the house. Probably the kitchen."

I let a few seconds pass then pushed the bell button again. "What do we do if he answers?" I asked.

"No idea, but I guess if he doesn't answer we're stepping it up to breaking and entering."

After another minute, we both realized Dalfour wasn't home, or wasn't answering. We walked around the side of the house. The grass here was overgrown and weeds had taken a good hold against the foundation. The backyard was in similar shape. Apparently, Dalfour wasn't much of a gardener.

We walked to the back porch. The kitchen door stood open.

"He may have run out this way when he saw us pull up," I said.

"Possible," Sidney replied, turning to look over the ragged yard and the tall fence rising between Dalfour's property and a low field running out to a stand of trees. Without further hesitation, he started up the stairs, and I followed.

Dalfour's house was hot, even muggy as if it had been sealed up, rather than left wide open. No breeze moved in the house and the air baked. If he was hiding here, he wasn't overly concerned with comfort.

Thick sweat, just another layer to add to the many already soaked into my collar, broke out on my neck and brow.

"Aaron!" I called. "Aaron Dalfour? This is Mick Harris."

"Don't touch anything," Sidney whispered.

"Sure," I said. "Why?"

"Because this could be a crime scene," he said, setting off toward the swinging door separating the kitchen from the dining room. "Maybe I got a bit of the gift myself. This place feels wrong."

And I knew what he meant. The house's temperature was a single part of a more complex discomfort. Violence hung in the air, clung to the heat. It followed us through the first floor where we searched the dining room, the spare room, closets and a half bath nestled off the kitchen. The feeling of brutality rode our shoulders up the stairs and into Dalfour's master suite. We checked everything. After the second floor was ruled out we checked the third and the attic, which was sparser than Dalfour's living room. Up there, we found four boxes, all containing old toys–mementoes of Dalfour's childhood. But no jars or bowls or anything that might have served as a vessel.

"There's probably a basement," I said.

"Yeah," Sidney agreed, holding an ancient Raggedy Andy doll in his hand. Most of the yarn serving as Andy's hair had been cut, plucked out or burned. Sidney dropped the doll on top of the other items held in the box and turned away.

The sound of footsteps rose to us as we descended to the first floor. I stopped on the stairs and threw my arm back across Sidney's chest, stopping him in mid step. A board groaned below. The soft press of shoe soles on wood rolled up toward us. Whoever shared Dalfour's house with us wasn't even attempting stealth, which made me believe Jody or one of his people had tracked me down again. That or Dalfour had armed himself and was ready to bring an end to our pursuit. I signaled for Sidney to back up the staircase and immediately regretted it when I heard a step complain under his weight.

"Come down," a familiar voice called. "This is Doug Richmond with the Celebration Police Department."

"Damn," Sidney said, exhaling with relief.

I called to alert Richmond to our presence, and we hurried down the stairs to meet him. He'd already drawn his service revolver, but it hung at his side. Beneath his uniform hat, a band of white bandage showed. Nervous exhaustion brought a twitch to his weighed down features.

"I thought the car out front looked familiar," he said. "Sidney, what the hell are you doing with this guy?"

"Just trying to help," Sidney replied.

"Yeah well, you could be helping yourself to a lot of trouble."

"True enough."

"What are you doing here?" I asked of Richmond.

"My job. After finishing up at the Wertimer's last night, I spent a few hours at the hospital and then I got to thinking about what you told me. I may not have believed all of this shit before, but I'd be as dumb as a stump to ignore it now, and since Dalfour is about the only name on my list, I came here. Have you found anything?"

"Nothing," I told him.

"We were headed for the basement," Sidney said.

"I'll take it from here," Richmond replied.

"The hell you will," I said. "I know it's your job, and you like following your regulations, but I'm looking for my daughter, so get used to having me around until I do."

Richmond thought about this for a moment and shook his head. Then he turned around and led us down the hall, back toward the kitchen. At the end of the corridor he stopped and pointed at a door.

"This is it," he said. "I want you two to stay behind me. Anything moves down there, and I mean anything, you get your asses back up the stairs."

Without waiting for our reply, he opened the door.

A sharp odor–sweat and smoke and shit and raw meat–rolled over us in a thick cloud. It shocked me into a momentary paralysis. The reek frightened me, because I'd smelled death before; you couldn't mistake its odor for anything else. Richmond also knew the source of the odor, but he wouldn't let it interfere with his duty. He nudged up the light switch with the barrel of his gun and stepped into the stairwell.

"Learning to hate this," Sidney said.

We followed Richmond down. A single bulb burned from its socket above the steps. More light spilled over the concrete at their base. My heart raced faster with each step. It skipped a beat when I reached the cellar floor and saw Aaron Dalfour.

"Damn," Richmond whispered.

I thought I was going to vomit. I nearly did, but managed to calm my mutinous gut before it launched. Sidney's reaction was a little more forceful.

"I can't…" he said, then turned around and raced back up the stairs.

Dalfour lay propped against a wall. His legs splayed out in front of him. A large red hole was opened in his stomach. A crimson stain ran from it to his knees. The right side of his face was gone as if hacked away by a dull blade, leaving jagged fragments of skull and dangling flesh, all painted with his blood. His jaw hung, unhinged. All but torn away. Fanning out from his ruined face was a great splash of blood, acting as adhesive for bits of hair, shattered bone, and gray matter.

"Shotgun did that," Richmond said, walking beside the stairs. He ducked low to check beneath them, service revolver raised and ready. "No hoodoo involved in this." He continued to the wall facing the one against which Dalfour's body rested, then disappeared for a moment around a corner made by the L-shaped cellar.

I stood where I was, inhaled the vile atmosphere. My stomach flipped and I threw a hand over my mouth. My leg began to throb again. Racing thoughts collided in my skull, making me dizzy. I reached out to the wall for support and grasped a wooden shelf.

"No one's here," Richmond called, having completed a quick search. He worked his way back through the basement to where I clutched the shelf for support.

I nodded, not yet able to speak through the sick lodged in my throat. I squeezed my eyes closed, tried to compose myself.

"This is fresh," he said. "Happened in the last few hours."

"How do you know?" I managed, refusing to open my eyes.

"The blood hasn't dried."

"Great," I said, swallowing hard against the lump in my throat. I drew in shallow breaths through my mouth, held tighter to the shelf. My head was getting lighter.

Then a hand fell on my shoulder, shocking me out of my swoon. It was Richmond. Over his shoulder, I saw Dalfour's corpse, and I quickly looked away.

"I have to call this in," he said. "Do you want to search around down here? Once it's an official crime scene, you won't have access, so if you're looking for something, now's your chance. The place looks cleaned out, but you never know."

I nodded my head and opened my eyes.

"You okay?" he asked.

"Not in the least."

"One suspect down," Richmond said. "I wonder if there's any chance this is unrelated. I did some checking on Dalfour, like I promised. You were right; he was big into gambling. Word was, he owed some mean motherfuckers a lot of cash."

I remembered the man I'd seen on Dalfour's stoop–the burly man with the loud Hawaiian shirt and a son's birthday to attend.

"You might want to check out a guy named Ryan," I said.

"Ryan?" Richmond asked. "Richard Ryan?"

"I didn't get his full name. A big guy. Bad taste in shirts."

"Sounds like him," Richmond said. "But he didn't have anything to do with this."

"You sound awfully sure."

"Yeah well, state troopers hauled his body out of a car wreck yesterday afternoon. He drove his SUV into a pine tree at about eighty miles an hour."

★   ★   ★

Searching the basement only took a few minutes. Doug's news about Richard Ryan clung to me, made me wonder if he too had gotten caught up in the world of Jody Mayram. At that point, it seemed perfectly logical that he'd received a note, a simple folded scrap of paper with a name scrawled in blood. As I walked along the concrete, I imagined him whispering the name, laughing it off before meeting Jody or another revenant out on the highway, perhaps swerving to miss the creature, ending his life with a steering column piercing his chest. Another victim on the growing list. I needed to find the vessels Granny Tierney had mentioned. They had to be here somewhere. It was a large space, but it was also open and well lit. The floor was concrete and the walls, brick. I found no boxes or jars of any kind. Rows of wooden shelves ran along two walls, the one at the foot of the staircase and another longer wall at the back of the room. I checked in the corners and behind the water heater and beneath the stairs, but found only dust. In fact, the only things down there were Aaron Dalfour's corpse and me. But then I remembered something I'd seen on the back shelves.

Averting my eyes, so I didn't have to look directly at Dalfour's corpse, I walked across the cellar to the first set of shelves, the ones I'd leaned on for support. These were nearly clean. This in and of itself wouldn't have struck me as terribly odd. After all, these would be the shelves he saw every time he came into the cellar. But the dust that had covered the shelves was worked into the wood grain, worked in deep.

Two rectangular ghosts, completely free of dust, were cut at the end of the shelf. Up until recently, boxes had covered the wood there. They'd been removed and the shelf hastily wiped down. I was putting together the series of events when I heard a sound like someone stumbling on the floor above me. I figured Richmond or Sidney had tripped while hurrying back through the house. I listened closer, and finally made out the sound of footsteps overhead. The cellar door opened, squeaking lightly.

I called out to Richmond, wanting him to see the marks on the shelf.

The bulb above the stairs went out, then came back on. It went out a second time, and the darkness was filled with the trilling giggle of a little girl. A great shadow filled the doorframe. I didn't need a sixty-watt bulb to identify the person standing above me.

Jody Mayram lumbered down the stairs. His followers poured through at his back, choking the doorway and the staircase in a matter of seconds. I ran to the back of the cellar, away from Dalfour's body, the staircase that the revenants descended. But there was nowhere to go; no nooks or vents in which to hide.

"He's dead," a little girl's voice said, drawing my attention to the stairs.

Jody Mayram stood by the shelves, a monstrous storm carved into a human form. Fury rolled off of him in palpable waves. The air around him rippled with heat. His shoulders trembled. His chest heaved.

At Dalfour's body, a little girl with gnarled teeth and a hunchback knelt over the corpse. She poked at the side of Dalfour's head, the side that still had flesh on it. The head canted, and the little girl giggled again before standing up and returning to Jody's side, reaching out for one of his massive hands.

All along the staircase, Jody's people watched with anticipation like Romans awaiting a bloodbath on the Coliseum floor.

"You do this?" Jody asked, his voice a quivering basso.

"No," I said, surprised by the strength of my own voice. It echoed back to me from the basement walls, the concrete floor. "He was like that when I arrived."

"Tell us who did this."

"I don't know."

"Was it the men upstairs?"

"No. They haven't done anything to you or your people."

"Who did this?" Jody asked again.

"I don't know. I told you that. What the hell do you want from me?"

Jody trembled all over, like a junkie watching his fix brew, aching to have the smack in his veins. He wanted to charge me, to touch me. He wanted me to show him the way back into death, but he fought it. The strain showed on every inch of him.

"This must end," he said, releasing the girl's hand.

""Yeah, it must, and I know how to end it, but I can't do anything for you if you murder me."

"You know what we are?"

"I know you're trapped. Your souls are chained to this world. Now, I don't give a shit what you did when you were alive. Your punishment was inhuman, and you've suffered enough."

"What we did when we were alive?" Jody asked, sounding bitter.

"You were cursed when you died. I know how to break that curse. If you'll give me a…."

"You don't know anything," Jody said. He reached out and touched the back of the girl's head, patted lightly. "Matilda, show him."

This was the moment before my death; I accepted the fact with the same certainty I would if I'd stepped onto a freeway in front of a semi-truck barreling down on me at ninety miles an hour. Giggling and eager, the girl ran forward. Her feet clapped happy applause on the concrete floor. In her eyes, I saw the desperate need, the promise of release. I stumbled into the shelves behind me. She sprang.

And hit my torso like a cannonball.

Her legs wrapped around my waist.

Her horrible face floated before mine; her wild eyes looked into me and through me.

Her hands, the cold steel hands of a bronze statue, clamped to the side of my head.

And I was falling, backward and down.

I was...

       ★   ★   ★

...her.

Flickering images of daylight.

Sun filtered through a mesh of pine needles. My body had shrunk, narrowed, become light and full of energy, as I ran through a forest, leaping stones and branches, chasing my brother down the path. In my hand, I carried Greta, my favorite rag baby, and she leapt along with me as Colwin led us through the woods. I felt a stitch in my side as we broke through the trees into the scrub grass to the back of Jefferson Dalfour's place. Colwin skidded to a stop and fell down into the weeds at the edge of a rise that dropped into the Dalfour pasture. He waved, motioned for me to get low.

Then, we looked down into the ditch that broke the hillside from the pasture, and I wrapped a hand over my mouth to keep my giggle quiet. Colwin's eyes were as big as mama's plates as he stared, and I could see why.

Two folks was sexing down there. It was funny, seeing the big man's butt moving around. For a minute I thought he was alone all

by himself, just humping at the weeds and dirt, but I noticed the tiny
legs poking out from either side of him and knew he wasn't alone at
all. But something wasn't right. Someone was crying, real soft and sad
from down there. Feeling bad, I stopped looking for a bit. Instead, I
gazed over the pastureland at the big white Dalfour house and thought
how pretty it looked, surrounded by willow trees and neat plots of
grass all fenced off in shrubs and pretty flower beds.

Then, I was looking down again, and the big man, turned out to
be Mr. Jefferson Dalfour himself. He was busy strapping his belt and
looking at the girl in the mud. From where I was, I thought she looked
like Colette Dalfour, Mr. Dalfour's grandgirl who'd come to stay for
the summer, but she was only my age, and she was kin, so I figured I
was seeing wrong because you don't sex with kin.

Turned out that the crying was coming from Mr. Dalfour. He
nudged the girl that looked like Colette with his boot. Did it again.
One more time. She rocked to the side with his foot but then wouldn't
move, and she was looking right at me. But I don't think she saw
nothing. Next to me, Colwin started tapping at my shoulder, and I
slapped his hand away.

Below, Dalfour was really and truly crying now. He rocked back
and forth on his knees, and slapped at Colette who just kept looking
at me, with her dress up around her middle and her tiny legs poking
to the sides. Dalfour looked around all scared like he heard people
come for him from all sides.

Colwin yanked my arm. He looked real frighted and wanted to go,
but I was trying to figure out what I was seeing, so I looked on back
down to the ditch.

And realized that the-girl-who-looked-like-Colette wasn't the only
one staring at me now.

*   *   *

Colwin pouted through dinner. He made me promise not to say nothing about what we saw out behind the Dalfour place, and I promised

because he was my brother and all. After dinner, Jody was going to have a sing-a-long out in the square for everybody, and those were a lot of fun. Jody had a real pretty voice and so did mama and daddy. Colwin didn't finish his supper, but I did because the afternoon of running had made me real hungry. I helped mama with the dishes. Daddy took Colwin's hand because he seemed afraid to go outside. I grabbed Greta my favorite rag baby and we went out to sing.

★   ★   ★

I heard the men coming, even through the singing. Jody pretended not to notice, but he must have heard them too, because Jody heard everything. Mama said Jody could hear my prayers at night even though I kept them inside my head and just moved my lips, and I believed her.

But I heard the men, and I turned around and saw the lanterns and torches coming through the trees. Their big boots crushed and crunched and stomped. Their voices were loud, calling out Jody's name and the name of our home.

"Mayram Ellyn," they called. Then something exploded and Colwin dropped down right next to me, like he just fell asleep. I giggled and shook his shoulder but he didn't move.

"Colwin," I said, insisting he stop acting silly. I rolled him over, and he stared at me like the girl had that afternoon, except Colwin had a hole in his face where his nose should have been.

I got real scared then. Everyone was screaming and running. Everyone except Jody. He stood at the far end of the camp, facing me and the men coming through the forest at my back, and he looked real mad. Daddy ran up and screamed Colwin's name. He lifted me up into his arms and then dropped me back on the ground. I looked up at him, and one of the men had cut daddy with a wheat scythe. The hooked blade was buried deep in daddy's shoulder and I cried because they were hurting him. The man with the scythe yanked it out, and daddy dropped to his knees.

More explosions came and my friends fell–Deeder, Frank, Thomas, Nollie, Pork, Sally and Scarlet and Rose–they fell down or were chopped down by the harvest blades. I couldn't move I was so scared. I watched a bunch of folks run into the woods behind Jody, running off toward the river. Mama was there and she kept trying to run on back but Claude, he was a big man, had her arm and was yanking her toward the trees. I screamed for my mama and then felt myself being lifted into the air.

Mr. Dalfour had me. He squeezed me so tight that it hurt and kept pointing his pistol at folks and making his gun explode.

"This is what you get for attacking my people," he screamed at me. And I didn't know what he meant at all. We didn't attack anybody. "Take her," he said, and another man lifted me from his arm. "Tie her up."

Jody was fighting three men on the far side of the fire. He threw one right into the flames, and the man screeched and rolled out onto the ground, his hair all lit up and smoking. One of the other men cut at Jody's leg with a gutting knife. The other hit him on the head with a club and Jody stumbled around, all dazed and wobbly like he was drunk. Mr. Dalfour walked right up to him and shot him in the knee.

"You sonofabitch," Dalfour screamed. "Why'd you have to kill her? Why?"

"I killed no one," Jody said.

"My grandgirl. Why?" Then, Dalfour shot Jody's other knee and he dropped to the dirt.

I struggled against the ropes they had me in, but a man saw me and put a knife under my chin. "You'll be dead soon enough," he said, spitting in my face as he talked. "It'll only happen faster if you get loose. So, just settle down."

He grabbed the knot at my back where my hands met and dragged me. Oh, it hurt so bad. Pain shooting up my arms and into my shoulders, and it made my head hurt too. I got dirt in my mouth and a small rock because my face was being dragged along. On the other side of the fire, the man dropped me and walked toward the group of men standing around Jody.

"Get their blood," Jefferson Dalfour said. "Put it in them jars we brought. Any that's still alive, I want their blood. Get their names, put 'em on the jars, then take the lot of it back to Ms. Leslie. She'll know what to do."

I looked all around the camp for help, but my friends and my brother and my daddy were all lying in the dirt, shaking and twitching and crying, and I thought they were all going to be dead. I didn't really know what dead meant exactly. Once Colwin and I had walked up to a coon in the forest and it just laid there and Colwin said it was dead. He said everything died eventually.

Dalfour's men walked around the camp. If someone tried to run away, like little Pork Deschield, they cut his legs out from under him. The men held little jars, much smaller than the ones mama used to can peaches and preserves, and they gathered up blood from the wounded folk; sometimes they made a fresh wound for it, even if plenty was running from the body already. Once they had themselves a good amount in a jar, they etched the lid with their knives. I watched them draw my daddy's blood from a cut they made in his wrist. He tried to fight them, but they planted boots alongside his head, then they cut his arm and filled their little awful jar. When they was done with him, the big man with the scythe returned. Daddy tried to get to his feet, but the man swung the blade, caught daddy in the neck and cut him real deep. His head didn't come off but almost. It hung from a piece of skin and some muscle, just dangled like a piece of fruit from its stem. Then he fell on over.

Everything died eventually.

Was my daddy dead? Was Colwin? Mama? Someone help.

I rolled over and got back on my backside. I couldn't stop crying because everything hurt. My hands and wrists where the rope rubbed and my face where it had gotten scraped on the ground and my whole darned body.

They tied Jody to a tree. They used wire on his head, wrapped it around the tree trunk half a dozen times so that the fire flames danced over the metal threads dimpling his brow, his nose and his cheeks and chin. All the men gathered around Jody. They kicked and spit at him and called him a monster for "what you done."

Dalfour stepped away from the crowd of men and walked over to me. He knelt down and grabbed my hair in a fist and that hurt real bad, too.

"You like to watch?" he whispered through gritted teeth. "You like spying on other people's business?"

'I know you did it," I said real angry. "I know you were sexing…"

But his fist came round and knocked the rest of the words back down my throat.

"You like watching. You watch this!"

And I didn't want to. I tried closing my eyes, but Jody was in so much pain. He faced me. They used a knife to cut off his pants and stood around staring at him, while he sat there naked and bleeding.

"Freak," one of the men said, pointing at Jody's privates.

Old Jefferson Dalfour began sobbing and screaming "How could you? She was just a child. How could you?" And he took a knife from another man and started stabbing at Jody's privates, cutting and slicing and screaming the whole time.

One of the men, Mr. Carter from the bakery, I think, stopped Dalfour and said, "Don't let him die too quick. That's no kind'a punishment."

Jefferson Dalfour nodded his head, wiped lying tears from his eyes. He looked back at me and smiled. He pulled one of them little jars out of his pocket and leaned in close to collect Jody's blood.

Those horrible men tortured Jody for so long, cutting at him with their knives and burning his hands and feet with their torches. After a few minutes, Jody couldn't even scream anymore.

Mr. Buncy, the nice man who lived in the house next to my mama and daddy's came running out of the woods with a tree branch raised over his head like a club, but Mr. Carter shot him before he made it five steps into the square. The men all laughed.

By that time, Jody had stopped moving. All of his nice hair was tangled up in the wires around his head. I thought they might leave him alone now. If he was dead there wasn't no point in hurting him anymore. But Jefferson Dalfour pulled the pistol out of his pants, and he aimed at Jody's nose.

"For my dear, Colette," Dalfour said.

He pulled the trigger.

All the men stood quietly then, heads down like they was praying. One of them turned around and looked at me.

"What about this one?" he asked.

"Get me her blood," Dalfour said. "Then toss her on the fire."

I tried to roll away from the man. He showed me the long arched blade of his knife, let a bit of firelight dance along its edge. He put the blade to my neck and I felt it bite into my skin. At first it tugged, but didn't hurt much. He wrestled with his little jar, shoved it under my jaw. He pushed me away so he could put the lid on, and I looked at all the red blood inside the glass and wondered if all of it had come out of me. It didn't seem possible. Surely it would hurt more to lose so much blood. The man drove the point of his knife into the metal lid.

"What's your name?" he asked. He kicked me hard in the leg and yelled at me. "What's your cocksucking name?"

I told him and he set to work making marks on the lid with his knife blade. All around me, The Glen was getting fuzzy. I could hardly see my daddy, and he was only a bit aways from me. The trees seemed to have all sprouted twice as many branches and needles. Even the fire seemed to be different. Not flames at all. More like a floating orange pond, recently disturbed by a stone. Voices buzzed all around, but I could no longer understand words. My neck hurt then. Really hurt. I tried to reach up and touch the sore place, but my hands were still tied.

Then the man with the knife put the jar in his pocket. He leaned forward and lifted me up, just like daddy did when he wanted to set me on his lap to tell me a story. Only this man didn't set me in his lap. He didn't even bring me close. He turned and threw me into the orange lake.

★   ★   ★

Panting, terrified, I opened my eyes, confused by the exposed beams overhead and the hard concrete against my back. My entire body ached and bolted with pain as hers had, feeling a sharp stick jabbing into my shoulder and flames biting through my clothes, my skin. The reek of burning hair filled my nostrils. I heard it crackling. My back was an agony of burns, but the pain and panic were fading. I stopped writhing on the floor, stopped struggling completely, leaned back and let the cool concrete soothe me.

Jody stood at my feet, holding the little girl. She squirmed in his arms and hissed, like a feral beast yanked from a meal. She kicked and growled, wanting to complete the journey from the land of the living.

"You said you could end this," Jody said, backing away with the unhinged child held tight against his body.

"What about my daughter," I asked, finally returning to rational thought. "Is she still alive?"

"I couldn't say. We did her no harm."

Was my denial so complete that I was willing to take this creature at its word? After the scenes I had witnessed through the eyes of a deformed little girl; my answer was *yes.* Because I wasn't merely viewing a series of events. I was experiencing the world as she'd experienced it, and I felt her/my innocence and decency, just as I felt with complete certainty that her family and her friends were equally moral.

These weren't monsters, or at least, had not begun that way. In Mayram Ellyn Glen they were good people, surviving the only way they knew how. Their vilification was a fabrication of the incestuous Jefferson Dalfour, making monsters to assign guilt so no one would suspect his perversion. From the beginning, they were victims, even before birth: victims of the poisonous effluent of Jefferson Dalfour's mill. Once born, they suffered the fear, intolerance and repulsion of their own families, so much so they created their own community, bothering no one, living with a peace woven of their own hands. But even that was not enough. Falsely accused, these estranged people were murdered and cursed, so that even in death they remained victims, forced to exist in agony and serve whoever held the chains keeping their souls from peace.

As Jody and his people observed me from the stairs, I struggled to incorporate what I knew of these creatures with their appearance. They would never be beautiful in my eyes, and pitying them would deny the nobility they had exhibited in life. I didn't know what to feel.

"Keep your word," Jody said earnestly.

Then they filed out of the cellar, moving slower than they had upon entering. This sad parade kept my attention, until the last of them, Jody Mayram, disappeared onto the landing.

I lay back on the poured stone and gazed at the wooden planks above, the gentle swirls of grain, the play of dark and light, the cobwebs and the dust. Villains past and present walked through my thoughts. Dalfour and his obscene ancestor were there, but they weren't the sum of this tragedy's designers.

Dalfour's murder had been an act of betrayal. Perhaps he'd lost his taste for murder and had threatened his accomplice with exposure. This scenario didn't play, mostly because I firmly believed Dalfour was responsible for Richard Ryan's death. So the likely answer revolved around Dalfour's usefulness. Whomever he worked for no longer needed him and the man who'd been instrumental in the summoning of Jody Mayram had been demoted to the status of a loose end. His manner of death had been brutal. Either one of the shotgun wounds would have been sufficient to kill him, but the murderer had pumped another shell into the chamber and delivered a second blast. Why? Spite?

Slowly, I lifted myself from the cool concrete floor.

I knew almost everything I needed to know.

Sidney met me at the top of the stairs. He wrapped his arms around my neck and held me tightly as Doug Richmond looked on confounded.

"Stay with Doug," I told him. I pulled away and tried to smile for him but sadness made the gesture impossible, allowing little more than a smirk.

"Where are you going?" Sidney asked.

"I have one last thing to check out," I said. "And then I'm going to see my daughter."

31

The stunning white plantation house rose on my left. It was built by the ancestor of a man I'd found dead in a dusty basement. Behind this house, far out in the eastern field, below a steep rise, Jeffereson Dalfour had raped and murdered his granddaughter. You can't blame a place for the things that happen around it, but as I pulled into the drive, I had an overwhelming urge to burn the house to the ground.

I rapped on the front door, pounding the brass ring against the angry lion's mane. Movement inside made my muscles tense.

Darrell Wertimer opened the door. I had not gotten a good look at him the last time we'd met. I remembered that he was a pleasant looking gentleman with a round, boyish face perched above narrow shoulders and a paunch, neatly secured behind a crisp starched shirt. Our previous encounter had not allowed me to see the cool intelligence of his sky blue eyes.

"You're Isley's father," Wertimer said.

I didn't reply. Instead, I walked over his threshold as if he didn't exist and into the house. The lights were not as bright as they had been. The chandeliers were dark so the only light came from lamps and through the windows. In this illumination, the home appeared normal, even comfortable.

"What has she done now?" the man asked.

I turned on him quickly. "Don't," I snapped.

"Please keep your voice down, Mr. Harris. My wife is in bed. Last night upset her terribly, and she's quite ill."

His serene delivery of this request startled me. His reasoned tone did a lot to quell my tirade and reminded me why I was there.

"Now, please, is there something I can do for you?"

My anger train had been derailed. I looked at this guy and tried to find my voice so that I could accuse him of the crimes I wanted to believe he'd perpetrated, but damned if I could find a single thing about him on which to hang my accusations.

"Isley told me," I began and then stopped.

"Yes?" Wertimer looked at me with patience and warmth in his eyes. He looked like a man that had already seen the worst in the world and had accepted that nothing else could affect him again.

"I want to see your basement," I said, unable to verbalize my charges against him.

"My basement?"

"Is that a problem?"

Wertimer shrugged. "I can't imagine what you'd find interesting down there." But he led me down the hall. I paused for a moment to look at the locked door, the place Jody had struck while chasing me and felt an uneasy tickle at the back of my neck. Wertimer pulled a ring of keys from the pocket of his slacks and jabbed one into the lock.

The basement stairs were carpeted in a fine Berber. I'd used the same model of carpet on a house in Cherry Hills a couple of years back. I followed Wertimer down into the shadows, tensed for a moment until the man flipped a toggle and brought the basement into the light.

"It goes on for quite a ways in either direction," he said.

And it did. The carpet from the stairs spread out into the wing on my left. Here there was a pool table, a dartboard, a small bowling game and a television set mounted high on the wall. Across the room was a wet bar with an Old English pub motif. I looked around for cameras, even a computer, something to indicate that Wertimer had the ability to broadcast his indiscretions, but saw nothing of the sort. At the back of the game room, two doors flanked a standing marble ashtray.

"What's in there?" I asked.

"The room on the left is a storage closet. The one on the right is private."

"That's the one I want to see."

"Mr. Harris, that was Lance's room. I would think that under the circumstances you might show a little respect."

But I was desperate. I had to find something in that house to corroborate Isley's story. I had to. Even if it meant breaking through every lock in the place. The crazy wife and psycho butler had been real. The doped-up matron of the house had made a fine display of announcing that her servant had murdered a man. But what if the rest had just been a story?

Then I reminded myself that I wasn't expecting to find any proof of Isley's claims. More than anything I wanted to find some basement porn studio or a dungeon where the bad children were sent for punishment, but this was a last desperate grasp at denial.

"Please," I said. I couldn't find the strength to make demands. My watery convictions evaporated fast.

"Very well. Just don't touch anything. Lance was always very particular about his room."

Again Wertimer produced his keys and again a door was opened to me.

Lance's room was spare to the point of being monastic. The long room made an L at the end and disappeared into a broad opening, but what I saw was a simple bed with a beige comforter. A flat screen television bolted to the wall, with a DVD player in a bracket beneath. On the wooden desk across from the bed, notebooks had been stacked in neat piles. A cup of pencils. A sharpener.

"What are those?" I asked, pointing at the notebooks.

"Lance kept journals," Wertimer said. "He wrote poetry as well, but I believe these are mostly his thoughts. Lance had something of a breakdown. His therapist thought it might help him to write everything down, so he did."

"A breakdown?" I asked.

"Many years ago, Lance stopped by for a visit and found Mrs. Wertimer being attacked. I was out of town on business, as always seems to be the case, and he walked in to find two men…" Wertimer winced with pain. "He saved my wife, but one of the men was killed. The guilt and what he'd seen happen to his sister pretty much broke an already fragile mind."

"Lance is your wife's brother?"

"Yes. They were very close. They had a difficult childhood, but that's hardly your business. When he recovered, I invited him to stay so

Frances wouldn't be alone. I could tell it was difficult for him, seeing his sister's decline every day. It hurt him and embarrassed him. Sometimes, he'd throw people out of the house just so he didn't have to endure the things she said. But he loved her very much, and we loved him."

I looked at Wertimer and searched his face for deceit. Found none. But his story had been so damned neat. It answered every argument I could have raised. He didn't know me from a Brazilian manicurist and yet he was more than happy to share these intimate details of his life?

"I need to see one more thing," I told him.

Wertimer led me upstairs, through the hall and to the staircase in the foyer. "I have to ask you to be very quiet up there. Frances is really quite ill."

I did as I was told, going so far as to walk on the balls of my feet to keep the sound of my steps muffled. At Isley's room, Wertimer opened the door and then stepped back into the hall. He didn't seem to have any interest in the room or what I might find there.

A beautiful canopied bed, with tiny yellow roses printed on the fabric occupied the center of the room. A large window with a lemon-colored window seat allowed a flood of late morning light into the room. An intricately carved secretary's desk sat on the wall on my left. A new Hewlett Packard computer with a flat panel monitor occupied the otherwise empty desk. The chest of drawers matched the desk. It was polished to a high, impeccable shine. The room had another flat screen television and DVD unit like the one in Lance's room, a telephone. Priceless antiques butted up against state-of-the-art gadgetry, and they worked well together. The room was amazing. Beautiful. Everything a kid could want. The Wertimer's had gone out of their way to pamper their wards.

I went to the bathroom door and pulled it open, already knowing that I'd find no bolt on the back of the door.

The wood was white and smooth. The only lock was one of those flimsy buttons in the doorknob, the kind that was easily jacked with a paperclip or a coat hanger. I looked at the claw-footed tub and frowned bitterly.

"I'm sorry," I told Darrell Wertimer, whose brow creased at the apology. "Thank you for doing your best with Isley."

"I'm afraid it didn't do much good."

I nodded. "When I came in, you asked what she'd done now. Did you mean anything in particular?"

He waved me out of the room and I followed along the hall and down the stairs. In the foyer, Wertimer shoved his hands in the pockets of his slacks.

"She's a very disturbed young woman," he said. "Noelle did what she could. We all know that, but Isley's behavior is such that I can't believe it's simply a result of the recent tragedies. When she came back here this morning… "

I had to interrupt him then. "She came back?"

"A little over an hour ago. I tried speaking with her, but she ignored me. Pretended I didn't exist. Didn't say a word."

Of course not. She knew that Jody would home in on her voice. By that time, she would also know that I had survived, and she'd imagine that the threat to her was still quite real. She wouldn't speak to anyone. Not even Aaron until she knew all of the residents of Mayram Ellyn had moved on.

"She did give me a note," Wertimer said. "It had a name written on it."

"I know what it said."

"Do you know what it means?"

"Yes."

"When I was a boy, Reginald Dalfour was my best friend, despite some family jealousies. My father had bought the Dalfour home because Reginald Sr. had fallen on hard times. The Dalfour's claimed bad foreign investments, but most of us knew Reginald Sr. had more than a few expensive vices. At any rate, Reginald Jr. was Aaron's older brother, and he used to talk about Freak Town and the people who'd died there. Foul, evil tales of perversion and sickness, and he told me that if you ever spoke the true name of one of those people, you died that very same night. One day he handed me a note in class with those words on it. He taunted me all day. Called me a baby for not saying them. Finally, in exasperation, Reginald said them. He laughed and said it was all a great joke."

"And he died," I said.

"That very same night. So, when I saw those words again, I thought about what had happened here with Sandy and Noelle and last night when Lance was killed, and I knew she'd done those things. I know you're her father, and you don't want to... "

I waved away the denouement of that sentence. "She doesn't mean a thing to me." Again, I thanked Wertimer and left his home.

I thought about Sandy Winchester and Noelle Vale. I thought about the Wertimer house, once belonging to Aaron Dalfour's family. What I wanted to believe didn't matter anymore. I was a fool, with the aspirations of a fool. All of my beliefs had been tainted and stained by ridiculous hopes, dreams I'd carried from Denver. They were songs played on broken instruments, out of tune. Inharmonious. Discordant. Distorted.

32

I was no actor. When Palace made videos that required me to do anything but play my bass the fact came through loud and clear. Unlike Ricky, I didn't have the showman's gene. I had none of the film star aspirations he did. My face always showed exactly what I felt. It was a block of wood carved by my emotions, inflexible until a new set of sharp-edged feelings hacked a fresh expression.

So as I drove to Amaryllis Street, my face was a blank mask, empty, weathered and wooden. Emotions had worked so hard that their edges were dull and my face whittled down to its barest components. The house was peaceful from the outside, the yellow and white paint clean and inviting. The frame of smeared putty, which I'd never had the chance to clean, was still around the front window. Shadows covered the porch like a swaddling blanket, offering coolness instead of warmth. In front, I saw the white Ford Escort Isley had inherited from her mother.

Why didn't she just leave? I wondered. *Who the fuck cares?* I answered.

I tried the front door and found it locked. Dazed and overcome with the cold void in my gut, I crossed to the window and shattered the glass with my elbow. My arm was cut, but that hardly mattered. I cleared the lower frame with my shoe and stepped through a blast of freezing air into Noelle Vale's house. I expected Isley to find me then, perhaps racing into the room with the shotgun she'd used to blow Aaron Dalfour's face off, but the house was silent, except for the stomping of my feet.

In the kitchen, I paused at the sink and stared down at the rusted drain surrounded by stained porcelain. This entire, agonizing trip had begun in a kitchen with a phone call from a stranger. That kitchen had been pristine. No rust. No paint chipped away from the cabinet doors.

I looked out the back window and remembered a couple of boys who'd played catch under the gentle drops of a yard sprinkler.

"It took you long enough," Isley said at my back.

I turned and found her in the doorway, a shotgun aimed at my chest. She had showered, dressed in one of the outfits I'd bought her the day before and done her hair. She never looked more beautiful. It was grotesque.

"Yeah. I got held up."

My response, the desolation in my voice, obviously surprised her. She stood there, aiming down the barrel at me, her brow knit. "You should have let them kill you."

"They had their chance," I said. "Obviously, they thought I might be able to help them."

"Like you helped me?"

"Fuck you," I sounded so bored, so beyond caring about anything she had to say her face went crimson with anger.

"You're the one that's fucked," Isley whispered into the stock of the gun. "I thought you might actually be a challenge. But you're as stupid as Aaron. At least he got his dick sucked a few times, and he thought he was going to get rich. What in the hell did you think you were going to get?"

"Nothing," I said.

"Then I guess you got what you wanted."

"What about Noelle. Did she get what she wanted?"

"She wouldn't say the name," Isley said. "But she knew what it meant. Aaron hadn't expected that. Then she started doing research, just like you, so I moved things along."

"You killed your mother." The news didn't surprise me.

"So?" Isley asked. "She took my life away long before I put those pills in her dinner. She couldn't give me shit, except a recipe for peach cobbler and an old sewing machine. With you, I might have actually had a life, seen the world. You could have introduced me to rock stars and movie stars. Real people. Important people. I could have actually done things that mattered, but no, I was trapped here, in fucking Celebration, watching the grass grow and attending church socials. I was cheated out of my life, out of my father."

"Remind me to thank her for that." I expected those to be my last words. I didn't close my eyes or wince; I just looked at this deranged and deluded little girl, wondering how anything so monstrous could exist.

Isley's eyes narrowed, her face still burning with a furious blush. She lifted the barrel of the shotgun a fraction, aimed down its length.

I looked on passively. My accusations had dried up, confirmed in the most terrible manner I could have imagined, and no words of protest sprang to my lips. I'd lived a life that had swung between the flamboyant, loud, and public to the all but hermetic, and had found lasting happiness nowhere along the spectrum.

Isley screamed then. Her body jerked back, pulling the barrel of the shotgun upward and away from me. The gun flew out of her hands, clacked on the floor, and her body twisted violently, pushing at the kitchen door and revealing those who stood beyond it.

They had gathered in the living room. Jody, the one who had knocked the gun from her hands, stood only a foot away from her. Isley kept screaming, but it had no effect on the revenants, except to excite them further. They all trembled and moved from side to side in a lazy dance, eager to be released. Isley backed into the kitchen and let the door swing closed. They followed, one after the other sliding into the kitchen.

"We have to get out of here," Isley cried in my ear. She was pawing at me, clawing at my shoulder.

I didn't move, just watched as the revenants walked into the room. There was Jody and Nollie and Pork and Lucida and Mr. Stemps. Matilda, the little girl who had shared her last moments with me, flitted back and forth in front of Jody. Sensing I was going to be no help to her, Isley fled toward the kitchen door, but Nollie was quick. He sprang across the kitchen, blocking her escape. Six of the other revenants converged on her, forming a tight semi-circle. I could see the desperation in their eyes. They wanted out of this painful world, away from the cruel hearts and minds that surrounded them.

"Is she the one?" Jody Mayram asked.

Isley spun on me. Terror and panic playing over her face like tics. Her lips quivered. "Daddy," she said, her voice a thin plea.

"Yeah," I said. "That's her. But keep your hands off of her."

Jody stepped forward and a question knitted the brow above the trenches where his eyes should have been.

"If you want me to set you free, you let her walk out of here, now."

Isley regarded me with confusion. She thought I was saving her life, and she wanted to know why, but she didn't dare speak.

I looked away, turning my attention to Jody. He faced me, head down; his long hair, black and gray, veiled his eyeless face. Around him, his followers continued the strange dance, fighting their urge to lunge at me, to use me as their friends had used Bump Carter and his wife, to carry them out of this harsh realm.

"I can end this," I told him.

"Forever?" he asked.

"As I promised. All I need are the vessels. Once those are destroyed, you'll be free."

Jody's expression didn't change but he moved his head from me to Isley as if he could see us and nodded.

Isley's face lit up with gratitude. She ran to me and threw her arms around my neck, whispered thank yous into my shoulder. I shoved her away.

"Don't touch me," I said. "Are the jars in your mother's car?" I asked.

"What jars?" Her question was all soft and childish innocence. She even managed to give me a doe-eyed look of virtue that made me want to slap the expression from her face.

Instead I grabbed her shoulders harshly. "Tell me where those jars are or I'm walking out and leaving you with them."

"They're in the car," she whined. "In the trunk."

"Give me the keys."

Isley hesitated, tried to pull back.

I yanked her forward and shouted, "Give me the fucking keys."

Arms restrained by my grasp, she dug in the front pocket of her expensive new jeans and produced a simple keyring. I snatched it from her fingers and shoved it in the pocket of my shorts. Then I turned to Jody. "I'll be done here in a minute. Meet me in the Glen."

Jody took a step forward and his people became agitated. "You're playing games."

"No," I said. "If I'm not there, it will be because of her, and you can
do whatever you want to her if I don't show."

"If you don't, her death will be unpleasant," Jody warned.

"I'm counting on it."

Hesitantly, Jody led his people out of the kitchen. Matilda paused
in the doorway and flashed me a warm smile, like a child who'd been
promised a precious gift for her birthday. Despite the jagged display
of her overlapping teeth, I found the little girl beautiful.

"I'll see you soon," I told her.

She released a stream of giggles, then waved and scurried out after
her family.

"Daddy…" Isley began and I shoved her away from me. Her attention immediately went to the discarded shotgun. And the loathing I
felt for her vanished into a deep, icy void.

I walked across the kitchen and picked the weapon up by the barrel.
"This is evidence in the murder of Aaron Dalfour," I told her. "I'm
calling Doug Richmond to let him know I have it, along with a good
set of fingerprints so he can ID Dalfour's murderer."

"But I didn't…" Isley said.

"Shut up. Just shut your fucking mouth. You have two options right
now and trying to bullshit me isn't one of them. You can call Richmond yourself and the jury might take your confession into account,
which could keep you off death row, or you can run. You can get away
from me and this place and disappear, and maybe they'll never find you."

"Where am I supposed to go?" Isley asked.

"Straight down," I told her. "You murdered a mother that loved you
and worked her ass off to make a good life for you. And for what?"

"You don't know what it was like."

"You'd better leave," I said. "And for the record, you're not getting
away with anything. Even if you manage to beat the murder rap for
Dalfour your life is going to be one layer of shit on top of another,
and I can't wait to watch it happen."

Isley rolled this around in her head, and as cruel and hollow as
that bitch was, she still tried to play the victim with me. "You're my

father," she said. "You can't leave me with nothing. It was Aaron's fault. He made me help him." Tears filled her eyes in a tremendous show of talent. "I didn't want anyone to get hurt. I *didn't*. It was all Aaron. That's why I killed him, for what he did to Sandy and Mom. You can't punish me for what he did. You can't. It's not fair."

"Goodbye," I said, unable to listen to another second of her performance. I limped past her to the kitchen door, keeping my body between her and the shotgun in my hand. She reached out and grabbed hold of my shirt.

"Daddy," she whined.

"Don't ever call me that again." I couldn't even look at her.

I slapped her hand away and continued into the living room. Then I left the house on Amaryllis Street.

★   ★   ★

At least Isley hadn't lied about the jars. I found the two boxes in the trunk of the white Ford Escort. Inside, nestled in straw were the vessels, over two dozen short round jars, similar in size and shape to those that hold minced garlic. I plucked one out at random. The rough etching on its metal lid had rusted through, and I could just make out an initial, N. and the abbreviation of a last name, M. The blood inside had not congealed, had not even thickened. It remained fluid, cresting over the insides of the jar as I rolled it in my hand. Across the side of the vessel, a label had been affixed, with the full name of Nollie Mayram—apparently Jody's son—printed in the same jerking hand that had written Jody Mayram's name on the note left for me at Faye's Inn.

I closed the trunk and started my final journey to Freak Town.

Too numb to think about Isley, I instead followed the path of her crimes. I already knew all I needed to about Sandy Winchester and Noelle. I'd run the motivation for their deaths through my head a dozen times. But the night before, the night she actually bloodied her hands was a different matter.

After we were separated in the woods, Isley had paid a visit to Aaron Dalfour. She knew he would be the only likely suspect, and if he were cornered he might reveal his association with Isley Vale, the way she'd seduced him into committing murder. She didn't need him any longer, but she needed the vessels.

I thought you might actually be a challenge…

I might have managed to live, but Isley had clearly played the game better. Somehow she'd known that I wouldn't trust kindness from her or anyone else. She was insane and cruel and bitter. She was the most evil person I'd ever met in my life, and she knew me better than anyone else ever had. How fucked up was that?

I drove past the diner where I'd first met Isley. The live bait machine stood out front, holding its writhing cargo, oblivious to the fact that their lives would end there in the dark or at the end of a hook. Trucks filled the lot.

It was just another day for the residents of Celebration.

At Faye's, I unloaded the two crates, ignoring Faye LaMarche who glared at me from the porch of her office. With the vessels in my arms, I limped onto the path between cabins 9 and 10. When the path made a T at Cabin 3, I turned left and began shambling upstream. The air was filled with the pure scent of pine and earth and river water. I felt stronger with each step, even as I approached the bend, beyond which a blue flame did its flickering dance, denoting the boundary of Mayram Ellyn Glen. The miserable sickness that I'd felt on my first visit returned, though. Suddenly the two crates seemed to triple in weight, slowing me as the palpable dread built in my gut. By the time I reached the wall of flame, hardly noticeable in the light of day, sweat coated me, made my clothes tight and abrasive against my skin. I stumbled, barely kept myself from crashing to the ground. With two deep breaths, I stepped through the flames and into the Glen.

I forced myself to its center. Even now, three quarters of a century after its destruction, a handful of foundations remained. Their edges were no longer blackened, the soot and burn eroded by rain and wind. I remembered what the Glen had looked like before Jefferson

Dalfour's attack, remembered the small comfortable looking homes, the smiling faces of the people. Children had played here. Men and women cared for one another. They cooked meals. They made love. They squabbled, and they cried.

The crates became unbearably heavy; so I set them down in the damp, overgrown grass. Even my own body felt too heavy, so I dropped to my ass and lowered my head. I sat and I waited for Jody Mayram as the generations-old misery seeped through my flesh and into my bone.

33

The revenant souls of Mayram Ellyn Glen emerged through the trees an hour later. Still confined to the limitations of their bodies, they had journeyed on foot from the house on Amaryllis Street to their home.

Upon seeing Jody Mayram I stood, heavily burdened by the emotion of this place. He paused before me, his people gathered tight at his back. There was nothing to be said. No reason to prolong these moments, so terrible for us all. I thought it only right that their souls be freed in this place, and now that we were together, I would make it happen.

I lifted a jar from a nest of straw, and read the name on the label: "Hollis Meade." I tried to unscrew the lid, but time and rust had affixed it to the glass. Instead of wasting any more time on the task, I threw the vessel at a low wall of foundation stones. It made a dull pop, breaking apart on the rock. From over Jody's shoulder, came a deep, nearly orgasmic sigh. A tall man with no hands and one leg significantly shorter than the other turned to dust, then to a blue gray mist.

Then he was gone.

Destroying the vessels, setting the residents of Mayram Ellyn Glen free became a ritual. I pulled a jar from the crate. I read the name on the label, and then I smashed the damnable thing against the foundation stones. With each shattering of glass another of those euphoric sighs rose, even if the named soul was not manifested before me. With the first crate empty, I discarded it, spilling straw into the tall damp grass. The first jar I pulled from the second crate carried Jody Mayram's name. I spoke it, but was not allowed to crush it against the stones.

"After," Jody said, reaching out a hand and nearly touching my arm. Only a sudden realization stopped him from grabbing my wrist. "When the others are gone, then I'll follow."

And so it went. Names were uttered. Jars were smashed. Released souls cried out in joy. Finally, I was left alone in the Glen with Jody and a small round jar, carrying his name.

Jody Mayram stood up straight. His massive chest pushed his suspenders out to the sides. Instead of speaking his name, I handed him
the vessel, carefully avoiding any contact with his hand. Jody looked
at the jar. I expected some final statement, his last words. But Jody was
eager to move on, wherever he might go.

He dropped the vessel on the ground, broke it under his foot.

Then disappeared.

★   ★   ★

The miasma engulfing Mayram Ellyn Glen vanished with Jody. The
flame faded, and the air felt hot and clean, finally purged of the dread
that had captured so many lost souls. I walked away, back to the path.

On the trail, I found a boulder to lean against, and I cried. Sobs
punched my ribcage. Tears streamed over my face, joining the per-
spiration at my collar. I wanted it to stop. I wanted the cold void to
open up again and consume all of the pain, but it refused me. It was
gone as surely as Jody Mayram was gone. Noelle was dead, Isley was
on the run. Despite her cold-blooded manipulations, I missed her,
not for who she was, but for what she might have been. More to the
point, for what she would have meant to me. I wanted the comfort of
numbness that had served me so well over the last ten years to return.
I wanted anything but to feel.

But I sat on that rock and bawled until my tear ducts were dry
and my throat ached. My chest still hitched. Emotion burned there.
White hot.

Finally, I was able to move. I pushed myself away from the rock and
returned to the path.

When I emerged into the parking lot of Faye's Inn, I stopped, startled by the man waiting for me there. I considered turning around and
fleeing back down the path, thought about saying nothing and just
going to the Escort, driving it back to Amaryllis Street and trading it
for the rental car. From there, I would drive to the airport, climb on
a plane and put Celebration behind me forever.

It didn't work that way.

"I was so worried about you," Sidney said. He wrapped his arms around my neck, and my tears returned.

END OF THE LINE

I left Celebration that afternoon. Doug Richmond took possession of the shotgun and told me to stick around for a statement. I didn't. Instead, I drove to Little Rock. Sidney followed in his truck. Who knows what he was expecting? He said he wanted to make sure I didn't drive off the road, and he made a good point, since I could hardly focus on a single rational thought let alone the highway ahead, but we made it to the airport without incident. I turned in the rental car and immediately realized I'd already missed the flight I'd booked upon leaving Celebration. Fortunately, Sidney had hung around and he drove us to the Wyndham Riverfront Hotel, where I took a room.

"You feel like getting a drink?" he asked from where he sat by the room's window.

I sat silently on the edge of the bed. Unsure what to say, but certain I didn't want him to leave, I stared at the floor, digging through my head for any bit of relevant trivia, but found nothing but a mire of dark images and darker emotions.

"Mick, there was nothing you could do," Sidney said. "Whatever messed with Isley's wiring happened a long time ago. Noelle went to a lot of trouble keeping you out of that girl's life, so you can't blame yourself for what she became."

"Noelle kept me out of Isley's life because Isley wasn't my daughter," I said.

Sidney's eyes narrowed. "Excuse me?"

I couldn't respond. Instead I remembered a long ago night, when I hit the first major bump on the rock star highway.

★   ★   ★

We were in Austin, Texas on a three-day break before heading up to Dallas for a gig. Noelle and I had been togethers for weeks, and she'd slowly immersed herself in the distractions of the road—some weed, a little blow, a lot of Jack Daniels and Stoli. Compared to most of the girls we met along the way, she was a teetotaler, but on that night–our last night–she had thrown herself into the party like a seasoned rocker. I was so blasted myself, I hardly noticed. She was smiling, laughing and dancing; she was having a good time, and that's all I needed to know. Ever since meeting her, I'd been worried the road life would drive her away, so seeing her embracing the bacchanal actually eased my mind. We ended up in bed at sunrise, both of us too wasted to fuck, but holding each other like icebound explorers, clutching tightly to keep away the cold.

I'd booked an afternoon at a local recording studio to get a few ideas for the next album on tape, and since my sleep requirements were minimal, I woke at noon, did a few bumps of blow to get the blood flowing and snagged an acoustic guitar on my way out of the room.

The session wasn't terribly productive. In fact it sucked. A lot of the riffs I'd worked out on the bus and in hotel rooms sounded flat and amateurish when I heard them on playback. One tune stood out. It was a typical power ballad progression–just another attempt to recreate "Stairway to Heaven"–but there were a couple of interesting parts that I figured I could work with. The rest of the bits and pieces struck me as useless.

Apparently the engineer agreed. He was an ancient fucker with a white beard down to his nipples and an old man mullet that would have made David Crosby proud. As he boxed up the tape, I made the mistake of asking his opinion.

"I don't have one. All you did was lay down chords–soulless white noise. When you're ready to bleed me some music, I'll tell you what I think."

The rock star ego kicked hard and fast, but I managed to get out of the place without making a complete ass of myself, not that I didn't treat the geriatric hippie in a less than civil manner, but I did manage to keep from beating him unconscious with a mic stand. In front of the studio on the sidewalk, I nearly tossed the reel box into the trashcan.

On the walk back to the hotel, the old man's words sank in deeper, needling a long ingrained sense of inadequacy. My mind twisted the whole thing into anger, but the truth was I agreed with the engineer, and it hurt like a bitch to carry his confirmation of my mediocrity down the street and into the hotel.

I thought about stopping in the hotel lounge for a shot of Jack to kill a bit of the agitation, but it hadn't opened yet, so I continued on to the elevator and up to the fourth floor. Every time I think about that afternoon, I wish the damn lounge had been open.

At the room, I slid the card key in and threw open the door, ready to vent my frustration to the one person who I felt certain wouldn't laugh about it. But Noelle wasn't in any position to comfort me.

She knelt on all fours on the bed, facing me. Ricky Blaine fucked her from behind. Noelle was drunk again or high again or both. I could see it in the dreamy expression on her face. The source of her euphoria didn't really matter. My mind shut down, went into that cold place. Whether it was the dull, slow recognition that swam into Noelle's eyes, or the satisfied grin cutting Ricky's face as he got off that shut me down completely, I couldn't say. The scene faded. Turned white.

I remember crossing the room to the nightstand and picking up the vial of blow and shoving it in my pocket. I vaguely remember throwing the guitar case, and though I want to believe I threw it at the wall, more times than not, I remember aiming for Ricky Blaine.

Then things went white again. The next thing I'm sure of was sitting in the hotel lounge with a flock of shot glasses circling the table. Noelle slid into the booth across from me and tried to speak, but after acknowledging her presence, I returned my attention to the oddly mobile glassware.

The conversation went something like this:

"I'm sorry, Mick."

"This the first time?"

"No."

"Fuck you."

Silence. Alcohol.

"I can't do this anymore, Mick. I don't like what I'm becoming."

"So become something else."

"Can we please discuss this like adults?" I think she was crying at this point, but that might have been something I imagined to make myself feel better.

"Is that what he did?" I asked. "Did he talk to you like an adult? Did he make you feel like a real grown up?

"Mick, don't."

"You know… fuck this. Plenty of fish in the sea, right?" I struggled to get out of the booth.

"Would you just wait a minute?" she pleaded—or at least that's how I remember it.

"I don't think so."

Then she asked me where I was going, and I said, "Going fishing. See ya."

I left the hotel and flagged a cab. I came to sometime late the next afternoon in a bathhouse, and by the time I managed to get back to the hotel, Noelle had cleared out. No note. No message of any kind. I was so angry, it took me days to understand exactly what I'd lost.

That was the story I didn't dare tell Isley. Her mother, the good country girl, the pure force that would cleanse my soul, was fucking Ricky Blaine, cheating on me with an empty piece of shit who until that moment, I'd considered my best friend.

Once I recovered from the initial shock and fury, I actually tried to win Noelle back, rationalizing that I'd put her in this situation, had made her comfortable in a world of easy ecstasy. It wasn't her fault that Ricky had targeted her as a yet another fuck you to the one guy in the band who'd never worshipped him. I tracked her down at her school. I made her sit on a bench and tried to speak with her. She looked sick, completely unnerved by my presence. Of course, she was already pregnant with Isley, but I didn't find that out until later.

"We have to work this out," I told her.

"I can't."

"Look, this kind of shit happens. It shouldn't, but it does. We forget ourselves and pretend we're something that we aren't. For fuck's sake I've been doing it for the last ten years. We can work through this. I love you."

"I can't, Mick. I don't like who I am when I'm with you. I have to go."

"Did you hear what I said? I love you."

"And I feel alone with you," Noelle said. She got up from the bench, turned her back on me. And then she walked away.

I went back to the hotel and bled out a song.

★   ★   ★

"I think she told me Isley was mine because she hated the idea of what she and Ricky had done," I told Sidney. "My name was on the birth certificate, probably another lie."

"But you don't know for sure?" Sidney asked.

"No. I mean Noelle is the only one who knows for sure. I only found out about the pregnancy from a friend of hers, a friend that Noelle told I was the father."

"So, why did she freeze you out?"

"Guilt," I said. "Noelle could accept me as the lesser of two evils for the birth certificate, but even so, she would have felt wrong taking my money to raise another man's child."

"You've known this all along and you still went through hell for that kid?"

"The thing is, Isley didn't know. She believed she was my daughter, and there was no reason she couldn't be. I wanted her to be. In a way, I needed it."

"And all of this strikes you as *normal?*" Sidney asked. "Damn. I'm going to need a new dictionary hanging out with you."

"The truth is, I don't know. She could be my daughter. She could be Ricky's. Right now, after everything that's happened, I'd rather believe she was his."

"Do you think Richmond will catch her?"

"Somebody will."

"And you're not worried about her coming after you?"

"Not much," I told him. "By this time tomorrow she'll be dumped from my estate and I'll get things underway to dismantle her trust. I'll call my lawyer first thing in the morning, just in case the plane goes down or I get struck by lightning or I choke on a chicken bone. I don't want there to be any chance she'll see a penny from me, and my guess is she'll figure that out pretty fast. If she realizes there's nothing to gain, she'll figure laying low is a better option."

"And then what?" Sidney asked.

"How do you mean?"

"What are you going to do?"

I told him I didn't have a clue.

★   ★   ★

Two weeks after returning from Celebration, Arkansas for the second time in my life, I sat in the kitchen with a mug of coffee. Edwin stood on the other side of the counter, eyeing me curiously.

"What are you doing?" I asked.

"Looking for signs of life," he said.

"Meaning?"

"Well, aren't you even a little excited?"

"You seem to have that covered for the both of us."

"Sometimes I wonder why you even bother getting out of bed," he said. He lifted his mug of coffee, shook his head, then took a sip. "If I were you, I'd be bouncing off the walls and cleaning house."

"The house is clean," I said.

"It's never clean enough for this kind of guest."

"Ed, just chill, okay? It's a weekend. It's not a wedding."

"Not yet."

"I barely know the guy," I said.

"You've been on the phone with him every night for two weeks."

"How in the fuck could you know that?"

Edwin's face lit up, and he hopped in place twice like a kid waiting for an ice cream cone. "I knew it. Mick's got a boyfriend. Mick's got…"

"I'll hurt you."

"Well, it's about fucking time you settled down again," he said.

"Look, I don't need this right now. I don't even know what I'm thinking. No way in hell I'm moving to that place, and he's got two kids down there. His whole family lives in that town. He's not going anywhere."

"You can make it work."

"I don't see how."

"But you want to."

Yeah, I wanted to.

★   ★   ★

Nearly ten years have passed since I received Aaron Dalfour's call, telling me that my daughter was in "terrible trouble." Sidney and I were serious for a while, and we tried to keep the relationship going, but anything spanning such a great distance gets stretched too thin and is bound to break. He visited me and then I flew to Little Rock, and we did that for a year. The one time I stayed in Celebration, I took a room at the Celebration House, a quaint inn just off the town square, because Sidney had his kid's for the weekend. During my visit, Mr. Rowley Twain was more than happy to share the story of Herbert "Baby-leg" Kole, who'd been a guest at the inn for a single night. Listening to Rowley spin the yarn got me to thinking about writing all of this down–Isley, Noelle, Jody, the lot of it–and I called Doug Richmond to see if he'd mind filling in some gaps.

He was more forthcoming than I would have expected. We met on two occasions and he explained that Baby-leg had been working for Richard Ryan, and he'd come to Celebration to collect a thirty thousand dollar debt from Aaron Dalfour. Of course, he'd gotten nothing but a note with a name on it, and like the rest of us he'd been compelled to speak the name aloud, summoning Jody or one of his followers to Baby-leg's room at the inn. At the second meeting, he produced crime scene photos–Baby-leg's and Aaron Dalfour's–that

I could have lived a lifetime without seeing. Less forthcoming were Sandy Winchester's parents. In fact, that's not even his real name as I was threatened with a variety of legal actions should I mention Sandy in any way. The descriptions of the boy are accurate and I imagine anyone in Celebration would know Isley's first victim by name, but you won't find it here.

A few months later, Sidney told me the long-distance thing wasn't working for him. I shouldn't have been surprised. I'd had the conversation with myself so many times that it was almost like experiencing déjà vu when he laid it all out over dinner: he couldn't afford to spend so much time away; his friends and family were asking too many questions about his increasingly frequent trips; he didn't think it was fair to me because he couldn't come out of the closet. Even though I'd seen it coming, the hurt and anger still blindsided me. I spent the rest of the night wandering through town–even considered moving to Celebration–but that only solved the problem of distance and did nothing to address the issue of Sidney's fear of exposure.

So I left town, and I haven't been back. Sidney emails every now and then. I see him when I'm in the area. It's good. It's okay.

As for Isley, she's still out there. I'd underestimated her, and though I'd told Sidney that I wasn't worried about her seeking me out for revenge, the longer she remained free the greater my concern grew. Some nights a noise would sound in another part of the house, and I'd leap out of the bed, certain the deranged girl would be in my room, taking aim with a new shotgun to collect on an old debt. Edwin tried talking me down from my increasing paranoia more times than I can count, but the dread seeped in and took deep root.

I spend a lot of time out of town these days. Edwin and I hired a couple of guys to take over the finish work I used to do, and we still manage to make a decent profit on most of the properties. I've joined on for the occasional tour, mostly nostalgia gigs with other metal bands. I even played on a cruise ship with a bunch of bands that used to fill arenas back when the hair was high. Half the guys wear wigs now. Some replaced their Jack Daniels and amphetamines with organic kale shakes and vitamins; others, those who still have a taste for the suicide spice, maintain their worship of Hedon.

I don't think I was ever meant to stay in one place too long. As for men, they still move in and out of my life, but the few I let close, like Sidney, mean something. Maybe they feel the same. Maybe not. The picket fence, the husband, the two-point-three Pekinese don't figure into my future anymore, at least not my dream of the future. The music is there. The music is enough.

I looked up that quote John mentioned the night we'd met. He'd said it was from Aristotle, and I found it online. It reads:

"But he who is unable to live in society, or who has no need because he is sufficient for himself, must be either a beast or a god..."

I don't really know what to make of that, but it seems like a good enough place to end this story. In the words of Ricky Blaine, it's time to get back on the road.

THE END

CPSIA information can be obtained
at www.ICGtesting.com
Printed in the USA
LVHW041157141118
596829LV00008B/150/P

9 781590 213575